W9-CUW-012

QUICKSAND

ALSO BY IRIS JOHANSEN

Pandora's Daughter
Stalemate
An Unexpected Song
Killer Dreams
On the Run
Countdown
Blind Alley
Firestorm
Fatal Tide
Dead Aim
No One to Trust
Body of Lies
Final Target
The Search
The Killing Game
The Face of Deception
And Then You Die
Long After Midnight
The Ugly Duckling
Lion's Bride
Dark Rider
Midnight Warrior
The Beloved Scoundrel
The Magnificent Rogue
The Tiger Prince

Last Bridge Home
The Golden Barbarian
Reap the Wind
Storm Winds
Wind Dancer

QUICKSAND

IRIS JOHANSEN

**Doubleday Large Print
Home Library Edition**

ST. MARTIN'S PRESS ≈ NEW YORK

This Large Print Edition, prepared especially for Doubleday Large Print Home Library, contains the complete, unabridged text of the original Publisher's Edition.

This is a work of fiction. All of the characters, organizations, and events portrayed in this novel are either products of the author's imagination or are used fictitiously.

**This Large Print Book carries the
Seal of Approval of N.A.V.H.**

QUICKSAND

ONE

SOMEONE WAS WATCHING HIM.

Henry Kistle's hand tightened on the curtain as he looked down, careful to stay hidden from view. There, in the shadow of the elm a short distance down the street, was a tall, thin man. He was talking on a cell phone. Who was he talking to? Who had managed to track him down this time?

Don't be nervous, he told himself. It didn't matter if one of them had found him. He had occasionally been found before and managed to survive. It was only a matter of removing the immediate threat and then running. But he saw to it that those bastards who made him run were always punished for it when he was safe again.

And the immediate threat was standing down there waiting for him to make a mistake. A surge of anger tore through him. It wasn't fair. He had a right to live and take whatever pleasure he could find in this crap yard of a world.

Who was it? A father, a brother, a cop? Which one?

It didn't matter. He'd find out. But he had to be ready to go. Grab a few clothes. Pack his guns, his precious memory box, and have everything in the car.

He turned away from the window.

Damn him. He didn't want to have to run now. He hadn't had his fill yet of this small, sleepy town. Cities were safer, but pitting his wits against these yokels was exciting. They felt so safe that he could walk into their lives and take whatever he pleased.

Oh, well, there would be another time.

Another town.

Another child . . .

Yes, another child . . .

"HE WENT INTO THE HOUSE at seven this evening and hasn't come out," Jedroth said into his cell phone. "The lights are still on. It's only eight-forty. They went out at eleven last night."

"And you're sure he didn't leave the place all night, Sheriff?" Joe Quinn asked.

"I may not be a big-city cop, but I know my business," Jedroth said sourly. "I wouldn't let a scumbag like that out of my sight."

"And surveillance during the day?"

"I have a deputy keeping an eye on him. But we can't keep spending the tax-payers' money without evidence. One more night and that's it."

"I don't have evidence. I just located Kistle late yesterday. I need more time."

"Look, I didn't set up this surveillance without checking you out. I have an idea why you're so hot to get your hands on this bastard. I'm going along with you because Kistle may be a threat to my town. But I've got to have more than your say-so."

"I understand. I'll be up there by eight tomorrow morning to take over. If you need to contact me again, don't use this number. The cell phone number I gave you will reach me."

"Get here as quick as you can." The sheriff paused. "But we're not going to quibble about a few hours. Kistle isn't going anywhere. I have a few questions to ask him. We had a little boy go missing three weeks ago. Bobby Joe's tennis shoes and shirt were found on the bank of the river and he was presumed drowned."

"No body recovery?"

"Not yet. It's a fast-moving river and there are branches on the bottom carried down from flooding up north. It would be easy for a swimmer to get trapped."

"It could happen."

"That's what I thought until you called me yesterday and asked me to order surveillance on Kistle. I hate child molesters. We know how to treat them in my town."

"I'm sure you do. Call me if he makes a move."

"If he makes a move on any of the kids in this town, he won't make another one." Jedroth hung up his cell phone, his gaze on the lights beaming from the second floor of the house across the street. The glow of a TV set was flickering against the wall now. What kind of programs did sick sons of bitches like Kistle watch? Old classic movies of Shirley Temple? Or maybe *Cold Case Files* or *CSI* to keep himself from making mistakes. When Jedroth was working in Chicago when he was a younger man, he'd run across a killer who'd studied all of those kinds of shows for that very reason.

And the system had let him learn and go free. Jedroth had seen it happen time after time. It wouldn't happen in his town. That's why he'd come back to Bloomburg after ten years. He could make a difference here.

Quinn was an Atlanta detective and dealt with red tape every day, but Jedroth had an idea that he'd understood and condoned his attitude toward Kistle. He'd gotten the impression Joe Quinn would slice through red tape with the force of a machete.

Machete. Hell, yes, that's what he'd like to use on that prick in that upstairs bedroom. Cut off his dick and then slice him to pieces.

Make your move, you slimeball. Give me a chance to bury you.

Lake Cottage
Atlanta

"YOU'RE LEAVING?" JANE MAC-GUIRE stood in the doorway of Joe's bedroom, watching him throw clothes into a suitcase. "Hey, I just got here yesterday. Is it something I said?"

"I have business in Illinois." He smiled over his shoulder at her. "With any luck I should be back in a few days. Don't act as if either you or Eve will miss me. The two of you will be too busy catching up. She hasn't seen you in four months."

"We'll miss you." Jane frowned. "What business?"

"I have to interview a suspect." He changed the subject. "Will you drive me to the airport? I have to leave right away and I want Eve to have the Jeep."

"You're leaving without telling Eve good-bye?"

"She's at her mother's apartment for the day. It will be okay. I'll call her when I get to Bloomburg."

"Bullshit. What's happening, Joe?"

He should have known Jane wouldn't be deceived. His adopted daughter had grown up on the streets and she was very shrewd. Jane had been with them since she was ten years old and could read both him and Eve like the proverbial book. She'd recently graduated from college and was making a name for herself in the art world. Yet that artistic streak was balanced by toughness. "Okay, it will be easier if I don't have to talk to her. I don't want her asking questions."

"Why not?" She stiffened. "You've found Kistle?"

"I think so. I've found *a* Henry Kistle. I tracked him to Bloomburg, Illinois."

"He's the man who might have killed Bonnie?" she whispered.

"So Eve's been told. Montalvo's investigators unearthed three possible suspects. Kistle is one of them and the only one we were able to trace." He fastened his duffel bag. "It could all be a bunch of crap. I don't want Eve's hopes raised until I investigate Kistle."

"I don't think she thought it was crap. She trusted Montalvo."

"That she did," he said curtly. "He played her like a song."

"No one plays Eve," Jane said. "You

should know that, Joe." She studied his expression. "What the hell happened down in Colombia?"

"Eve told you when she got back."

"She told me she was on a forensic sculpting job for Montalvo and that you were shot and almost killed." She paused. "She didn't tell me you hated his guts. Even though he was once a weapons dealer, she doesn't feel that way."

"We have an entirely different take on Montalvo." He started toward the door. "And we agree to disagree."

"You don't generally disagree on many things."

"Then this is the exception that proves the rule. Are you taking me to the airport?"

"Of course I am." She stood aside so that he could pass. "I need some more answers before you get on that plane."

"You won't get them."

"I can but try." She grinned. "I've been out of the loop too long because I've been closeted finishing those paintings for the last show. I should never have accepted Eve's story at face value. I had a hunch that there was something brewing . . ."

"Only in your imagination." He moved toward the front door. "Eve and I are just plodding along doing the same old things."

"Plodding? No way." She followed him out on the porch. "You're streaking out of here to go after Kistle before Eve can get into gear. She's not going to like it, Joe. She felt terrible that you were wounded because you came after her to Colombia. Bonnie was her daughter, not yours. She believes it's her job to find Bonnie's body and her killer. She won't be closed out."

"Watch me," he said. "She's not going to go after Kistle until I find out whether we have the right man. Montalvo could have pulled a name out of a hat, for all I know."

Jane gave a low whistle. "My, my, we are bitter, aren't we?"

He gave her a cool glance over his shoulder. "I don't know about you, but, yes, I'm bitter as hell. Let's get to the airport."

ONLY TOBY RAN TO MEET Eve Duncan when she drove up to the cottage. The house was dark and only the Jeep was in the driveway. Jane's rental car was gone. Joe could be working late, but where was Jane?

She patted the dog's head absently as she got out of the car. "Did Jane leave you, boy?" She moved up the steps and opened the screen door. "Have you been fed?"

Toby gave a mournful woof.

"I don't know if I believe you. You like food too much." She turned on the lights. "And you lie a lot." She headed for the kitchen. "But we'll start off with a snack until I call Jane." She filled Toby's bowl half full of dry food and set it down. She dialed Jane's cell but only got voice mail. Well, maybe she was at a movie or something. She had grown up here in Atlanta and had old friends with whom she kept in touch. "Okay, you win, Toby." She poured the rest of the food into his now-empty bowl. "Now be good while I get some work in on Carrie's reconstruction." She moved across the room to the skull on the easel in the studio area. She had been chomping at the bit to get back to Carrie all afternoon. She was nearing the end and she was always intense when she got close to the point when an identity revealed itself beneath her fingers. But she didn't spend enough time with her mother these days and during their last phone conversation she had seemed needy.

She took off the drape covering Carrie's skull and tossed it on the table. Another few days and, hopefully, Carrie would no longer be her name. Eve always gave her reconstructions names because it seemed more respectful and it helped her to draw closer to them. This child had been close to ten years old when she had been murdered and buried near a freeway in southern Kentucky. The local police had no missing children of that age in their files, but if she could put a face to that skull, then she might be able to bring Carrie home.

Might.

So many children victimized by the beasts that prowled the earth remained lost from everyone who had loved them.

Don't think about it. She could only do what God had given her the talent to do. Sometimes identifying the children helped the police to find their murderers;

sometimes the killers were never caught. But at least she could give these children a chance for proper burial and their parents the opportunity to come to some kind of closure. Eve had never had that closure when her own seven-year-old daughter had been kidnapped and presumed murdered several years ago. She knew the pain those parents were feeling.

"Come on, Carrie," she murmured as her fingers began to mold the clay. She had spent days before this carefully measuring the tissue depths and then marking them. Then she'd taken strips of plasticene, applied them between the markers, and then built them up to the tissue depth points. After that it was an excruciatingly fine balance between concentrating on the scientific elements of depth and contouring until she was ready to let instinct take over. She was almost there. "Let's see what we can do before Jane gets back. I'll have to stop then. You're very important to me, but if I've learned anything over the years of working with you and the other children, it's that you have to cherish every single moment of life with the ones you love . . ."

THE KNIFE SANK DEEP in the man's back.

No scream.

Kistle twisted the knife as he drew it out. He hoped the bastard was still alive enough to feel it.

The man wore a sheriff's uniform. He was a cop. That meant that there might be others nearby. He'd have to move quickly. He rolled the body into the bushes and searched his pockets. A notebook, ID that identified him as Sheriff James Jedroth, a cell phone, a couple pictures of a woman and a teenage kid. He grabbed the cell phone and headed for his car. He checked the last number. Not local. So he hadn't been checking in with his wife when Kistle had noticed him on the phone. Who had tipped off the police he was here? Who had forced him to run?

He didn't try the number until he was a few miles from town.

No answer. On the fifth ring the voice mail picked up.

Joe Quinn. Eve Duncan.

He went still as he made the connection.

Eve Duncan.

He drew a deep breath. It had been a long time, but it was all coming back to him. An explosion of pleasure tore through him. He had to talk to her. He had to tell her how glad he was that she had come back into his life.

THE PHONE WAS RINGING again, Eve realized impatiently. It was the third time in fifteen minutes and she supposed she'd have to answer it. It couldn't be that important. Joe or Jane would have called her on her cell phone when she hadn't answered. They knew how absorbed she became when she was working.

She glanced down at the ID. Bloomburg, Illinois. Sheriff James Jedroth. It had to be another police department asking her to do a reconstruction. Since she'd become so blasted famous, those requests never stopped. But it was nearly ten at night and evidently Sheriff Jedroth didn't understand the concept of business hours. Well, Eve didn't either, so she might as well answer.

"Eve Duncan."

"Do you still miss your little Bonnie?"

Shock jolted through her. "I beg your pardon."

"She had curly red hair and on the last day you saw her, she was wearing a Bugs Bunny T-shirt."

"Is this some kind of sick joke, Sheriff Jedroth? I'm not amused."

"I'm amused. Amused and excited and full of anticipation. I haven't felt like this for years. I didn't realize I was getting stale and that the kill was losing its luster. Then I heard your name on your voice mail and suddenly I felt reborn."

"Kill." Her hand tightened on the phone. "Who is this? You're not a sheriff, are you?"

"I impersonated a sheriff once. It was in Fort Collins, Colorado. Children are taught to trust policemen."

"Who are you?" she repeated. "I don't know you. Why are you calling me?"

"Bonnie knew me. She knew me very well before the end."

Don't show him the wrenching pain his words are causing. "You son of a bitch. What are you trying to tell me?"

"You shouldn't have tried to track me down. Now I'll have to punish you. I never let myself be victimized without making sure that my pain is reciprocated." He chuckled. "Though this time I'm not feeling nearly so bitter. I've been following your search for Bonnie for years and it's lightened many a dull moment."

"I didn't try to track you down. I don't even know your name."

"Henry Kistle."

Kistle. The name of the man Montalvo had given her as one of the possible murderers of her daughter.

"Yes, you know me. You set that asshole, Jedroth, to watch me."

"Where are you?"

"It would be no use to tell you. I've just left town. I'll be hundreds of miles away from here before you can call and get someone to try to find me. I know about red tape."

"What . . . do you know about Bonnie?"

"That she was seven years old and a beautiful child. Do you know how many pretty little girls I've killed since your Bonnie died? Though I always regard her as my inspiration. She was like a burning arrow lighting the darkness. I remember how—"

"Shut up." She couldn't take any more. "Don't talk about her."

"I'm done for the time being. I just

wanted to touch base with you. I needed something to keep me up and zinging."

"Zinging?"

"That's what life's about. You have to keep on top of it, keep excited and moving. I got a little buzz earlier tonight but nothing like the one I'm feeling now. It's not as good as a kill, but maybe you could make the next kill extraordinary."

"What kill?"

But he had hung up the phone.

She was shaking.

She had curly red hair and the last day you saw her, she was wearing a Bugs Bunny T-shirt.

Kistle.

Joe. She had to call Joe.

Her hand was shaking as she dialed his cell number. No answer. The voice mail picked up immediately. His phone had to be turned off.

She hung up. Dammit, she *needed* him. Where the hell was he?

Stop whining. He was a cop. There were all kinds of situations where he'd turn off his cell. Okay, she had to handle it alone. She'd reach Joe as soon as he was available.

She was like a burning arrow lighting the darkness.

Bonnie.

Block out the pain. She had to try to catch that bastard before he was out of reach.

Sheriff James Jedroth. Kistle had used Jedroth's telephone and Jedroth was located in Bloomburg, Illinois. Call information and get the number for the sheriff's department. Move.

Five minutes later she had reached the sheriff's department and been transferred to three different extensions before she reached a Deputy Charles Dodsworth. "I'm sorry, ma'am"—he had a distinctly midwestern twang—"but Sheriff Jedroth isn't on duty. May I help you?"

"I was afraid he wasn't on duty. I only used his name to get through to anyone in authority." Eve continued urgently, "That's why I've been trying to contact someone, anyone. I received a phone call this evening from Sheriff Jedroth's cell phone. Only it wasn't the sheriff. It was Henry Kistle."

There was a silence on the other end. "Kistle. You're positive that was the name?"

"Dammit, I'm positive. You know who he is, don't you? I can tell by your tone."

"I'm familiar with the name," he said cautiously.

"Then go get him. I think he was in a car and on the move. He boasted that you wouldn't be able to catch him. But it's been less than ten minutes. He must have been under investigation by you or he wouldn't have been able to take the sheriff's phone. Can't you call the highway patrol and try to stop him?"

Silence. "He really had Jim's phone?"

"That's what it said on my ID."

"Shit." The deputy's tone was now curt. "I'll get back to you." He hung up.

Good. She was encouraged that he had wanted to get rid of her so that he could take action. At least there was a hope that Kistle could be intercepted. Hurry, she prayed. Don't let him get away.

She called Joe again. His phone was still turned off. She left a message for him to call her as soon as possible.

But there was a car driving up the road to the cottage.

She ran out on the porch to see Jane getting out of the rental car. "I can't get in touch with Joe. Have you heard from him?"

"Yes." She gave Toby a hug in greeting and pushed him aside. "And you can't get in touch with him because he probably had to turn his phone off on the plane." She grimaced. "Though he might not have answered you anyway. He didn't want to have to deal with you until he was sure."

She stared at her. "Deal with me? Plane?"

"I told him he wasn't handling this right." Jane was climbing the porch steps. "But you know Joe. Stubborn. He had to get on that damn plane to Bloomburg."

Eve stiffened. "Bloomburg?" she whispered. "Kistle."

"Yes." Jane's gaze narrowed on Eve's face. "How did you know?"

"Kistle just called me," she said numbly. "He was telling me what a beautiful child my Bonnie was."

"Damn." Jane's arms slid around her and she held her close. "I wish I'd been here with you. You shouldn't have had to be alone."

She wasn't alone now. She had Jane, and the healing comfort was like a blessing. "I'm okay." She hugged Jane before letting her go. "And we have a chance of getting the bastard. He called from an officer's phone and I was able to notify the sheriff's department pretty quick."

"Come on." Jane took her arm and pulled her into the cottage. "I'll make some coffee and you can tell me about it."

CHARLIE DODSWORTH HESITATED, staring at the phone after he'd hung up from talking to Eve Duncan. She'd sounded scared and desperate, but who knew if she wasn't some kind of nut? He was only a deputy. He had no business calling the highway patrol and setting up roadblocks. That was a sheriff's job. Jim's job.

He dialed Jim's cell number. No answer.

Jim always answered. Unless his cell was no longer in his hands, as Eve Duncan had claimed.

Damn, that scared him.

He punched the number for Torrance with the highway patrol and while he was waiting he called out to Annie Burke in the front office. "Get that report Jim requested on Joe Quinn." After he had read the report, the sheriff had thought Quinn might have valid reasons for suspecting Kistle and had started the surveillance on him. He needed to know everything Jim knew.

"Ten minutes," Annie said. "I'm on my lunch break."

"Now!"

Annie would probably give him hell later. He couldn't worry about it. Torrance had picked up and Dodsworth was telling him what had to be done.

"By whose authority?" Torrance asked. "I'm not about to send my guys off on a wild-goose chase at this time of night."

"Sheriff Jim Jedroth," Dodsworth lied. "I'm just relaying his orders."

"Got you." Torrance hung up.

Annie was standing in the doorway holding a folder. "You lied to him. What's got into you, Charlie Dodsworth? Jim's going to have your ass."

"I hope he does." Dodsworth got up from the desk. "I haven't got time to read that report. Walk me to the patrol car and fill me in, Annie."

"Where are you going?" She fell into step with him as she took out the report.

"I can't get in touch with Jim."

"He could still be okay. That doesn't—"

She broke off, her gaze scanning the report. "Joe Quinn is a lieutenant with ATLPD. Lots of commendations, formerly with the SEALs and FBI. There's a photo."

He glanced at the picture. Quinn appeared to be in his late thirties, brown hair, square face, broad mouth, and wide-set brown eyes.

Annie went on, "He went to Harvard and is supposed to be very, very smart. He lives in a lake cottage outside Atlanta with an Eve Duncan."

He punched the elevator button. "Tell me about Eve Duncan. Is there anything on her?"

Annie nodded. "Yeah, evidently they've worked together on several cases. She's a forensic sculptor, one of the best in the world, and does work for police departments all over the country. Several years ago her daughter, Bonnie, disappeared and was presumed killed by a serial killer who was later executed. Her body was never recovered and later it was suspected that the man who was executed for her death was innocent of that particular killing. Though he was guilty of several more child murders. Eve Duncan went back to school to study forensic sculpting and has been searching for the killer and the remains of her murdered daughter ever since. Joe Quinn has taken several leaves of absences from the department over the years to investigate possible suspects."

"Like Kistle," Dodsworth said grimly. "And this time he may have hit the jackpot." He was going down the steps toward the patrol car parked in front of the building. "Why the hell couldn't he have stayed out of our town?" He jumped into the car. "If Torrance calls back, cover my ass, Annie."

She frowned. "What's happening, Charlie? Where are you going? It must be pretty serious if you're willing to risk your job like this."

He backed out of the parking spot. "Dead serious."

FLASHING LIGHTS. HIGHWAY patrol cars drawn across the highway ahead.

Roadblock.

This was farm country and a roadblock was big stuff, Kistle thought. Those cops weren't going to be checking for seat belt violations.

He stomped on the brake, made a U-turn, and pressed the accelerator to the floor.

He could hear the sirens behind him.

He should have had more time. He'd hidden the sheriff's body and he should have had a chance to get out of the county before the police were able to martial their forces.

Eve Duncan had done this.

He knew he'd shaken and sickened her, but she must have rallied quickly, to get this fast a response. He felt a thrill of excitement as he went around a curve in the road. He could feel the blood pumping in his veins. He hadn't been this close to capture in a long time. He'd forgotten the adrenaline rush, the feeling of being alive. These days it usually came only with the kill.

They were getting close.

But according to his GPS there was a forest up ahead. Clayborne Forest.

He put on more speed and skidded around the next turn. Then he turned off his lights, left the road, and drove into the woods, bumping along on the rutted ground, branches swatting the windshield of his car.

The two highway patrol cars raced past him and around the curve, sirens blaring.

But they'd be back.

This car was a handicap now. He'd have to abandon it and go it on foot. He grabbed his duffel, rifle, and memory box and jumped out of the car.

No one would be able to catch him once he took to the woods. As a kid, he had spent all his free hours in the forest near his home. Later, in the Army, his skills had been honed to supreme sharpness. None of these country bumpkins could touch him, much less catch him.

If they got close, he'd just take them out one by one.

He splashed through a stream. He was acutely aware of the power of his muscles, the wind in his face. He was beginning to feel a sense of primitive joy. They thought him prey, but he was really the hunter. As a child, he'd seen a movie about a werewolf and in the forest he'd always pretended to be that monstrous, lethal entity. Now that he was grown he'd gone far beyond those fantasies and become far more deadly.

No one could catch him.

No silver bullet could kill him.

Hurry. Put distance between himself and the car. The first patrolmen after him would probably be novice trackers, but they'd pull in more experienced woodsmen if they didn't catch him. He had to have time to mask his signs.

These stupid cops won't catch me, Eve. I told you I'd get away from them.

He could feel again that surge of excitement.

Eve Duncan. Eve Duncan. Eve Duncan.

The name repeated in his mind like a mantra, he could hear the rhythm of it in his heartbeat as he ran.

Are you thinking about me, Eve? You shouldn't have done this to me, you know. You'll have to be punished.

The thought brought a swelling wave of pleasure. There were so many ways she could be hurt. He had hurt her tonight, but she had bounced back immediately. It would take time and study to find a way to bring her to her knees. But he didn't want to wait that time. He wanted that exquisite satisfaction now.

So what do I know about you, Eve Duncan?

You're a tough bitch who grew up in Atlanta's slums. Let's see, you're illegitimate and so was your Bonnie. Then when she was born, you turned your life around. You finished school and went on to college. What a sparkling example for those other street kids. But all that drive didn't help you, did it? Your Bonnie died and you couldn't do anything about it. Take away a child and the world stops turning, and the one who takes her away is all-powerful. It's the ultimate way to play God. You were helpless. And you're helpless now, but you don't know it.

But you'll know it soon.

TWO

"KEEP BEHIND THE YELLOW tape," the policeman said roughly. "If you're that curious about forensic procedures, watch *CSI* or *Bones*."

"I'm sorry, sir," Miguel Vicente said sympathetically. "I heard the victim was a sheriff? One of your own. I can understand how you'd be upset. I was in the military and the bond is much the same."

"You don't look old enough to have been in the military. You can't be more than nineteen or twenty." The officer's gaze traveled over Miguel's slender body and lingered on his thickly bandaged hands. "Iraq?"

"Not all wars are in Iraq. But I've had friends die fighting beside me. I know how you must feel."

"Jim Jedroth was a damn fine officer and a great guy. We'll get the pervert who killed him. We're hunting the woods for him now." He turned and walked back toward the forensic team, who were making a chalk mark around the body. "Stay behind that tape, kid."

"Yes, sir. Whatever you say." Miguel pushed his way back through the crowd cordoned off from the crime scene. He didn't pull out his phone until he was on his way to his rental car parked down the street. He slowly dialed Montalvo's number, wincing with pain as he tried to make his fingers work. "We're too late, Colonel," he told Montalvo when he picked up the phone. "I think Kistle's on the run."

Montalvo muttered a curse. "You're sure?"

"There's a dead sheriff outside Kistle's flat and a deputy who's swearing vengeance on the pervert who killed him.

He said they were hunting the woods for him now. I'd say that was a pretty good indication. I'll find out more, but I thought you'd want a report."

"Dammit, I thought we'd be able to rope Kistle in and hand him to Eve on a plate. We were so close."

"Evidently so were the local police. He must have been under suspicion."

"Why? Kistle is smart as hell. I'd bet they were alerted to watch him."

"Joe Quinn?"

"Probably. We knew he was doing his own investigation. I just didn't think he'd get there before we did."

"And you wanted to be first."

"I always want to be first."

"Particularly where Eve Duncan is concerned," Miguel said softly.

"I made her a promise."

"And she told you to forget it. Could it be you just want to be her hero? My, under the same circumstances I believe you'd accuse me of being sickeningly sentimental, Colonel."

"I keep my promises, you scamp. Now back off."

"Yes, sir." Miguel recognized by the

thread of steel in Montalvo's voice it was time to change the subject. He had served under him since he was a young boy in the military compound Montalvo had run in Colombia and he would serve him again anywhere, anytime, for the rest of his life. That didn't mean he didn't know how tough Montalvo could be if he stepped beyond the allowed limitations. "Just an observation. What do you want me to do next?"

"Find out all you can about the sheriff's investigation into Kistle. I'll get a flight out tonight."

"Do you want me to go into the woods after Kistle? I may still be able to rope him in for Eve if I can keep from stumbling over the sheriff's deputies."

"Hell, no. I spent a small fortune on those operations on your hands. You're not even supposed to open a book, much less try guerrilla warfare."

"I'm bored. My hands are fine." He amended, "Well, not fine, but functional. An ingenious man like me can compensate."

"An ingenious man like you could end up with gangrene. Stay there, keep watching, and stay out of those woods."

"**YOU THINK IT'S BONNIE'S** killer?" Jane gazed down into the coffee in her cup. "You told me once that you had dozens of crank calls confessing to Bonnie's killing right after she disappeared. Could this be another one?"

"Yes." Eve leaned wearily back in her chair. "The investigators Montalvo hired tapped a lot of prison inmates, who gave them information about friends or acquaintances who had actually told them they had killed Bonnie. They came up with three possible suspects. Maybe they were like the creeps who called me at the time. They could have wanted some sick glory among their peers."

"But you think it's possible?"

She nodded jerkily. "He called her a burning arrow in the darkness. Bonnie was— He sounded like he knew her."

"Or a clever sadist who wanted to make sure he'd hurt you."

"Yes, he definitely wanted to do that." She lifted her cup to her lips. "He didn't like Joe setting the police on him, and I was the nearest target." She thought about it. "No, it was more than that. He sounded . . . exhilarated."

"What do you know about Kistle?"

"Not as much as I'd like. The report Montalvo gave me was pretty scanty. There were three possible suspects his investigators turned up. Kistle was one of them. They traced Kistle from the time he was running drugs in Atlanta at the time of Bonnie's death to last year when he was living in Detroit. There were big gaps in the report. He must have moved around a lot and been smart enough to be able to change identities and obtain false documents whenever he liked. He just disappeared from view for long periods. We don't know where in the country he was living. Though he mentioned Colorado to me on the telephone."

I impersonated a sheriff once. It was in Fort Collins, Colorado. Children are taught to trust policemen.

The memory brought back the same shock and sickness as when she'd first heard it. She wearily shook her head. "I need to know more. He used the name Kistle again when he showed up in Detroit

last year. A few months later he left Detroit
and there was no word until now."

"No prior arrests? No school records?"

"Nothing."

"Then Kistle can't be his real name."

Eve nodded. "We were trying to check
his background, but we weren't getting
very far. And we wanted to know where
the bastard was *now*. Evidently Joe found
him." Her lips tightened. "And didn't tell me."

"It was a wrong move," Jane said. "But
he only wanted what was best for you. He
didn't want you to go through all that pain
if Kistle wasn't the right man."

"I know that. It doesn't help. Bonnie is
my daughter. He should have shared
the—" She broke off as the phone rang.
She jumped up to answer it. "It's Deputy
Dodsworth," she told Jane as she picked
up the handset. "Eve Duncan. Please. Tell
me you got Kistle, Deputy."

"Not yet." His voice was grim. "I called
the highway patrol and they set up roadblocks, but he drove into Clayborne Forest and abandoned his car. We're
searching for him now. We're combing the
entire area. We'll find him."

"And Sheriff Jedroth?"

"Dead. I jumped in the patrol car myself and drove over to Kistle's place where Jim was doing surveillance. The bastard stabbed him in the back. I don't know how the hell he did it. Jim was sharp, real sharp. He would have been—" The deputy cleared his throat. "He was a good man."

Eve said gently, "I'm sure he was. I'm sorry, Deputy."

"Yeah, me too. We grew up together." He drew a deep breath before he said, "I have questions to ask you. This telephone number is the same one the sheriff was using for Detective Joe Quinn. I want to speak to him."

"You'll be doing that in person in a few hours. He's on his way there. You can meet him at the airport. There can't be that many flights into Bloomburg."

"And you are Eve Duncan?"

"Yes, I told you that before. I live with Joe Quinn."

"And why should Kistle have—"

"Look, Joe must have told you or your sheriff enough about why we're after Kistle to satisfy you. I'm sorry, but I don't want to talk about it right now. If you need to know anything else, ask Joe. Good-bye, Deputy." She hung up and turned back to Jane. "He got away. They still think they may be able to get him. He's running around in the woods somewhere." She sank back into her chair. "And Sheriff Jedroth was murdered, stabbed in the back while he was doing surveillance on Kistle."

"You're not surprised, are you? It wasn't likely that he'd have picked up the sheriff's cell phone in the lost and found."

"No, I'm not surprised." Eve lifted her cup to her lips. "Kistle was incredibly ugly. If you could have heard—" She broke off. She couldn't talk about it. Not now. She set her cup down and pushed back her chair. "I'm going outside for a walk."

"I'll go with you."

"No, I'll take my cell in case Joe calls me, but I need you to answer the house phone and call me if you hear anything about Kistle."

"And you want to be alone."

She nodded jerkily. "No offense. I'm grateful you were here. I just need—"

"For God's sake, you don't have to explain yourself to me. After all these years I'd think you'd know that. Get out of here.

I'll hold down the fort." She nudged Toby with her foot. "Go with her, you lazy lug. Being with Toby is like being alone and yet he's good company."

"If you can get him moving," Eve said as she headed for the door. "I won't be long, Jane."

"I know."

Toby got to his feet, yawned, and trotted after Eve.

Eve took a deep breath of the sharp, clear air as she went out on the porch. That was better. She had needed something to brace her. She had needed to be alone. She didn't want to worry Jane any more than she had already. She was no longer shaking, but the muscles of her stomach were locked and tense and she felt a terrible sense of foreboding. It was stupid. If Kistle had killed Bonnie, there was nothing worse that he could do to her. Taunts were painful, but they paled in the reality of her little girl's death.

She went down the steps and started down the lake path.

A beautiful child.

Like a burning arrow.

Bonnie.

She stopped to look out over the glittering surface of the lake. She had spent so many years here since she had come to live with Joe. So peaceful and lovely. It had never failed to bring her a sense of serenity and inner strength. How Bonnie would have loved to be able to play and run beside this lake. She had missed so many things.

"*NOT SO MANY,* Mama."

Eve stopped on the path as she saw Bonnie sitting cross-legged on the ground beneath the oak tree to the right of the path. She was wearing her Bugs Bunny T-shirt and the moonlight was tangled in her curly red hair.

"Of course you did," Eve said. "What do you know? You were only seven when you were taken from me."

"And can you be sure that what I've got now isn't better than those years you're so sorry I missed?"

"Well, if you have it so good now, why are you flitting around haunting me? You must like it here."

Bonnie's smile illuminated her face. "No, I just like being with you, Mama."

Eve felt an aching melting deep within her. "Oh, and I like being with you, baby."

Bonnie suddenly chuckled. "You said I was haunting you. Ghosts haunt. Are you finally admitting that I'm a grade-A, genuine ghost?"

"Not necessarily. I'm sure hallucinations can haunt. Figments of the imagination are—" She shook her head. "I don't want to argue about it now. You're here and that's all I care about."

"You let him hurt you. You shouldn't have done that. Mama. He . . . likes it."

"Is he the one, baby?"

"I don't know. I don't let myself think of that night. I've told you that before, Mama."

"He wants me to believe he did."

"Truth or lie. He knows it hurts you. He's going to keep on trying to hurt you. Stay away from him." She frowned. "And stay away from the woman too. She can hurt you more than anyone."

"What woman?"

"I don't . . . know. The box. The woman with the box." She shook her head. "Just stay here where you're safe."

"I can't do that. I have to find Kistle

and make him tell me where you are. I have to bring you home."

"I'm home where I am now. You're the one who is lost. That's why I come. I can't let you stay lost. It hurts me when you hurt."

"Is that why you came tonight?"

"Maybe. But it's been a while since I was with you. I was missing you."

"And I always miss you, Bonnie."

"Yes, but you have Joe and Jane. You love them too." She looked back at the lights of the cottage. "Jane is waiting for you to come back. She's worried about you. She wanted to come with you, but she decided to give you your space." She paused. "She knows about me, doesn't she, Mama?"

"Yes. It was accidental. I didn't even know she knew."

"But you've still not told Joe?"

"I will someday. He's a realist. It would be . . . difficult."

Bonnie smiled. "You're being defensive."

"And you're being pushy. I'll tell him when the time is right."

"Well, this isn't the right time. He'll be

getting off that plane in Bloomburg soon and he's not even going to be able to take a breath before he's pulled down into the quicksand." She lifted her head. "Jane's answering the phone. You'd better go back to the cottage."

Eve's gaze followed hers to the cottage. "Quicksand. What do you mean, quick—"

BONNIE WAS GONE.

Eve didn't need to look back at the oak tree to know that that small, beloved figure would no longer be there. She felt the familiar rush of sadness that seemed to fill the world. Yet with the sadness she could feel a sort of serenity and healing that was always present after Bonnie came to her. From the time a year after Bonnie's death when Eve had first begun to dream, or fantasize, or whatever term she could find to use for seeing Bonnie, it had been the same. No matter what she called the experience, it had saved Eve's sanity and perhaps her life. She had been spiraling downward into deep depression and had not been able to fight her way out. Then

Bonnie had been there and life had begun to be bearable.

"Good-bye, baby," she whispered. "Come back soon."

Even if it meant dire warnings about a madman and a lethal woman with a box. She didn't care if Bonnie's visits were the outpouring of the mental ramblings of her own mind. She would cling with all her strength to these moments, since she could no longer cling to Bonnie.

She turned and started back up the path. "Come on, Toby." She whistled for the retriever. "Let's go back and see if Jane's heard anything."

JANE HANDED HER A POST-IT note when she walked into the cottage. "Luis Montalvo."

Eve stiffened. "What?"

"I said that he could call you on your cell phone, but he said after consideration it was better that he leave you a message. He wants to talk to you." She paused. "But only if you want to talk to him. He said to tell you he's going to be boarding a plane for Bloomburg in the next thirty minutes."

"Bloomburg," Eve repeated. "Dammit, of course I want to talk to him. He leaves a message like that and he wouldn't expect me to do anything else. Crafty bastard."

"He sounded very . . . sincere."

"Oh, Montalvo is very sincere." She started to dial the number. "When it suits him. You just have to be careful what he's sincere about. He never gives up. It can be anything from attacking a drug king's stronghold to stealing a skull from a grave." His phone was ringing. Answer me. Don't you dare leave me hanging. He finally picked up. "What the hell do you know about Bloomburg, Montalvo?"

"Hello to you too, Eve," Montalvo said quietly. "I'm glad you called."

"You knew I would."

"Only if you were aware of what was going on in Bloomburg. There was a possibility that Quinn might not have told you that he'd located Kistle. He's very protective of you." He paused. "But he did tell you?"

She ignored the question. "The deputy said that they would be catching Kistle soon. Why are you going?"

"Why is Quinn going? He is on his way, isn't he?"

"Yes. But how do you know he isn't there already?"

"Miguel would have told me."

"Miguel's in Bloomburg? Is he all right? How are his hands?"

"Not good. He's going to have to have at least one more operation. But I couldn't keep him from going when we found out Kistle had surfaced. He likes you, Eve."

And she liked Miguel. The young man was a law unto himself and she'd had problems with his complete devotion to Montalvo, but no one could help liking him. "You should have told him to stay in that hospital."

"Tell him yourself . . . when you get to Bloomburg." He paused. "You are going, aren't you?"

"Yes. But you didn't answer me. Why are you going when the sheriff's department is sure he's going to be caught anytime now?"

"My life hasn't given me much faith in anyone but myself. And I've been unearthing some additional information lately about Kistle that's made me uneasy."

Her hand tightened on the phone. "What information?"

"I have to board my plane. We'll get together in Bloomburg."

"I don't want to get together with you. I want to know now."

"But Quinn probably uncovered the same facts and shared them with you." He added, "Just as he told you about Bloomburg."

"Damn you."

"I'll see you soon. I did want to tell you I'm calling Venable with the CIA and asking him to get the FBI on site in Bloomburg. Kistle has been crossing state lines for years and even a suspicion that he's a child murderer should give them an excuse to intervene."

"It won't be easy. There's no evidence yet."

"I can bargain with Venable. I'm a storehouse of information about the underbelly of crime in Colombia. And he owes you, Eve. That should be enough for him to be very persuasive with the FBI."

"Why are you so determined to get the FBI involved?"

"I want all the help I can get. The best, most experienced help."

"You really don't believe the sheriff's men are going to get Kistle, do you?"

"I hope they do. I have to go now. I'll see you in Bloomburg." He paused and then said softly, "I would have told you, Eve. It's your right. I would have taken you with me. I'd take you with me now if you'd come."

"Good-bye, Montalvo." She hung up.

It had been months since she'd seen Montalvo and yet it seemed like only yesterday. Their time together in Colombia had been fraught with danger that had bred a closeness that had dominated her life for that short period. The intimacy that had grown between them while she was working on his wife's skull had been too strong, too sensual, and she'd shut him out of her life.

"My God." Jane's gaze was on her face. "No wonder Joe doesn't like Montalvo."

Eve was jerked back to the present. She should have been more guarded. She hadn't wanted Jane to be aware of the fallout from that reconstruction she had done for Montalvo. "That's putting it mildly."

"Did you have an affair with him?"

Eve felt a ripple of shock. She wanted to

back away, change the subject, but she wasn't going to lie to Jane. "No, it wasn't like that."

"It might have been better if it had been. He disturbs the hell out of you."

She couldn't deny that either. "I love Joe. Joe is smart and sexy and we . . . mesh. We complete each other. I know how lucky I am. He's everything I want." She moistened her lips. "Montalvo is just . . ." How could she explain it to Jane when she had trouble understanding it herself? "He *knows* me. Maybe it's because he went through the same pain with his wife that I did with Bonnie. Maybe it's just that there are some people who are instinctively in tune. He said we were mirror images of each other."

"And do you believe it?"

"Sometimes. We shared pain and obsession. No one can actually understand how that feels unless they've been there."

"Joe said Montalvo plays you like a song."

"He tries. And he's good at it." She stared Jane in the eye. "That's why I told him that I didn't want his help finding Bonnie's killer. We made a deal when I did his wife's reconstruction, but now that he's given us a lead, Joe and I can find Kistle by ourselves. I value the life I have with Joe and I won't have it turned upside down."

"You sound determined."

"I couldn't be more determined. As long as Joe wants me, I'll never leave him."

"He'll always want you."

"I hope so. He's put up with a lot from me over the years. Sometimes I think he's getting a little tired."

"People don't get tired of you, Eve. Joe wouldn't. I wouldn't. Now stop talking nonsense." Jane reached out and touched Eve's cheek. "But if I can help you work it out, let me know."

"There's nothing to work out. That's not what this is about. It's about Kistle . . . and Bonnie." She turned toward her bedroom. "I'm going to pack. Will you call and make me a reservation to Bloomburg?"

"Two reservations," Jane corrected. "I'm going with you."

"You said you had to start the work for your next show."

"I can paint anywhere. Do you really believe I'd let you go after that son of a bitch without having me in your corner?"

She smiled. "I guess not. Whatever was

I thinking? By all means, come along. It seems as if my entire world is flocking to Bloomburg."

"Right, I'll pack a bag. We can drop Toby off at my friend Patty's, so she can take care of him while we're gone."

"Let's hope that won't be long." She closed the bedroom door. It would be good to have Jane with her. They were so much alike in spirit and background that they might well have been mother and daughter. Jane had appeared years after she had lost Bonnie, and her presence had warmed and enriched her. Jane always insisted that she wasn't hurt that Bonnie dominated Eve's life. She said that friendship was enough. Maybe it was, when the friendship was this close. Daughter or friend, Eve had been lucky to have Jane come into her life.

And to have Joe come into her life and choose to stay.

She reached for her phone and dialed Joe again.

Still no answer. The phone was still turned off. Surely the plane must have landed by now.

He's not even going to be able to take

a breath before he's pulled down into the quicksand.

She felt a chill go through her as she remembered Bonnie's words.

She moved over to the closet and pulled out her duffel. Pack and then call Joe again. Dammit, answer me this time, Joe.

Quicksand . . .

QUICKSAND.

Kistle could feel his muscles strain as he pulled himself hand over hand through the trees twenty feet above the bog. Most quicksand wasn't as dangerous as most people thought, but it could slow you down.

And it made an excellent trap.

He'd left a few scraps of his shirt material on the branches of the path leading here as bait. Then he'd covered the first few yards of the bog with branches. Everything was working out splendidly. The sheriff's men had split up and were scouring the entire forest and he hadn't had to isolate them individually. Two of the pricks were heading this way now, trotting like cattle to the slaughter.

"Come on," he whispered as he settled

in the crook of a tree and lifted his rifle, checking the silencer and the scope. "Just a little farther. Come and get me."

A minute later a man burst from the shrubbery at a run. The next instant he was followed by a second man. They were three yards from the camouflaged bog.

A few more steps.

He took aim three feet ahead of them.

Into the quicksand!

He didn't wait to watch them flounder helplessly as they sank.

Two shots.

One bullet in the head of the first officer. The other in the throat of the second man . . .

He was already moving toward them as they fell. He grabbed the two men by the shirts and dragged them out of the bog, dripping with mud and sand. They had been nothing, no challenge at all. Just as he'd thought. Cattle to the slaughterhouse.

He could feel the excitement tingling through him as he reached into his pocket and pulled out the messages he'd scrawled on scraps of paper he'd ripped from his notebook.

It was starting.

"DETECTIVE QUINN?"

Joe looked around to see a uniformed officer coming toward him across the terminal. "Yes."

"Deputy Charlie Dodsworth." He shook his head wearily. "No, that's not right. They've made me acting sheriff until the next election. I talked to an Eve Duncan at your phone number and she told me—"

"Eve? You called Eve? I told Sheriff Jedroth to call me on my cell phone. Why the hell—"

"I didn't call her. She called me," the deputy interrupted. "The sheriff is dead and Kistle had his phone and contacted her." He turned toward the exit. "I'll give you a ride into town. I have some questions to ask you."

"Jedroth's dead? How did—"

"Not now." Dodsworth waved his hand to stop the flow of words. "I've got to have my questions answered first. You'll have your turn. I've had one hell of a night. I lost my friend. And we lost that damned child killer in the woods. Now I've got to find a way to catch the bastard. What you know, I have to know." He went ahead of Joe through the door and out into the parking lot.

Joe hesitated and then followed Dodsworth toward the patrol car. It was clear all hell had broken loose since he had talked to Jedroth earlier tonight. Kistle had called Eve. My God, it was the last thing Joe had wanted to happen. He should call her and ask what that—

"Detective?" Dodsworth had opened the passenger door. "I want to get this over with quick. I have to go and see Maggie Jedroth and try to explain why her husband died tonight."

How many times had Joe had to break that news? Whether in a big-city precinct or a sheriff's office in a little town, the life of a cop still sucked sometimes. "Fifteen minutes. Ask your questions. Then I have to ask a few of my own and make a phone call."

"I DON'T KNOW ANYTHING about Kistle's background," Joe said impatiently. "I told you, I traced him by his cell phone he bought in Detroit. If I knew any of his friends or family, I'd be on my way to see them, since you lost the bastard."

"We'll get him back. Why did Kistle call Eve Duncan?"

"My number was the last number on the sheriff's phone."

"But he talked to her. She said he was taunting her, telling her he could never be caught."

"How could I know anything about that? When I call her, I'll ask what he said." And he needed to make that call right now. Find a way to skip over the unessential questions and give the sheriff a quick summary. "Look, the reason that we're after Kistle isn't only that he may be a child killer. He could have killed Eve Duncan's child, Bonnie. That makes it very personal. If he did call to taunt Eve, it may mean that he's the one we're searching for."

"It wasn't hard to figure out that it was personal after we read the report on you. You may be in luck," Dodsworth said. "Because we're not going to let him slip away from us." He parked in front of the sheriff's office. "Now come inside and sign a statement and we'll—"

"No way. I'll do it later. I told you that—"

The deputy's radio blared out. "Charlie. Where are you, Charlie?"

"Dodsworth," he answered. "Have you got him, Pete?"

"No. God, Charlie. It's bad here. You gotta come and—"

"What the hell is going on?"

"Bill Parks and Lenny Brewster. They're dead, Charlie. Shot."

"Kistle?"

"I guess so. You gotta come and see them."

"I'm on my way." Dodsworth was backing out of the parking space. "I should be there in ten minutes."

"Where are we going?" Joe asked.

"Clayborne Forest." Dodsworth pressed the accelerator and put on the siren. "That was Pete Shaw, a deputy, on the radio. Parks and Brewster were in the posse tracking down Kistle."

THE PATROL CAR WAS MET at the edge of the forest by a lanky young deputy whose face was pale enough to show the freckles scattered on his thin cheeks. "They're dead, Charlie. I was talking to them ten minutes before we found them. We split up, but there were two of them and—"

"Take it easy, Pete." Dodsworth got out of the car. "You did the right thing. Where are they?"

"Still at the bog. I called the medical examiner and told him to come take a look."

"Take me there." He glanced at Joe. "Coming?"

Joe was already out of the car and shedding his jacket. "You bet I am." He threw the jacket on the hood of the car. "Let's get out there."

"Pete Shaw, Joe Quinn," Dodsworth said. "He's Atlanta PD, Pete."

But the young deputy was already yards away in the brush ahead of them.

The forest itself was pitch-black, but Joe could see beams of flashlights dotting the darkness as he moved after Dodsworth. "How big is this forest?"

"Over a thousand acres."

"And how many men do you have out here?"

"Twenty, maybe twenty-five. We had a

lot of volunteers. Everyone liked Jim Jed-roth."

Eager young men like this Pete Shaw who wanted to catch the monster and had no idea what they were up against, Joe thought. "The victims were shot in the bog?"

"We think so." Pete had stopped to wait for them. "But we found them on the bank. It's ugly, Charlie." He pulled aside a bush to reveal an area lit by lanterns and teeming with men, some in uniform and some in camouflage hunting garb. "I don't understand why— See for yourself."

"God," Dodsworth murmured. "What did he do to them?"

The two dead men were propped up against a tree. Their eyes were wide open and staring into nothingness.

"Bill was shot in the head. Lenny has a bullet wound in his throat," Pete said. "But after he killed them he set them up like that and pounded short wooden stakes through their hearts. It looked like he was using them to fasten those messages on their chests." He swallowed hard. "Son of a bitch."

Joe could see the scraps of notebook

paper, but they were stained with blood and he was too far away to read what they said. He had to get closer. He shouldn't compromise the crime scene, but it had already been trampled by the ten or twelve searchers at the scene. He'd just be as careful as he could.

He moved toward the victims. "Do the notes both say the same thing?"

"Yeah." Pete followed them. "Same thing."

Joe squatted down a few feet from the dead men. "Give me your flashlight."

He shone the beam on one of the bloodstained notes. Some of the ink had smeared and run, but he could still decipher the letters. It appeared to be three words. The first one started with an F . . .

He stiffened.

For you, Eve.

THREE

EVE FINALLY RECEIVED A CALL back from Joe when she was at the gate in Atlanta ready to board her flight. Her first reaction was profound relief, the second was anger. "Why the hell didn't you tell me you'd located Kistle?"

"Jane must have told you my reasons by now. Nothing I can say is going to make you like it any better. I did what I thought was best for you."

"Stop sheltering me, Joe. How many times have I told you that I won't have it where Bonnie is concerned?"

"I can't do anything else," he said simply. "I won't watch you be hurt unnecessarily."

She felt melting warmth mixed with frustration. "Joe, it was wrong. I have to—" She broke off. Arguing would get them nowhere. "Have they caught Kistle yet?"

"No, the bastard has to be pretty woods-savvy. He's been running the deputies ragged."

"Maybe he's not in the woods at all. Couldn't he have made his way to another road or major highway?"

"Maybe. They have guards patrolling around the perimeter of the forest, but he might be able to avoid them if he wanted to do it."

There was a note in Joe's voice that Eve recognized. "But you don't think he's left the woods, do you?"

"No. I think he may be enjoying himself too much."

"Enjoying? With those deputies on his heels?"

"Dodsworth told me Kistle had called you. What was your take on him?"

She was like a burning arrow lighting the darkness.

"Evil." She tried to get past that pain to be more analytical. "He seemed exhilarated, almost happy. He didn't like that you'd set Jedroth on him, but he was supremely sure of himself. He said he was glad I'd come back into his life."

"Did he confess to killing Bonnie?"

"No, not in so many words. But he knew what she wore on the day she disappeared. He spoke of her with a sort of horrible . . . intimacy. And he said he'd killed other little girls after Bonnie." They were calling her flight. "I'll be in Bloomburg in four hours. Jane and I are getting on the plane now."

"No," Joe said sharply. "Dammit, stay where you are."

"No way." She stood up. "Four hours, Joe. Good-bye." She hung up and turned off her phone.

"They still haven't caught Kistle?" Jane asked as she picked up her carry-on.

Eve shook her head. "But Joe doesn't think he's left that forest." She frowned. "And there was something about the way Joe . . . He's keeping something from me." She headed for the jetway. "But you can bet I'm going to find out what it is."

"SHE'S COMING?" DODSWORTH asked as Joe hung up the phone. "Good. I have a few questions to ask her. What the hell kind of relationship does she have with that sicko, that he'd kill two good men to please her?"

"The relationship of a victim," Joe said. "It wasn't to please her, it was to hurt her. Anyone who knows anything about Eve knows that she spends her life trying to find a way to catch murderers and save lives. Kistle killed those men to show her that what she was doing was futile and just by existing she was causing deaths." Lord, he was going to hate telling Eve about those notes. In spite of the years of dealing with murdered children in her work, she had never developed callousness. Eve was strong, but her sensitivity was both her strength and her weakness. He treasured that fragility as much as he did her honesty and her intelligence.

"You didn't tell her about what happened at the quicksand."

"I will." He stared him in the eye. "And if you try to tell her before I get the chance, I won't be pleased, Dodsworth."

"Are you threatening me?"

"Take it how you will. Just don't upset Eve any more than she has to be upset." He got out of the patrol car. "What's the best hotel you have in this town?"

"We've got a pretty nice place on Spruce Avenue, the Brown Hotel."

"I'm making reservations for Eve and my adopted daughter, Jane MacGuire. I want twenty-four-hour protection for them."

"Is that necessary? You told Jim that Kistle is supposed to be a child killer."

"He killed two of your deputies in that bog and stabbed your sheriff to death earlier. Kistle doesn't seem to be narrowing his field of operation at the moment. I want Eve—" His cell phone rang and he picked up. "Quinn."

"Les Braun. What the devil are you doing up there, Joe?"

He felt a ripple of surprise. Les Braun was with the Atlanta field office of the FBI and he'd worked with him several times in the past, but he hadn't been in contact with him lately. "What do you think I'm doing?"

"Causing us a lot of trouble. We're spread pretty thin as it is. We didn't need to be pulled into this case."

"I didn't pull you in."

"No, you had Venable and his CIA buddies talking sweet and making deals with the director. Okay, you've got what you want. Cassidy from the St. Louis field office is on his way to Bloomburg now. The director is leaving it up to Cassidy to decide if we're needed on the case. I've given him your number and he'll contact you as soon as he gets in. My office is supposed to offer you any assistance if Cassidy decides that we're needed. Who's the local police contact?"

"Charles Dodsworth. Acting sheriff."

"I'll call and pave the way for Cassidy. Small-town cops don't like interference from us."

"Neither do big-town cops."

"Come on, Joe. Years ago you were an agent too."

"A lifetime ago. Cooperation is great, interference sucks."

"Either way, you've got us for the time being. And Cassidy isn't going to like it any more than you do. They jerked him off a case he'd been building for the last six months. See you." He hung up.

Joe turned to Dodsworth. "You're going

to be contacted by an Agent Cassidy, FBI. He's going to assess the situation here."

Dodsworth frowned. "You called the FBI?"

"Not me." And Joe didn't know how the hell Venable had known about Kistle, much less decided to pressure the FBI. "But they're on the case anyway."

Dodsworth slowly nodded. "I'm glad."

Joe's brows lifted. "You are?"

"Did you think I'd tell them to go to hell? Dammit, I'm only a deputy in spite of what they're calling me. I'm feeling way out of my depth. I was in charge when two men died tonight. They were my responsibility. I want Kistle caught before he kills anyone else. The FBI's got all kinds of gadgets and databases that can help us, right?"

"Right." He paused. "But you might remember that all the manpower and techno wizardry didn't help at all when everyone was tracking down Eric Rudolph in North Carolina. He lasted two years and they had an army of agents after him. If a man is good in the woods, then the game often reverts to the basic laws of nature. He could last for months."

"How do you know?"

"I was a Navy SEAL. I've survived in worse environments than that forest with men after me." He changed the subject. "Go and have that talk with your sheriff's widow and then go get some sleep. You're going to need it once Cassidy and his agents appear on the scene."

"You don't like them coming?"

"I don't know. They may help. They may get in the way." Joe turned away and started dialing his phone. "But I don't like the idea of Venable sticking his oar in without my asking. I need to talk to him."

DAYLIGHT.

Darkness was safer. Darkness was his own, Kistle thought.

But should he go and kill to prove he could do it in broad daylight? It would take those country bumpkins off guard and maybe frighten them.

No, he'd already sent a chill through them with those kills at the bog. He could afford to rest and plan his next move.

Have they told you what I did for you, Eve?

It's not every woman who has the power of life or death.

Well, not life. But death, definitely death.

Are you coming? Of course, you are.

I'll have to rest now and then decide what to do to welcome you.

EVE SAW JOE AS SOON AS she got off the plane.

He kissed her quick and hard, and then gave Jane a hug. "Neither one of you should be here. Eve's obsessed, Jane, but you don't have that excuse." He grabbed their bags and headed for the exit. "What do you think you're going to do? Trek out into those woods and hunt the bastard down?"

"It's a thought," Jane murmured.

"A lousy thought," Joe said curtly. "If Kistle doesn't shoot you, then one of those trigger-happy deputies will do it. They're nervous as hell."

"I'm not planning on going hunting," Eve said. "I just want to be close to wait until Kistle is caught." Something he had said caught her attention. "Why are the deputies so nervous?"

"Because they're not used to dealing with creeps like Kistle." He opened the door of the rental SUV and threw in their bags. "They were all full of moral indignation and piss and vinegar and thought they'd run him down in a few hours. Now they're probably scared and trying to pretend they're not."

"It's only been one day," Jane said. "And Kistle is the one on the run. No one should be scared yet." Her gaze narrowed on Joe's face. "Isn't that true?"

"Ask them." Joe started the SUV and backed out of the parking space. "I'm sure they think they have reason."

"And so do you," Eve said. "What's been happening here, Joe?"

"I've made reservations for you at the Brown Hotel," Joe said. "Its about four blocks from here. Dodsworth recommended it."

"Joe."

"And the FBI should be in town later today to assist. That forest should be crawling with agents by tonight."

"And you're not happy?"

"No." His lips twisted. "That local posse is enough to worry about. The FBI can be a hell of a lot more efficient and lethal. I don't want Kistle dead before he tells you what you want to know. I'll be damned if Bonnie is going to haunt us for the rest of our lives."

Eve stared at him in shock at the harshness of his words. "She doesn't have to haunt you, Joe. It's my problem."

"No, it isn't." He pulled into the parking space in front of the hotel. "What you feel, I feel. That's the way it is." He got out, opened the car doors, and handed them their luggage. "I'll call you later. I'm going back to Clayborne Forest." He glanced at Jane. "Take care of her."

Jane nodded. "Always." She glanced from Eve to Joe and then started toward the entrance. "I'll check us in, Eve. Ask the desk clerk for the room number."

"She's being diplomatic. She thinks we're going to argue." Joe started to turn away. "I'll call you later."

"Don't you drive off," Eve said. "You didn't answer me. There's something going on that you're not telling me." She braced herself before adding, "And there's something I should tell you. Montalvo nudged Venable into getting the FBI involved. He said that he wanted the best and most experienced men after Kistle."

Joe turned to look at her. "Montalvo called you and told you that?"

"Yes."

"And did you tell him it was none of his business?"

"No, I don't care who is involved if it means we can catch Kistle." She met his gaze. "I did say I didn't want to meet with Montalvo."

"But he wouldn't listen, would he? Is he on his way here?"

"He might already be here by now."

Joe nodded. "Why not? It's the perfect opportunity for him to bond with you. When Venable told me that Montalvo had made a deal with him, it was clear as glass."

She stiffened. "You already knew that Montalvo was responsible for the FBI being here? Why didn't you tell me? Was this some kind of test?"

"No."

"I think it was."

He shrugged. "Maybe I was curious."

"For God's sake, after all these years don't you know I wouldn't lie to you even by omission?"

"Yes, you would. Maybe not about another man, but you'd do it for Bonnie."

It was the second time he'd mentioned Bonnie with that same bitterness. "Not if I felt you were on my side, Joe."

"I'm always on your side," he said roughly. "And that sometimes means I have to be against Bonnie. Because your damn obsession is going to kill you someday." He opened the car door. "And that day could be today or tomorrow or next week. Kistle is fixating on you like a mad dog. It's only a matter of time before you end up with a stake through your heart too. I won't stand by and wait for it to happen."

"Stake? What are you talking about?"

"Kistle killed two deputies last night. He led them to a bog and when they were struggling in the quicksand, he shot them. Then he left notes on stakes he stabbed into their hearts."

"Quicksand," she whispered.

"Aren't you interested in what he wrote on those notes? Just three words." He paused. "*For you, Eve.*"

The words tore through her like a knife thrust. "No!"

"He wanted to hurt you. It does hurt you, doesn't it?"

"Of course it does," she said unevenly. "It makes me feel . . . responsible."

"I knew you'd feel like that." He added bitterly, "That's why I didn't want Dodsworth to tell you. I wanted it to be done gently by someone who loved you. I do love you, but I can't be gentle right now." He started the SUV. "So I end up by hurting you too. Kistle would be proud of me."

She watched him back out of the parking space, filled with a bewildering mixture of horror, sadness, anger . . . and fear.

Quicksand.

Those two men had died in that bog and Joe was on his way to Clayborne Forest now. She wanted to call him and tell him to come back.

It would be no use. She had never seen Joe this driven and bitter. She could almost feel the explosive emotional energy that was tearing through him.

And she was in little better shape. The shock of Joe's revelation and the raw harshness of his words had shaken her. Get over it. She was here in Bloomburg for a purpose and that purpose would be accomplished. She had to believe that Joe would be able to take care of himself.

Yeah, since she could do nothing about it anyway, she thought dryly. Joe wasn't about to do anything she asked him to do. He had his own agenda and believed she was some kind of fluttering, suicidal bird flying to destruction. He might understand that Kistle could be the one to bring her peace and closure, but he didn't really accept it.

"It's good to see you, Eve. Though I wish it was under kinder circumstances."

She whirled to see Miguel Vicente coming out of the hotel. The last time she had seen him he had been bedridden from the torture he'd received at the hands of the drug dealer who had also almost taken Joe's life during those nightmare weeks in the jungle. Though it was impossible to ever say Miguel was subdued, he'd definitely been under the weather. Now he looked like the young man she had first seen at that armed compound in Colombia. Tall, dark, handsome, and filled with a wicked sense of understated humor that could be both endearing and exasperating. "Hello, Miguel. Montalvo told me you were here." She frowned as she looked at his bandaged hands. "And I told him to send you back to the hospital."

"If I'm careful, all is well." He smiled. "For instance, I will not offer to carry your bags into this hotel. Though it offends my sense of gallantry, I will let you take them in yourself." He tilted his head. "Of course, I could go inside and prod the doorman, who should be out here to do his duty." He beamed. "Yes, that would be much less boring. Wait here."

"No," she said firmly. She knew exactly how lethal Miguel could be even with those wounded hands. "I'll do it myself."

"That one box looks very familiar," he said. "Another skull?"

"Yes."

"Anyone I know?"

"No, a child no one knows right now."

His smile faded. "I meant no disrespect. As you know, it's my nature."

"Why are you here, Miguel?"

"One, to make sure you're comfortable. Two, to make sure you stay alive. Montalvo said the latter was more important than the former." His boyish demeanor suddenly dropped as he turned to the bellman leaning against the reception desk and gestured to Eve's cases. "I believe you have a job to do," he said softly. "I'll be very displeased if it isn't done quickly."

The bellman started to smile and then blinked and rushed forward.

"Good." Miguel turned back to Eve. "Now you go up and tell your Jane that I'm here and that I'll be in the hall if either of you need me."

"How did you know I was with Jane? For that matter, how did you know I was at this hotel?"

"I followed you from the airport. I decided that I would not approach you when you were with Quinn. He does not have good feelings for me. I could see that he was not in the best of moods."

"He has reason."

Miguel nodded. "Montalvo is very tense also. Am I invited for dinner and to meet Jane MacGuire? I feel almost as though I know her already and I'm sure she would find me interesting."

"You can join us for dinner. I don't need you to stand guard over me. This isn't Colombia."

"No, I like it better here, but I prefer the

discipline Montalvo enforces. It's much easier to stay alive if everyone knows the rules and the consequences. In your country the rules keep changing and there are always exceptions." He inclined his head. "I will see you at six for dinner. Okay?"

She nodded. "But no lurking in the halls."

He smiled cheerfully. "As you like. I'll go to the forest and see what's happening. I think Montalvo may have only told me to guard you to keep me away from the bog. He keeps talking about gangrene."

She sighed. Manipulation? Probably. But it was working, dammit. "Okay, Miguel." She headed for the desk. "Lurk to your heart's content."

"You haven't asked where Montalvo is," he said behind her.

"No, I haven't." She glanced over her shoulder. "And you're invited to dinner. Montalvo is not."

"I WAS WONDERING IF I should come down and run interference," Jane said when Eve walked into the room. "My tactfulness can only last so long. You know I tend to dive in and try to straighten out a tangle when I see it."

"It's not a tangle." What was she saying? Of course it was. "Or maybe it is. Anyway, it's up to me to untangle it."

"Good luck. I've never seen Joe this way," Jane said. "He was almost combustible."

That had been Eve's thought too. She was once more aware of how much alike she and Jane were. "It's a difficult time for him." She was suddenly impatient. "But it's difficult for me too. We have to deal with it. He can't just drive away and let—"

"Shh." Jane shook her head. "Deal with it later. You haven't slept all night and you're on edge. Get some sleep and then we'll have dinner and talk about it." She nodded toward the adjoining door. "That's your bedroom. Take a shower and get at least a couple hours' rest."

"After I set Carrie up."

"I already cleared the desk over there." Jane smiled. "I knew you wouldn't let Carrie stay in that case any longer than you had to. But I think you should cover her when we have room service. It might be a little disconcerting to the waiter."

"Particularly since this entire town is probably edgy about the sheriff's death." She opened Carrie's case and carefully took out the skull and placed it on the desk. It wouldn't be ideal work conditions, but she could manage. She draped the cloth over the reconstruction and headed for the bedroom. "We're going to have dinner with Miguel Vicente at six."

"Vicente?" Jane frowned, processing the name. "Montalvo's friend?"

"Friend, second in command, thorn in his side. It's hard to describe Miguel's relationship with Montalvo. At any rate, he showed up downstairs and informed me he was on guard duty and wanted to meet you."

"Interesting. Does that mean I'm going to meet Montalvo too?"

"No. You probably will eventually, but I'm going to put it off as long as possible. Montalvo is an element I don't need to deal with right now." She shut the door behind her and headed for the bathroom. She didn't want to deal with Miguel either, but refusing his help might bring Montalvo in his place. Besides, though she didn't believe she needed a guard, she'd never refuse protection for Jane. She should have told her to stay in Atlanta but she'd been in no shape to argue. No, face it, she'd wanted Jane's company. No one understood her like Jane, and being with her was a comfort. There was nothing soothing or comfortable about anything else in this situation.

Including Joe.

She should have known Joe would try to keep any knowledge about Kistle to himself. These last months together had partially bridged the gap between them that had been growing even before she had gone to Colombia. But the abyss still remained and his recent move to shut her out wouldn't help.

She couldn't tear herself up worrying about relationships right now. She stepped into the tub and turned on the shower. What was done, was done. She was here and so was Kistle. How many miles was Clayborne Forest from this hotel?

For you, Eve.

She shuddered.

Would those two men have died if Kistle hadn't wanted to send a message to her? Killers were killers and they needed no excuse to murder. Easy to say, but who knew what would trigger a monster like Kistle? He might have gone dormant for months if he hadn't talked to her. She had to stop thinking about it. Kistle had meant to hurt her and she mustn't let him.

For you, Eve . . .

FOUR

CLAYBORNE FOREST WAS STILL teeming with searchers when Joe arrived at the command post the sheriff's department had set up near the road. And the cavalry had arrived, he noticed.

The scowling red-haired man who was talking to that young deputy Pete Shaw was dressed in a dark suit and Joe would bet he was FBI.

The deputy turned to Joe in relief as he approached. "This is Agent Hal Cassidy, Detective Quinn. I've been filling him in, but I've got to call Charlie and give him my report. You talk to him." He hurried away toward his vehicle.

Cassidy shook his head. "My God, if they have nothing but kids like him conducting this investigation, it's no wonder Kistle is using them for target practice." Cassidy turned and shook his hand. "Venable told me about you, Quinn. What the hell is happening here?"

"I'm sure the deputy gave you the bare bones. What else do you want to know?"

"What the FBI is doing here," he said curtly. "We have no proof that we're even needed. It's a cop killing, but they have so many searchers they're tripping over each other. They should be able to handle it. And the deputy mentioned another possible kidnapping and murder, but how can we investigate it when there may not even be a crime? All the deputy could say was that a little boy, Bobby Joe Windlaw, was missing and everyone had thought he was drowned." He stared Joe in the eye. "Until you contacted Jedroth and he began to wonder."

"I didn't say anything about any local killings. I don't know anything about Bobby Joe Windlaw." But he remembered Jedroth had said something about the little boy during that last phone call. "I just told the sheriff I had suspicions and asked him for surveillance. I'd say those suspicions were warranted, since Jedroth ended up dead."

"We haven't been able to track down any records on Kistle yet." Cassidy's gaze shifted toward the trees. "And this kind of case could stretch on indefinitely. We might be beating those bushes for the next year. I've seen it happen. The locals should take care of it."

"Do you expect me to argue? I didn't call you into the case. Go back to St. Louis."

"Easy to say," he said sourly. "I've got work there, damn important work to do. I'll be out of here in a heartbeat if I can persuade the director to stop playing pattycake with Venable."

"You've obviously made up your mind. Just give him your report."

Cassidy's gaze narrowed on Joe's face. "You don't want us here. Why?"

"I don't care whether you're here or not. It won't affect what I do." He walked away from Cassidy toward the bog where the two deputies had been shot. The bodies were gone, but chalk markings indicated where they had been found. The area was now cordoned off. Not that it would do any good after all the trampling that had gone on last night.

He moved closer to the bog and looked up into the trees. The men had been shot after they had entered the quicksand, and judging by the wounds, the bullets had come from the front and angled downward. That meant Kistle had probably been waiting for them in one of those trees. Which one . . . ?

"The big oak on the other side of the bog."

He stiffened but didn't turn around. "Hello, Montalvo."

"What a pleasure to see you looking so strong and well again, Quinn. I was most unhappy when you were ill and a mere shadow of yourself."

Joe turned to face him. Montalvo was dressed in the same type boots, khaki pants, and shirt that had been almost his uniform in Colombia, and he looked very much at home in these woods. "Bullshit. I was in your way and you would have loved it if I'd croaked."

Montalvo chuckled. "Not true. That would have guaranteed that you'd remain a part of my life. Eve would never have forgiven me."

Joe felt a surge of rage tear through him. He had hated those days in Montalvo's compound when he'd been hurt and helpless, and in contrast Montalvo had been everything that was vibrant and powerful. The memory was still a throbbing wound. Keep calm. Calm, hell, he wanted to break the bastard's neck. "You're right." He turned back to the bog. "Eve is completely loyal to the people she loves."

There was a silence behind him. "A wonderful quality. A wonderful woman."

"What are you doing here, Montalvo?"

"Keeping a promise." He moved forward to stand beside Joe. "Is that so hard to believe?"

"Yes."

"I can see how you'd have problems, considering the stakes. But in my way I'm an honorable man. One has to have some code to live by. I always keep my promises and I always repay my debts."

"And you don't have trouble collecting debts owed you," he said through his teeth.

He smiled. "That goes without saying."

"Do I have to ask why you're here?"

"The same reason you are. I want to bring in Kistle." He added softly, "I want to drag the dragon in front of the lady and cut off his head. And then I hope she'll think it worth giving me a prize. Isn't that what you want, Quinn?"

"That's simplistic."

"It's honest. Do I want to ease her pain? Yes. Do I want to give her the solace she gave me when she did the reconstruction on my wife's skull? With all my heart. Do I want to take her to bed and never let her go back to you? Absolutely." He looked out over the bog. "And this may be the way to do all three. So I'd be a fool to miss the opportunity that's offered."

"Why did you ask Venable to bring in the FBI if you wanted to go after Kistle yourself?"

Montalvo turned to him and smiled. "Can't you guess? If I don't catch Kistle, I don't want you to be the one to do it. I'd much rather the FBI pick him up than you be the hero. You're an ex-SEAL and I'm sure you can be very impressive when you're on the hunt. I'd really hate to see you slaying the dragon for Eve."

"You may be disappointed. Cassidy doesn't want to be here and he's looking for excuses to go back to St. Louis."

Montalvo nodded. "I gathered that from talking to him earlier. I'll have to find a way to change his mind."

"Then I assume that we'll get no cooperation from you tracking down Kistle."

"Yes, you will. That would be stupid of me. I'll help you all I can." He pointed to the oak tree across the bog. "For instance, that's the tree that Kistle used. It's the only one that would have given him the right angle."

"He was being chased and he had to take time to spread those branches over the quicksand. He would have had to run an extra quarter of a mile to go around the bog to get to that tree."

"He didn't run." Montalvo pointed to the branches of the three trees that overhung the bog. "He used the branches. He went hand over hand over the bog. It would have taken him practically no time to swing over the bog and settle himself in that oak tree."

"How can you be sure?"

"I'm not. But I saw two fresh scuff marks in the bark of that maple on this side of the bog. That has to be the one he used to climb and access the others. It makes sense."

Yes, it made sense, Joe thought. It shouldn't have surprised him that Montalvo would be able to work out the scenario. He had been a colonel in the rebel army before he had become an arms dealer and he had lived in the jungle for years.

"He would have to be extraordinarily strong and agile."

"Not so extraordinary. I could do it." Montalvo's gaze shifted back to him. "You could do it."

"We've had training and experience."

"So has Kistle." Montalvo smiled. "He spent six months surviving in the jungles of Nicaragua."

Joe stiffened. "How the hell do you know that?"

"Do you think I've been twiddling my thumbs since I left Colombia? I had to stay with Miguel during his surgery, but I've had investigators working nonstop on digging for information. I don't have your police contacts, but money is very persuasive."

"What else did you find out?"

"Not enough. Kistle has been brilliant about covering his tracks. But some of it may give us a clearer picture of him."

"Us?" His lips twisted. "Don't tell me you're going to share?"

"Of course. Eve wouldn't understand me doing anything else."

Damn, the bastard was clever, Joe thought bitterly. And he had studied Eve enough to know exactly how she would react. "And when are we going to be privy to this information?"

"That's up to you. Whenever you and Eve decide to set up a meeting with me. I'm entirely at your disposal."

"I could probably find out the same information if I worked at it."

"I'm certain you could. If you took the time." He glanced at Cassidy, who was talking to the deputies. "Perhaps he could help you. Oh, that's right; you'd prefer the FBI to do a quick exit."

"I didn't say that."

"No, but you want to catch Kistle and

wring the truth out of him. It could get very messy and the FBI could interfere."

"So could the sheriff's department."

"You'd have no trouble with them." He turned away. "Miguel is at the hotel guarding Eve. When you want to see me, ask Miguel to contact me."

"Don't hold your breath. Where are you going?"

"I'm going to join Cassidy and tell him we should go check out that tree. Who knows? We may find something interesting."

Joe doubted it. Kistle's moves so far had been smart and careful. His gaze returned to the overhanging branches of the trees. Yes, he could almost see Kistle moving across that bog. Joe had crossed a narrow river that way when he was on a mission in Libya. Hand over hand, hands gripping, moving, gripping again, muscles straining. His heart had beat fast, hard, but not with fear. Joy, fierce exhilaration in the celebration of his own strength and the conquering of the river below him. He could feel that same flow of heady exuberance now. He had a sudden urge to climb that tree and follow the—

"It brings it all back, doesn't it?" Montalvo said softly. Joe turned to see him standing a few yards away, staring at the branches as Joe himself had been doing. "Life was simpler then. A soldier has so few rules to live by. Kill or be killed. Survive the fires, the rivers, the bullets. Live for the moment and enjoy that moment. Sometimes I miss it."

So did Joe. Every now and then he welcomed the chance to break free and become that man again, to embrace the savagery. "It was a long time ago."

Montalvo nodded and turned away again. "Yes, for me, too. But today it seems like yesterday. Isn't that strange?"

Joe watched him walk away. Hell, for a moment he had actually felt a kind of bond with Montalvo. So they had a common military background and some of the same feelings and attitudes bred from those experiences. As he'd told Montalvo, those experiences had been a long time ago and the war they were now fighting was with each other.

Montalvo stopped again before he reached Cassidy. "I'll be waiting for you to contact me, Quinn." He smiled. "I'm sure that Eve would want to know everything I know. Don't you?"

Bastard.

"I'VE BROUGHT WINE," MIGUEL said when Eve opened the door at six that night. He handed her the bottle. "I'm assured it's much better than what is stored in the cellars of this hotel."

"And who assured you?"

"Mr. BlackJack Calahan. He owns the only liquor store in Bloomburg." He looked past her to Jane as he came into the room. "You are Jane MacGuire. I'm delighted to meet you. I'm sure Eve has told you what a fine, upstanding man I am."

"She told me you're interesting." Jane looked at the label of the wine. "But you have very bad taste in wine."

"That's because I grew up in the jungle and I have no social skills. BlackJack lied to me?"

"BlackJack must have seen you coming." Jane put the wine on the table. "Eve's already ordered dinner. It should be here soon."

"Too bad. I thought I'd have time to impress you with my stories of life in Colombia."

"I'd rather hear if you've had any news from Clayborne Forest," Eve said. "I know about your life in Colombia." She looked down at his bandaged hands. "And what you went through makes me sick."

"It wasn't bad. Montalvo made it challenging. He likes challenges." His gaze went to the reconstruction of Carrie on the desk. "Is she dining with us? Not that I'd object. But it's difficult to divide my attention between the two of you, and that would—"

"Have you heard anything?" Eve interrupted. "I haven't heard from Joe since this morning."

"Montalvo saw him and I assume he was well."

"Montalvo and Joe?" Eve said slowly.

"All is well. Montalvo didn't mention attempted murder or mayhem on either part." He was staring at Jane. "You're very beautiful. That red-brown hair and brown eyes are like Eve's, yet you're different. Same strength, same character in your face, but it's not the same."

"If we look alike it's pure coincidence. We're not related."

"I think you are in spirit. But you're a firecracker set to gloriously explode. She's a wonderful enigma that could take a man a lifetime to solve."

Jane shook her head in disgust. "Talk about saccharine. I believe I'm going to be sick."

Miguel beamed. "And you have a tongue that's as sharp as a machete. I believe I may be in love."

Jane blinked. "What?"

"I can't be in love with Eve. That would cause too many complications. You're much safer. Do you have a man?"

"That's none of your business."

"Do you?"

"I have a relationship."

"Why isn't he with you?"

"Trevor has his own life. I have mine." Jane frowned. "Back off, Miguel."

He sighed. "I'll try to contain myself. But it's difficult. I would really have liked to have been in love with you. It would have been beyond everything."

Eve was shaking her head. "Stop making Jane uncomfortable or I'll kick you out."

"She's not uncomfortable, she's tough like you." Miguel smiled. "And she likes me,

or she would have kicked me out herself."
There was a knock on the door and Miguel
swung around to open it. "That must be dinner. I'll get—" He broke off as he opened
the door. "Good evening, Quinn. Eve was
just asking about you. I told her you'd met
with Montalvo and survived." He stepped
aside to let him in. "I've been looking forward to spending the evening with your two
beautiful—" His smile faded. "You're very
grim. Does that mean that you're not going
to permit me to intrude?"

"I don't care what you do," Joe said. "I'm
going to talk to Eve and I want you to call
Montalvo and tell him to come here tomorrow morning at eight. Then I'll get
back to Clayborne Forest."

"Ask him," Miguel corrected. "I don't tell
Montalvo anything."

"Then ask him." He turned to Eve. "May
I talk to you?"

She nodded. "Hell, yes. That's what I've
wanted you to do since we got here." She
turned and headed toward her bedroom.
"I'll eat later, Jane. You two go ahead."

"We're being thrown together," Miguel
said as the door closed behind them. "It
may be fate, Jane."

"I doubt it," Jane said dryly. "I believe in fate, but this was Joe in tornado mode. Why don't you call Montalvo to set up that meeting for tomorrow? I think that would be more beneficial than all this chitchat."

"You're right. Montalvo will want to know. Will you lock me out if I step outside in the hall to phone him?"

"Privacy?" She raised her brows. "From me? When I'm the love of your life?"

He flinched. "Stung." He opened the door. "I'll make my call and then plead humbly to be permitted back in. You'll, of course, be impressed by my sincerity and—"

"Bullshit." She closed the door firmly behind him.

He was still smiling as he dialed Montalvo.

"Quinn is here. He wants you to come to the hotel at eight tomorrow morning."

"Good. I'll be there. I'm going back to see Cassidy again. I think he's been talking to his superiors about dropping the case."

"Are you going to be able to persuade him to stay?"

"I think I'll have to call Venable and see

what he can do. Cassidy's right, technically the FBI isn't needed here."

"Then why don't you let him go back to St. Louis? We'd have much more fun without them getting in our way." He paused. "You want them here because Quinn does not?"

"Not entirely. The picture is much bigger. Is everything well there?"

"No sign of any trouble. Evidently Quinn also thought Eve should have protection. I was stopped in the hall by a deputy because I was a suspicious character."

"Obviously a man of perception."

"There's no need for me to be here. Why don't I meet you at—"

"No."

"Oh, very well. Enjoy yourself in the woods. I suppose I'll have to go have a fine dinner and be entertained by Jane MacGuire. You didn't tell me what a beautiful woman she is."

"I haven't met her yet."

"She's like Eve. Guarded. But you don't see it until you study her for a while. And she's very protective of Eve. She doesn't make a big deal of it, but it's always there."

"Eve adopted her when she was ten. It

was a number of years after she lost her daughter, Bonnie. Jane was a street kid and probably as tough as you are, Miguel."

"I knew we were meant for each other. But she doesn't see it. She has other fish to fry." He heard the service elevator open. "Our dinner has arrived. I'll think of you in that damp hellhole of a bog while I drink fine wine and eat like a king. Good night, Colonel."

"I DON'T WANT TO TALK TO you, Montalvo," Venable said curtly. "I've just spent fifteen minutes talking to the director of the FBI, who wants to know what the hell his agents are doing in those woods when evidently half the population of Illinois is already stumbling around there. You said they were needed."

Evidently Cassidy hadn't wasted any time, Montalvo thought. "What's it going to take to get them to stay?"

"A valid reason. Proof that the local police can't do the job. Since it's a simple search and pursuit, you're going to get an argument."

"What about bringing up the possibility

of the child killing? The investigation of Bobby Joe Windlaw's disappearance might require sophisticated techniques and expertise."

"When even the sheriff's department won't commit to whether they're certain the boy wasn't accidentally drowned? Sorry, I'd like to help Eve Duncan, but there's no—"

"I'll give you the location of Nortano's weapons cache near Bogotá. You've been looking for it for the last four years."

There was silence at the other end of the connection. "You son of a bitch."

"That little boy was reported missing after Kistle showed up in Bloomburg."

"I know. I know. Bobby Joe Windlaw," Venable said. "No body. Cassidy says that everyone thought he drowned in the river. His shirt and shoes were found on the riverbank."

"Kistle shows up. The little boy disappears. I don't believe in coincidences."

"No body," Venable repeated. "Find the boy's body and then come back to me."

"No, you do it and come back to me. I'm not the one who wants Nortano's weapons."

Venable muttered a curse. "I thought you'd walked away from that life."

"I have, but that doesn't mean I don't know the value of an ace in the hole. Stall Cassidy until you can find a way to locate Bobby Joe's body."

"Cassidy won't help until he's ordered to do it. He'll call it a wild-goose chase."

"Then that leaves it up to you, doesn't it?"

"I'm CIA, dammit. We're talking about jurisdiction. You know we're supposed to operate only outside the country."

"And the CIA never does anything but exactly what it's supposed to do, never steps on anyone's toes? I'm not asking you to join in the hunt for Kistle. But the boy's body has to be found and it has to be done quickly. If the FBI is called into the boy's case, then they'll have to go after Kistle as a possible suspect."

"And give you the FBI presence you want in Clayborne Forest. I'll see what I can do." Venable hung up.

Montalvo put away his phone and got out of the car and moved toward the forest. He didn't doubt Venable would do everything he could. He was smart and experienced and the bribe Montalvo had dangled in front of him would be tempting enough to be nearly irresistible.

In the meantime, he'd do a little scouting of his own and hope those nervous deputies didn't take potshots at him. He could feel his pulse begin to quicken as his gaze fastened on the trees. Kistle was there. He wasn't trying to run. He was waiting. The prey was armed and dangerous and wanted to kill the hunter. It was the game Montalvo liked most. He couldn't blame Miguel for being disappointed that he'd made him stay at the hotel. Miguel understood the game.

And so did Joe Quinn, he thought suddenly.

Quinn had felt the same heady excitement Montalvo was feeling. He had seen it in his expression this afternoon. They were alike in that, if nothing else.

Except for their feelings for Eve. Yet even in that emotion they could not be more different. Quinn was the keeper of the castle, familiar with every battlement, and had the advantage of a passionate desire to keep what was his. Montalvo was the enemy at the gates who had nothing to lose and everything to win.

And Kistle might be the battering ram that would be the deciding weapon.

He melted into the shrubbery and began moving toward the distant trees.

Come on, Kistle. Let's get this battle started.

VENABLE LEANED BACK IN HIS chair after he'd hung up his phone. Dammit, Montalvo was twisting his arm and he wanted to tell him to go take a hike. If there was one thing he hated, it was getting into jurisdictional squabbles with other law enforcement agencies. It made him look ruthless and antagonized the organization he was riding roughshod over. He didn't want to make an enemy of the boys at Quantico. In his world you never knew when you were going to need a favor. Montalvo shouldn't have put him in this position.

Nortano's weapons cache.

God, he wanted to clean that bastard out. Nortano had been a thorn in the Colombian government's side for years and Venable's agents would have a safer path if he could be removed.

And if Montalvo said he'd give him the information, he would do it. He'd never reneged on a bargain in the years he'd known him.

Okay, the decision was made. He had to have Nortano's cache. How to go about getting it without obviously compromising the Company's jurisdiction?

Bobby Joe Windlaw. Find his body. Montalvo was right: if the kid had been murdered, then he had an excuse to draw the FBI back into the picture. If Bobby Joe had drowned, Montalvo would still have to agree that Venable had completed his part of the bargain.

All right, how to find Bobby Joe. Think. Make a plan. Keep it from looking like interference. He'd done this kind of sleight of hand before. It was just more difficult on U.S. soil. He'd call in any favors he could draw on and beg, borrow, and steal if he had to. Now who could do the job in the way he wanted it done?

He suddenly stiffened in shock in his chair as the answer came to him. "Holy shit."

He reached for his phone.

FIVE

"DO YOU MIND IF I USE YOUR bathroom?" Joe asked Eve after the door had closed behind them. "I need to clean up. You don't want me touching anything in this room. I've been out in the woods all day."

"Go ahead." Eve watched him as he moved across the bedroom. "But I thought it might be your bathroom too. You're not staying with me?"

"I've got a room on the next floor." Joe turned on the water faucet. "It will be more convenient."

Eve stood in the bathroom doorway

watching him as he took off his shirt and began to scrub. "Convenient for what?"

"I'll be in and out at all hours of the day and night. I don't want to disturb you."

"What the hell do you mean? I *am* disturbed. Every minute of the day and night I'm going to be disturbed until Kistle is caught. Do you expect me to sleep peacefully just because you've decided to barricade yourself in your own room?"

"I thought it best." He took the towel and began to dry off. "You're upset enough without me—"

"Bullshit," she said. "Get rid of that towel and talk to me. You've been closing me out since you got on that plane to come here. Disturbed? You're the one who's ready to explode. You can't even look at me."

"Oh, I can look at you." He threw the towel away. "But I don't want to talk. Tell me what I want to do, Eve."

His dark hair was tousled and his brown eyes were glittering in his taut face. He was half naked and his shoulders gleamed under the lights. His body was lean and tough and sleek with muscle. She could feel his tenseness, which was like a bolt of electricity. Lord, it was striking at her, stroking her,

readying her. "I'm not sure," she said unevenly. "Sex. But do you want to make love
to me or do you want to rape me?"

"When have I ever raped you?"

"Never. But then I've never seen you in
a mood like this."

"I've never been in a mood like this." He
started toward her. "And I may be rough. I
don't know if I can help myself. So if you
don't want me, tell me now."

He wasn't touching her, but she could
feel the heat move through her. It was a
mindless response. They were so far
apart emotionally that she should try to ignore it and try to talk to him.

She didn't want to talk. She wanted to
be mindless and only move, feel, be close
to him. No matter what else lay between
whenever they came together, the sex was
always fantastic.

He was standing only a few inches
away from her. She could feel the warmth
of his body flowing, surrounding her. Yet
she was still aware of violence held at bay.
He looked into her eyes. "Tell me."

She slowly reached out and touched
his bare chest. His skin felt fever-hot to
her palm.

A shudder went though him. "Eve."

"I do want you." She took a step closer and laid her cheek on his chest. His heart was pounding hard beneath her ear. "I always want you, Joe. Stop worrying about being rough with me. I can take care of myself."

"I don't want you to take care of yourself. I want to be there to meet every need. I've never wanted anything else since the day I met you." His hands were hovering over her shoulders, still not touching her. "And when I can't do it, I go crazy."

She felt an aching deep within her. She couldn't take it. She cleared her throat. "Well, you're driving me crazy now. If you want to address a need, I have one that's very urgent."

He was silent a moment. "Yeah, that's a problem I can usually fix, can't I?" His hovering hands fell to cup her shoulders. "Hooray for sex." He pushed her away from him and she could see the bitterness mixed with the desire in his face. "I may not have killed your dragon for you yet, but I can entertain you."

Dragon? What the hell was he . . . ?

Then she forgot everything as his fingers quickly unbuttoned her shirt and slipped inside to cup her breasts. She arched backward with a low cry.

"Bed," he said thickly. "Now." He was tearing off her clothes. Backing her toward the bed. "I have to—"

He was over her on the bed, shedding the rest of his clothes and recklessly casting them aside.

Beautiful, she thought hazily. She'd always thought Joe was beautiful naked. Lean and muscular and full of repressed energy.

Not repressed any longer.

Fierce. Desperate. And, yes, rough.

To hell with it. It didn't matter. Her nails dug into his back as she pulled him to her. She'd meet fierceness with fierceness, roughness with roughness . . .

"ARE YOU OKAY?" JOE'S CHEST was lifting and falling with the harshness of his breathing as he looked down at her. "Did I hurt you?"

"I've no idea." She couldn't catch her breath. "If you did, it didn't make an impression through the . . ." Through what?

The maze of wild erotica that was almost animalistic? "I didn't care."

Joe got off her and rolled over to the other side of the bed. He tucked his arm beneath his head. "I care. I lost control. I knew it would happen."

"If I hadn't wanted it, I'd have walked away." Eve pulled up the sheet. "Now come over here and cuddle me. I'm not having this separate-sides-of-the-bed business. That's not the way we do it and we're not going to start now."

"I should go up to my room and unpack."

"Bullshit." She rolled over and pressed her body against him. "Hold me."

He hesitated and then put his arm around her and drew her close. "It could happen again."

"Good. But not right now. I want to get my breath before the next storm." She pressed her lips to his shoulder. "Why are you fighting me, Joe?" she whispered. "You held me like this not four days ago. I thought everything was getting all right between us."

"Did you? I didn't. I knew that it was only a matter of time before it blew up in our faces." He brushed his lips over her forehead. "It was only a question of when I got word about Kistle. I knew that would be the trigger."

"It wouldn't have made any difference if you'd just not closed me out. We would have worked through it together. That's what we've done all these years."

He shook his head. "I can't do that any longer."

She stiffened and then sat up and looked down at him. "That sounds final. Are you trying tell me something, Joe?"

"I'm trying to tell you that I've changed and the way I'll react will be different."

"I see." She swung her legs to the floor and stood up. "Then I'd better find out what to expect, hadn't I?" She slipped on her terry robe and sat down in the easy chair across the room. She drew a deep breath. "Was it Colombia, Joe?"

"You mean Montalvo? He brought a few things to a head. But it's been going on long before you went to Colombia. We both knew you were slipping away from me. I couldn't seem to stop it. I didn't even know why it was happening." He stood up and started putting on his clothes. "I blamed it on you. Then I blamed it on Montalvo."

"I never slept with Montalvo, Joe. I'd never be unfaithful to you."

"But you told me you wanted to do it."

"You asked me, I'd never lie to you. I don't know why he had that effect on me. I felt close to him because he'd suffered the same loss and then it just became . . ." She wearily shook her head. "You know I haven't had much experience with that kind of sexual attraction. The kid who got me pregnant with Bonnie when I was sixteen and then disappeared? I believe you're the love of my life, but evidently that doesn't mean that I'm totally immune to feeling something for others." She stared him in the eye. "But I'm not going to apologize. I didn't do anything to hurt you but tell you the truth. I treated our relationship with honor."

"I know that." He smiled crookedly. "And I don't blame Montalvo for trying to snatch the gold ring. I'd do the same thing. But it doesn't stop me from hating his guts. I'm too primitive to do anything else." He shrugged into his jacket. "But blame is something else. The only reason I blamed either of you was that I didn't want to blame the person who rules our lives. I knew my chances weren't good of ever being able to fight Bonnie."

She stared at him. "You don't have to fight Bonnie. We only have to find her."

"I'm doing my damnedest. But what if it isn't Kistle? What if we don't find Bonnie? I don't know how many more times I can stand by and watch you be disappointed. Every time it makes me die a little." He paused. "And sometimes it makes me wish Bonnie had never been born."

She recoiled as if he'd struck her. "No."

"I realize that's a terrible sin to you. I can't help it. You love her. You know her. But she died before I met you. Maybe if I'd gotten to know her I wouldn't feel this bitterness. I used to try to feel some of the affection you feel for her because she was part of you. I thought it would help me go on with this hellish search. But I can't feel anything for her but pity." His lips tightened. "And lately when I see what's happening to you, I can't even feel that."

"How can you feel like that? She's innocent. She's the victim, Joe . . ."

"See, I'm hurting you again. God, I don't want to do that. I'm trying to work it out, but it's hard. I just hope to God it was

Kistle who killed Bonnie. We have to put an end to this."

"You could put an end to it," she said unsteadily. "You're worried about hurting me? My God, how I'm hurting you. I told you once I was damaged and obsessed and you should leave me. Maybe you're beginning to realize that."

"No way." He headed for the door. "I can't leave you. You're my center. We just have to find a way to survive."

"Where are you going?"

"I'm going to my room, shower, and get a few hours' sleep. Then I'm going to go back to Clayborne Forest. I'd bet Montalvo's already there."

"He's supposed to be here tomorrow morning, you said."

He nodded. "But he won't be wasting time. He has his eye on the prize."

"You mean Kistle?"

"Kistle's no prize, he's the target." He opened the door. "I'll see you in the morning, Eve."

She had to blink back stinging tears as the door shut behind him. So much raw pain had been in his expression when he had spoken about Bonnie. She had never wanted to cause Joe pain. He had been her rock, her lover, and her friend. He didn't deserve to be unhappy. She had been shocked by his bitterness about Bonnie, but she couldn't condemn it. Of course he couldn't love a child he'd never known. It was a wonderful thing that he'd fought so hard with Eve all these years to find her.

Yet she felt a twinge of loneliness that she couldn't share with him the love she felt for Bonnie.

And a sudden fear that she would have to choose between them or watch him walk out of her life.

Panic surged through her and she instantly rejected the thought.

Not yet. They could still work their way through this. The only positive thing was that they had both been totally honest with each other. Joe had given her hints of what he was feeling, but she had never believed him to be this close to a blowup. It had been Kistle who had set him off. But it could also be Kistle who saved them.

If Kistle had killed Bonnie. If they could

catch him. If he could be forced to tell where she was.

Too damn many ifs.

IT WAS QUINN STANDING across the little clearing, Kistle realized.

Quinn was in the shadow of the huge sweet gum tree. As soon as Kistle saw him, he was gone, vanished.

He had thought Joe Quinn would be coming after him, and he was glad that he hadn't been disappointed. Quinn knew what he was doing in the forest and would be an interesting challenge.

He could no longer see him and Quinn was making no sound. Silence and stealth. Kistle would have to be very careful. He knew Joe Quinn's background and respected it. It was good that he was going to be challenged by the best of the best. These other yokels would be a piece of cake and bore him in no time. But Quinn would not bore him.

And neither would the hunter who'd crossed his path earlier in the evening. He'd been bigger, more muscular, but just as silent. Kistle had barely caught a glimpse of him, but he'd had the same phantom elusiveness as Quinn.

A tracker they'd brought in to find him?

Possible. At any rate, someone to keep Kistle interested . . . until he chose to kill him.

Should he go after Quinn now? Excitement tingled through him at the thought. What a magnificently effective blow that would be to Eve. But devastation should be paced, build, until the final eruption.

He sighed as he reluctantly prepared to leave. No, he'd move away from the danger that was Joe Quinn and keep to his original plan.

What are you doing tonight, Eve? Are you waiting for me? You won't wait for long. I won't let you. You'll have to come after me yourself.

And then I'll wait for you.

"YOU'RE JANE? I'M LUIS Montalvo." Montalvo smiled as she opened the door. "Of course you're Jane. Miguel told me how beautiful you are. He's very disappointed that you won't let him sweep you off your feet."

"He'll recover. I think you're the only one he takes seriously." She stepped aside to let him enter. "Eve will be right out. Sit down. Would you like a cup of coffee?"

"Please. Black." He sat down on the couch. "Where is Quinn?"

"He'll be here. He was at the forest all night." She handed him the cup. "You were there too, weren't you? I'm surprised you didn't run into each other."

"It's a big area." His gaze went to the reconstruction on the desk. "Another child?"

"Yes. Eve calls her Carrie. She couldn't bear not to try to finish her if she got the chance."

He nodded thoughtfully. "I can see it. Food for the soul."

"What?"

"It keeps her going. Perhaps subconsciously she thinks of each child as a stepstone to get to her Bonnie. If she does enough good works, then someday she'll be rewarded by finding her daughter."

Oh, yes, Jane could see how Eve could have been drawn to Montalvo. Those high cheekbones and dark eyes were totally arresting and he radiated confidence and vitality. Looks, charisma, and what was more dangerous, intelligence.

"I never thought of it quite like that," she said slowly. "I think it's probably much simpler. She's a good woman trying to save others from pain."

He nodded. "You could be right. I have a tendency to overanalyze at times. Particularly when I need to know how someone is going to react. It's important to me to know how Eve thinks." He lifted his cup to his lips. "I bought a painting of yours a month ago."

Her brows lifted. "Why? You don't have to know how I think."

"I found it fascinating. I went to the gallery because I was curious about Eve's daughter and found myself caught."

"Which painting?"

"It's one of Quinn's lake cottage. Very serene. I tried to buy another one, but they told me it wasn't for sale. It was the portrait of a man. You titled it *Guilty*. There was a world of torment in that face. Guilty of what, Jane?"

"I don't know." She shrugged. "He doesn't exist. I just started sketching his face one night. It wouldn't leave me alone, so I thought if I did a portrait it would be a catharsis. It didn't work. I still paint him."

"Interesting. Perhaps it's not a person; it's the face of guilt."

"It could be true. We all have reason to be guilty in some area." She met his gaze. "But some of us aren't tormented by it."

He chuckled. "You're talking about me. You're right, I've developed a thick skin over the years. But I don't believe you're talking about my past. You're more personally involved."

"Very personally. I love Joe. Eve has a right to do what she wants to do. I'll back her all the way. But don't you make trouble for her."

His smile faded. "That's the last thing I want to do. I want her to be happy and at peace. I'm the one who can do that for her, Jane."

He was almost making her believe it. She shook her head. "She's happy with Joe."

"Is she?" He finished his coffee and set the cup on the coffee table. "There are degrees of happiness, just as there are degrees of guilt. As you said, Eve should do what she wants."

And he would do everything he could to make sure what Eve wanted was what he wanted, Jane thought. Persuasive as Satan, and yet she believed he meant every word he said. What a lethal combination.

He shook his head as he studied her expression. "Don't worry," he said gently. "I only want to give her what she—"

"Hello, Montalvo," Eve said as she opened the door. "I've just been on the phone with Joe. He'll be right down."

"Oh, that's right. Miguel told me he had another room." Montalvo rose to his feet. "Very wise. He doesn't need distractions." He smiled. "Hello, Eve. I've been getting to know your Jane. I feel as if I've run a gauntlet. She's very like you."

"I take that as a compliment."

Eve was tense, but Jane could sense the odd familiarity that was almost a bond between her and Montalvo.

He knows me, Eve had said.

Yes, he did, and that would be the most dangerous weapon Montalvo had in his possession.

"Would you like coffee, Eve? Or how about orange juice? It's pretty—" Jane's cell phone rang and she took it out of her pocket and checked the ID. "It's my agent, Eve. I can have him call back."

"No, go take the call. I'm not letting you put your life on hold for me." She went to the sideboard and poured herself a cup of coffee. "Shoo."

Jane hesitated. She was probably being idiotically protective. Eve wouldn't accept hovering from anyone. She punched the button on her phone as she headed for her bedroom. "If you need me, give a shout."

"IT'S GOOD TO SEE YOU, EVE," Montalvo said quietly. "They say anticipation makes pleasure more intense. I could do without the anticipation. I don't like doing without you."

"You never had me." She stared at him over the rim of the cup as she lifted it to her lips. She had hoped that when she saw him again he'd be less than she remembered him. He was the same Montalvo, dark eyes that gazed out at the world with intelligence and boldness, dark hair, full well-shaped lips, and a strength and vibrance that was like a living force. "I told you that I didn't want you involved in this, Montalvo. I want you out of my life."

"I'm not interfering. I felt duty-bound to have Miguel guard you, otherwise I've stayed in the background. Have I approached you?" He smiled. "After all, Quinn invited me here."

"Because you have information we need. Do you think I don't know Joe wouldn't have—" There was a knock on the door. "That must be Joe." She set down her cup and moved toward the door.

"What a polite knock," Montalvo murmured. "I approve."

Dammit, he was enjoying the fact that Joe wasn't staying with her. She threw open the door. "Did Jane forget to give you your key?" She took her own key from the chest by the door and handed it to him. "Montalvo's already here."

"So I see." Joe came into the room and shut the door. "Let's get to it."

"Certainly." He opened the portfolio he'd placed on the coffee table. "First, tell me what you've found out, Quinn."

"Not much. I was able to trace him by a credit card slip he used at the local

Wal-Mart. I was surprised he hadn't changed his name when he left Detroit."

"He wasn't under suspicion there and had no reason to change it. He had no idea we were after him." Montalvo spread documents and photos on the coffee table. "My investigator was able to gather quite a bit of information, but there's still a lot we don't know." He tapped a photograph. "This is the latest photo we have of Henry Kistle, Eve. It was taken two years ago at a barbecue given by his employer, Chad Pelham."

The photo was of a man sitting in a striped lounge chair holding a can of Budweiser. He was fortyish, well built, with large brown eyes and a thick shock of gray-brown hair. He was smiling into the camera. It seemed impossible to Eve that this was the man who had called her and spat out that poison.

"His employer?" Joe said. "What work did Kistle do?"

"He was a personal trainer. Pelham owned a gym and Kistle worked for him for over a year. His coworkers said that Kistle was very popular with the ladies. But there was no hint of indiscreet conduct with any of them. Then Pelham decided to cut

Kistle's commission, but he didn't give him an argument. Two weeks later Kistle said he had another job, resigned, and took off." He pulled a newspaper clipping out of the pile. "Pelham died in a car accident six weeks later. The brakes on his car failed him. No sign of tampering." Montalvo shrugged. "But then, the authorities weren't suspecting that he'd been murdered."

"How do you know he was?" Eve asked.

"Kistle doesn't like authority. He tolerates it because a loner is always suspect and it would interfere with his main goal."

"And what is that?"

Montalvo drew out three pictures and spread them out on the report. "Three children were reported missing in the year Kistle worked for Pelham. He didn't dirty his own backyard. The kids all lived in surrounding towns."

"They were killed?"

"They're still missing. No bodies. Evidently Kistle is clever and very careful. No bodies, no evidence."

Eve slowly picked up the photo on the top. The little girl was nine or ten, with blond hair in a ponytail. She was laughing into the camera.

Do you know how many pretty little girls I've killed since your Bonnie?

"Eve," Joe said quietly.

"It's okay." She dropped the photo back on the coffee table. "Go on, Montalvo."

"Kistle dropped out of sight for those two years. My bet is that he just settled somewhere else for a while and used fake ID. Only God knows how many killings he committed during those two years. Then, when he thought enough time had passed, he went back to Detroit and used the Henry Kistle name again."

"And why did he leave Detroit for Bloomburg?"

He threw another photo down. "Kevin Jacobs. He didn't show up from school one day. He lived in a suburb and again there was no body found. But he was a cute little kid and the media had a circus. Kistle probably felt safer exiting the scene again."

"God," Eve whispered.

"He probably gets fake ID every time he's forced to leave a town," Joe said.

Montalvo shrugged. "And he's been doing this for years. He's probably an expert at forging documents. I told you, he's very clever."

"And how do you know that?" Eve asked. "It wasn't clever of him to call me and run the risk I'd act fast enough to catch him."

"Maybe he didn't intend to talk to you until he heard your name. Then he couldn't resist." He gazed down at the photo of Kistle. "And he evidently likes to take chances. Not with the child killings. He probably realizes how crimes against children arouse the public and he's extremely careful with them. It's part of the joke he has on the world. As long as there are no bodies found, there's no crime and he can go on doing what he wants to do. But he didn't have to go back and kill his former boss, Pelham. It was petty. Why take the chance?"

"Revenge," Joe said. "And it made him feel superior."

"Good guess."

"It goes along with the profile on serial killers. In most cases it's all about power. Even the sexual abuse is a power play."

"Then Kistle follows the profile," Montalvo said. "He has to be best."

"You seem certain," Eve said. "You can't know what he thinks from these cases you told me about."

"No, there's something else." Joe's gaze was narrowed on Montalvo's face. "What?"

"I had my investigator go back to Murdock, the man who first tipped him that Kistle had told him that he'd killed Bonnie Duncan. He spent three days going over every detail of the time Murdock had spent with Kistle. He came up with a tiny bit of information. Kistle liked to go hunting. He boasted that he'd been dropped into a jungle and survived six months. What does that sound like to you, Quinn?"

"SEALS or Rangers."

"He was in the Rangers. My investigators spent a week trying to get permission to go through records and ended up using bribery. They had a photograph, or they would never had identified him. He was nineteen when he joined the Army under the name of Tim Hathaway. He later qualified for training to be a Ranger."

"That requires a hell of a lot of discipline," Joe said. "And if he made it, then his instability must have occurred later. Acceptance of discipline isn't in his profile."

"No, he was as sick then as he is now. He was just able to become what his officers wanted him to become. He showed that same talent later. He wanted that training and he would have done anything to get it."

"You mean he wanted to learn how to kill in the most efficient way possible," Eve said.

"And he liked proving he could survive when no one else could. He was superb during the survival tests in the jungle. He was strong and smart and never quit. His reports were glowing when he went on missions. He was polite and obedient and lethal. What else could the Army want?"

"He made it through his hitch?" Joe asked.

Montalvo nodded. "Honorably discharged." His lips twisted. "But curiously enough, three weeks later an Apache helicopter blew up carrying his commanding officer and two of the men Kistle served with. No evidence of anything but an accident, of course. Kistle was an expert by that time. I'd judge that he was releasing some pent-up malice. Maybe one of them was a little too good. As I said, Kistle had to be best."

"No other killings during that period?" Eve asked.

"Not at or near the base. Perhaps he was getting enough killing on his missions."

"Where did he go from there?"

"He disappeared from view again for a few years." He paused. "The next time he surfaced he was running drugs in Atlanta. He was on drugs himself for a while and I doubt if he would have boasted about killing Bonnie if he'd been clean. At first, Murdock thought he was just fascinated by the case. He read everything he could, talked about it a lot. His attitude was . . . weird. Feverish, bitter, obsessed. Bonnie was such an appealing little girl that the media wouldn't drop the story. Every time a mention came up, Kistle was glued to the TV set. He kept telling Murdock that everyone in the country knew about the man who killed Bonnie Duncan, recognized his power, and they'd made him a superstar. Then one night when he was stoned, he told Murdock he'd been the one who'd killed her."

Eve moistened her lips. "How? Where?"

Montalvo shook his head. "Do you think I wouldn't have told you? Murdock said he didn't tell him any more, and after he came down from the drugs he never mentioned it again. He might not even remember he told him."

"Murdock probably wouldn't be alive if he had," Joe said.

"I agree," Montalvo said. "Unless Kistle wanted Murdock to tell someone about Bonnie. Murdock said Kistle was totally fascinated by the case. Maybe he wanted to go back in time and revisit it."

"He said Bonnie was his inspiration," Eve said numbly. "A burning arrow in the dark."

"Anything else?" Joe asked Montalvo curtly. "She's been through enough."

Montalvo shook his head. "She can take it." He rose to his feet. "But that's it. I'll leave the reports and photos here with you, Eve."

"No bodies," she said slowly. "All those years and no bodies. And no hint of a crime except those officers here in Bloomburg. It seems incredible."

"He may not have been as tidy about cleaning up in other parts of the country," Joe said. "But we can concentrate on that later. Now we've got him in our sights."

"Not yet," Montalvo said. "And considering his experience, it won't be easy." He turned to Eve and said quietly, "But we'll get him this time." He didn't wait for an answer but headed for the door. "I'll be in touch."

Joe turned to her when the door shut behind him. "Don't get your hopes up. It still might not be Kistle, Eve."

"Don't tell me that," she said with sudden fierceness. "I'm going to keep on hoping. I *have* to hope." She sat down on the couch. "And right now I'm going through these reports and see if I can find anything to use against the bastard. All we know is that he has to be the best and he was some kind of Rambo." She looked down at the picture of Kistle. "And that he's been alive and laughing and killing all these years my Bonnie's been dead." She tried to steady her voice. "Can you get that FBI agent to check under the Hathaway name and see if he can come up with anything else? He might have used that name again later."

"Cassidy's bowing out of the case." He lifted his hand as he saw her open her lips. "It's okay. We don't need him. He could get in the way. I can still request the information from the national database at

Quantico." He moved toward the door. "I'll get right on it." He paused to look back at her. "How are you? Should I stay?"

She shook her head. "This is no real surprise. I knew he was a monster. I just didn't know he was such a clever one." She looked back down at the report. "Go on. Talk to Quantico."

SIX

JANE CAME OUT OF THE bedroom ten minutes later. "How did it go?" she asked as she saw the reports and photos spread out on the coffee table. "I gather Montalvo came through for you?"

"Yes." She couldn't look at these reports and newspapers stories anymore right now. They hurt too much. "He did what he promised. Joe's going to see if he can use them to get any more information."

"Cooperation between them?" Jane raised her brows. "Really?

"Really." Eve began to stack the information and put it back in the portfolio. "What did your agent want?"

"Nothing much."

"Jane."

She made a face. "He wanted me to go to Paris. A gallery there wants to exhibit the six paintings that didn't sell from the last show. He thinks it would open doors. I told him that a U.S. audience is just fine."

"Bullshit," Eve said. "Go. You don't have to sit here and hold my hand."

"I want to do it."

"Too bad. I'm feeling bad enough without guilt thrown into the mix. All I'm doing is sitting here while everyone else is trying to catch that bastard. You don't have to sit with me. One of us should do something productive." She got to her feet. "In fact, I'm going to start working on Carrie right now. You pack your bag and get out of here."

"No."

"Yes." Eve stared her in the eye. "I won't have Kistle spoil one more moment of my life. Everything around me is dirty and sad right now. You and your paintings are bright and full of beauty. I want to think of you in Paris. I want you to call and tell me what's happening in that world."

Jane gazed at her searchingly. "You mean it." She hesitated. "Will you call me when they catch Kistle? I'll fly back to be with you."

"The minute I hear." Eve gave her a quick hug. "Now get out of here so I can concentrate on Carrie." She moved toward the table. "Call and get me another pot of coffee before you leave, will you?"

Jane was still standing there. "I don't give a damn about Paris or the show, Eve. You're the only one who's important to me."

"The coffee," Eve said as she took off the drop cloth. "And Paris is important to me. Get out of here, Jane."

"Okay, I'm on my way." Jane went into the bedroom and closed the door.

Damn, she was going to miss her, Eve thought. But it was better for Jane to leave. She wouldn't have let her come with her to Bloomburg if she hadn't been so shaken. As she'd told Jane, it was ugly here and it was going to get uglier. After what Montalvo had told her about Kistle, it was clear that his behavior in contacting her was unusual for him. And those two poor deputies he had killed in her name were a message sent to frighten her. Kistle wasn't going to be content to keep his distance. He wanted to touch her, scare her, hurt her.

And Jane mustn't be here and get in his way.

She began to check the clay tissue depth beneath Carrie's cheekbone. "It's just you and me, Carrie," she whispered. "I have to work fast and finish you as quickly as possible. I don't think he's going to give me much time . . ."

"**YOU HAVE TO BE KIDDING,** Venable," Montalvo said. "If you think I'm going to give you any information for a harebrained scheme like that, you're mistaken."

"It's my best bet." Venable said. "I can't keep Cassidy on the hook for more than another day. Hell, I know it's a long shot. But I'm going with it. I've called that Sheriff Dodsworth and asked for his permission and cooperation and he gave it reluctantly."

"He didn't laugh in your face?"

"He's too polite. But he was damn skeptical."

"Amazing," Montalvo murmured.

"Be quiet, Montalvo. I'm doing the best I can. I have to keep this low-key. You don't have to pay me until we locate Bobby Joe. But I'd appreciate it if you'd give this option the benefit of the doubt." He paused. "Or else you might end up with egg on your face."

Montalvo hadn't expected that last remark. He'd thought it had been desperation that had led Venable to come up with this bizarre scheme, but he knew few men more clever or practical. "You actually believe this is a solution?"

"Hell, yes, I've seen it happen."

What the hell? At least, it would be interesting and he might be able to use it. "I'll go along with you for a while. What do you want me to do?"

"I can't be a party to this and, under the circumstances, I doubt if Quinn would want to stand in. Will you be out there at six in the morning to guide the process and bolster up the sheriff?"

"Very well, but if the place is teeming with media, I'm out of there."

"Don't worry, I was very solemn and impressive with our sheriff. He's not going to leak anything."

"He wasn't the one I'm worried about." He took out his notebook and pencil. "Okay, give me the details."

Five minutes later Montalvo hung up the phone and thoughtfully studied his notes. Incredible. Even more incredible that Venable believed it to be a true and valid solution.

But the premise definitely had possibilities. This morning he'd been able to see that Eve was on edge and frustrated that she was unable to actively participate in the hunt for Kistle. Even if this scheme didn't pan out, it gave him an opportunity to involve Eve in a way that would be safe for her. They'd be working together as they had in Colombia.

Yes, it was definitely worthwhile.

He began to dial Eve's number.

EVE THREW OPEN THE DOOR to Montalvo's knock. "Okay, what is it? You said Venable had a plan to help catch Kistle."

"In a way. Actually, it's to keep the FBI

on the job. We do want to have all the help we can get, don't we?"

"Of course we do. Though Joe says they may get in the way."

"I'm willing to risk it." He came into the room and closed the door. "But the FBI doesn't believe their expertise is needed to catch Kistle and the cop killings appear to be open-and-shut cases. But there may be a way to keep them involved. You knew about Bobby Joe Windlaw."

She nodded. "But he may not have been killed by Kistle."

"And he might have. I think there's a good chance. All we have to do is find the body."

"How does Venable think he's going to find this body when it's not been found by the local police?"

He grimaced. "There's the rub."

"What?"

"Venable is sending a psychic to that riverbank where the child's belongings were found. He asked me to be there at six tomorrow morning to meet with her. I thought you might want to go along in case they found something."

Eve stared at him in disbelief. "You have to be crazy."

"My reaction exactly."

"I can't understand how you could even consider this," Eve said curtly. "It's all bull-shit and I won't be a party to it."

"I understand your attitude. But Venable seems to be convinced that she's authentic. I thought you might be interested in checking it out."

"A psychic?" she repeated harshly. "Crooks. Charlatans."

"You seem to be very adamant about it." He paused, studying her expression. "Experience?"

Oh, yes, she'd had experience. It had been part of that nightmare. "They flocked like vultures around me after Bonnie was taken. At least once a week I'd have a phone call or a letter offering to help me find her, saying they knew where she was. Some of them said she was alive and happy, others said she was dead and buried. I was so desperate I even answered a couple of them. Joe tried to keep me from doing it, but I would have tried anything." Her lips curled bitterly. "They always had some reason why Bonnie wasn't coming through to them. But they gave a lot of interviews afterward claiming they'd given the police valuable leads."

"Venable assured me there would be no media. He says this woman wouldn't participate if there was any chance of that."

"Sure," Eve said. "And pigs can fly."

"He also said that he was having a hell of a time persuading her to come and do the job. She wanted no part of it."

"Good. Then there's one less con artist to stir up mud."

"I take it that you're not going with me tomorrow morning."

"For heavens sake, are you deaf? Of course, I'm not going."

"I just want to be certain. Since you're so familiar with this kind of con game, you could be a big help in debunking."

"There's nothing to debunk. No wires. No ghostly figures. They just 'feel' things. They 'sense' a presence or 'see' a vision. All very safe. They rely on some poor fool to want it to be true so badly that she'll accept anything they say." She still remembered standing in a forest in south Georgia and being torn by agony so intense she had felt ripped apart when she'd realized that the faint hope given by that psychic who had said Bonnie was alive was bogus. "And, dammit, I did. I *did*."

"Eve." He took a half step toward her and then stopped. "I'd like to comfort you, but I'm experiencing odd qualms of conscience. I can be very calculating, but believe me, I didn't mean to hurt you by this."

"I know." She had to get control of herself. It had all come flooding back to her with just the mention of that damn psychic. "I'd tell Venable to go jump in the lake if I were you. You're wasting your time."

"I gave him my word." He shrugged. "Who knows? Perhaps the sheriff will become inspired to bring in some of his officers to look a little deeper into the boy's case himself. It could happen. Sometimes good results come from bad actions." He turned away. "If you change your mind, call me."

"I won't call you," She started toward the reconstruction on the table. "It would be like going back to that hell I went through to hobnob with another one of those damn phonies."

THE BODY WAS HANGING thirty feet above the ground, a vine wrapped around his neck in a noose.

"Damn," Joe murmured as he played his flashlight on the man's face. "Who is it, Pete?"

"Don Astins." The deputy swallowed hard. "He's with the highway patrol. He volunteered to— God, another one. How does that bastard do it?"

Joe ignored the question. "When did you find him?"

"Twenty minutes ago. He didn't check in when he was supposed to do it, so we went looking for him. It took us a long time. We never thought to look up. Then someone saw the blood on the ground at the foot of the tree."

"Blood? He was hung."

"No, from the wound on his chest. I told everybody to leave him hanging. There might be evidence, right? He had to carry him up there."

"Could be." Joe moved to the left to get a better look at the front of the body. Wound on his chest, Pete had said. Dammit, don't let it be there.

He was in position to see the frontal area now. The stake driven into his chest and the—

"Shit!"

IT WAS CLOSE TO MIDNIGHT when Eve's phone rang.

"Did I wake you?" Joe asked when she picked up the phone. "Sorry, I just thought it was important enough to warrant a little loss of sleep."

"I wasn't sleeping. I was working." Her hand tightened on the phone. "You've caught him?"

"No." He paused. "He killed another police officer. According to the medical examiner he believes he was choked to death with a garrote and then hanged from the branches of the tree where we found him."

Eve closed her eyes. "Dear God."

"He had a stake through his heart."

She tensed. "With a note?"

"Yes."

"I don't have to ask what it said, do I?" she asked shakily.

"Same message."

She had known it was coming, but she still felt as if he'd struck her.

She could hear Joe cursing. "Dammit, I didn't want to tell you, but I was afraid someone else would get to you first."

"No, you were right to call me. I had to know." She steadied her voice. "How could it happen? You said there were so many deputies out there."

"You saw his history. He's trained to kill."

"And those deputies are like sitting ducks."

"I'll get him, Eve."

"Before he kills another man for me?"

"I'll get him," he repeated. "I'm tied up at the scene now, but if you need me, I'll come back right away."

She did need him. Another death . . . Who was the man who'd died in her name? Did he have a family?

"Eve, answer me. Do you need me?"

"I'm all right." What was she supposed to do? Take him away from the search because she was shocked and sad and felt helpless and weak? "Stay. Call me if you find out anything."

"Go to bed and try to sleep. It may take hours. These local forensic boys are doing their best, but they aren't exactly high-tech. I'll let you know if there's anything unexpected." He hung up.

She huddled on the couch and stared at the portfolio Montalvo had brought them this morning. Joe was right, Kistle was trained for guerrilla killing, and ordinary law enforcement officers had little chance in that forest. Even if they had even greater numbers, they could be picked off.

And there would be another killing. Kistle was enjoying proving how superior he was, how he could taunt her. There would be another stake through the heart, another note.

For you, Eve.

No!

She jerked upright and began to dial.

Montalvo answered on the second ring.

"Another officer was killed," she said. "Joe just called me."

"I know, I heard. I'm on my way there now."

"All those deputies and he's managed to kill three of them. For me, Montalvo. For me."

"No, you know better. He killed because he liked it. You're the excuse."

"I won't be an excuse for murder. It's got to stop. I have to do something."

He didn't speak for a moment. "Why did you call? What do you want from me?"

"I want that forest crawling with experienced men who aren't fodder for Kistle. I want the FBI back on the job. I don't want three agents. I want an army. I want them to bring in trackers and forest rangers and men like you and Joe. I want Kistle caught before he kills another man."

"That's a tall order. You know that Quinn doesn't believe we need the FBI."

"I won't see another man killed."

"Quinn is right, the FBI might not be the answer."

"Why are you arguing? You're the one who arranged for them in the first place."

"I'm not arguing. I want them on the job. I just want to be honest. I'm telling you that I'd bet on either Quinn or me getting Kistle. The FBI is just an ace in the hole."

For you, Eve.

"I want that ace in the hole."

"Then I'll get them for you. It has to be through Venable. You'll come with me tomorrow morning to the riverbank?"

She stiffened. "That psychic? No way."

"Venable set it up. If we go through his nice, safe scenario and come up with nothing, then maybe I can pressure him to forget about his jurisdictional red tape and help us."

"Why do I have to go?"

"You've been through this kind of charade before. Venable will listen to you if you tell him about your experiences and give him comparisons."

Her hand clenched in frustration on the phone. "Damnation, Venable's a smart man. I can't believe he's been taken in like this."

"Will you go?"

She didn't want to go. It would bring back too many hideous memories.

For you, Eve.

"I'll go." She drew a deep breath. "Pick me up at five. What's this psychic's name?"

"Let me check." He came back on the phone. "Her name is Megan Blair."

"FOR GOD'S SAKE, MEGAN, tell him to go to hell," Phillip Blair said. "You don't know what it will do to you."

"I can't tell Venable to go to hell." Megan

threw her computer into her duffel and fastened it shut. "He made me an offer I couldn't refuse, Phillip." Should she take her medical bag? She shouldn't be gone more than overnight, but she seldom traveled without it. Why not? She could never tell when it would be needed. Even though she wasn't practicing medicine at the moment, she felt a sense of terrible loss without it. She turned and smiled gently at her uncle. "Don't worry, Phillip. I'll be fine. I can get through it. I've done it before."

"I've heard how you got through it," Phillip said. "And I could choke Venable for insisting you do this."

That's the way she had felt when she had gotten that phone call from Venable. Not at first—her initial reaction had been sheer terror followed by the impulse to throw up. "He's not insisting. He just reminded me that he had ignored budget concerns in tracking down those kidnapped children from Molino's slavery ring. He promised me at least another year of fighting off the bureaucrats to keep the search going if I did this."

"Charming."

"He's a good man. He must need me."

"And what about you? You may end up in the hospital. Does Grady know?"

She shook her head. "Grady's still in Tanzania. He's having problems finding some of the children there." She turned and moved toward him. She could feel his anxiety, and it was hurting her. She laid her head on his chest. "It's only this one time. I'm not going to shatter and blow away."

"It's a little boy, Megan. You love kids. It will tear you apart."

"They don't even know where or if the boy was killed. I may go there and not hear anything."

"Lord, I hope so. I can't talk you out of it?"

"Nope." She brushed her lips on his cheek. "Now I've got to get out of here. Venable's agent will be here to pick me up any minute. I'm supposed to be in Illinois by six." She picked up her duffel and stopped in the hall to get her medical bag. "I'll call you when it's over."

"You'd better. Or I'll be heading to Bloomburg after you."

She could feel his worried gaze on her back as she went out on the porch. She wanted to run back inside to the safe haven her uncle had always given her. Had she been reassuring enough to him? Probably not. He knew her too well not to realize how frightened she was to go to that riverbank.

Please let it not be the place.

Please keep the voices away.

"HERE THEY ARE," MONTALVO SAID as he caught sight of the sheriff's car pulling up on the side of the road running along the river. "This shouldn't take too long, Eve."

"It might." It was cold on the riverbank. Or maybe it was she who was chilled by the memories of those other times. "How long do we have to put up with her play-acting before you call Venable?"

"We'll play it by ear."

Sheriff Dodsworth was opening the door and a young woman was getting out. Megan Blair had glossy dark hair and bright eyes and she radiated vitality.

"She's pretty," Eve said. "The media must love her."

"Venable said she was as media-shy as you are."

"Yeah, sure." She watched the woman

walk toward her. Megan Blair wasn't smiling and her hands were jammed into her
jacket. "I'll believe that in six weeks if she
hasn't given out any interviews."

The sheriff was obviously enamored,
hovering next to Megan, smiling and talking. She was nodding absently, her gaze
on Eve and Montalvo.

As she drew closer, Eve could see the
tightness of her lips and the rigid straight-
ness of her posture. Strange. She found
herself studying Megan as the sheriff
made the introductions.

"Eve Duncan, Luis Montalvo, this is Dr.
Megan Blair. Ms. Duncan is a forensic
sculptor, Dr. Blair."

"I know that. I'm from Atlanta and everyone there has heard about her. She's
world-famous. How do you do?" Megan
took her hand out of her pocket and extended it. Then, before Eve could shake it,
she jerked it away. "I'm sorry. I didn't
mean— I wasn't thinking." She jammed
her hand back in her pocket. She turned
back to the sheriff. "Where do you want
me to go?"

Good Lord, the woman was terrified,
Eve realized. Or if she wasn't frightened,

she was doing a darned good job of pretending.

The sheriff gestured down the bank. "Bobby Joe's tennis shoes and shirt were found by that big sweet gum tree."

"Then let's get it over." She turned and started down the incline.

"Unusual," Montalvo murmured as he took Eve's elbow to help her down the bank. "Why wouldn't she shake your hand?"

Unusual, but that didn't mean honest or not self-serving. "Maybe she has a phobia about germs. Or maybe she's feeling guilty."

They had reached the bank and Eve stopped and watched Megan Blair move toward the tree. "Aren't you going to ask the sheriff any questions? Won't it help you 'sense' what happened to him?"

"No." She looked over her shoulder at Eve. "Why are you so bitter? Do you think I like doing this?"

"You wouldn't do it if you didn't. What kind of doctor are you? Ph.D.?"

"Medical. I was in the ER at St. Andrew's."

"Then what the hell are you doing

here?" she asked. "Is this some kind of weird hobby?"

"It's weird. It's not a hobby." She moistened her lips. "Now back off. I'm upset enough. I don't know why you're angry and I don't care. I just have to make it through this so I can go home."

"Am I interfering with your concentration?"

"I'd bless you if you could interfere. Why do you—" She broke off and her eyes widened. "Oh, my God, your little girl. I'm not here for her, am I? Venable told me it was a little boy."

Eve vehemently shook her head. "Do you think I'd have another phony psychic spitting out garbage about her?"

"I'm sorry," Megan said gently. "Of course you would have tried even that, wouldn't you? You wouldn't have been able to help yourself."

There was such understanding and pity in her expression that Eve couldn't stand it. "Don't pretend. Don't talk about her. Just put on your show for the sheriff and get out of here."

Megan nodded. "I don't blame you." She

drew a deep breath. "I'm even grateful to you for distracting me. I was so scared I felt like throwing up." She started for the tree where Montalvo and the sheriff were waiting. "And I've no intention of putting on a show. I'd rather you all go away."

Eve followed her. "So that you can have a séance? Or do you need something that belonged to the boy so you can tell us where he is?"

"Knock it off," Megan said. "Good Lord, those vultures really did a number on you. I can see why you're such a skeptic. A few months ago I would have agreed with you right down the line." She didn't take her eyes from the tree. "Okay, do you want me to tell you what I do? I don't need any objects to tell me where Bobby Joe is. Someone who does that is called a Finder, and I have no talent in that direction. I'm a Listener. I hear voices. Whenever I'm in a place where something highly stressful or tragic happened, I can hear what took place, the conversations, the emotions . . . Oh, yes, definitely the emotions. I hear the complete echo."

"I've never heard anything like that."

"Good, then at least I won't remind you of one of the psychics who tried to cash in on your daughter's death."

"You're still bogus."

"I hope you'll be going away saying that." She went up to the sheriff. "This is the spot?"

"Yes, ma'am. Is there anything else I can do?"

She shook her head. "Why don't you all go back to the cars? I'll come up when I've finished."

"We'll stay," Montalvo said. "I find I'm very interested in all this."

She drew a deep breath. "Look, I've only done this once before and I don't even know if I'll draw a blank."

"But you're acting as if you hope you do," Eve said.

"You may not believe anything else I say or do, but believe that," Megan said.

"Only once?" Montalvo said. "Why would Venable trust you to—"

"Go away." Megan's hands were opening and closing at her sides. "Just leave me alone."

The fear was back, Eve could see it, feel it. "We'll wait for you on the slope."

"Whatever." She went to the tree and sank down on the ground.

"Do you mind if I go back to the car and check in with my deputies?" the sheriff asked as they started toward the slope. "I came straight from the forest to meet Dr. Blair and I need to see if there are any more developments."

Developments. Did he mean more bodies? Eve thought. "Go ahead. We'll call you if she suddenly comes up with something."

The sheriff glanced back at Megan. "She doesn't seem to be doing anything right now. I've never dealt with a psychic before. The sheriff in the next county invited one to a crime scene once, but nothing came of it."

"Imagine that," Eve murmured.

"I hope no one finds out about this. The guys will never stop rubbing it in. I'll be back in fifteen minutes." The sheriff took off up the hill.

She dropped down on the ground. "This is far enough. Too bad if our vibrations bother her from this distance."

Montalvo sat down beside her. "She didn't mention any vibrations."

"No, I was being sarcastic."

"I noticed. She took it well."

Yes, she had, Eve thought. So she was a class act. It was still a charade.

"She's not moving. What is she doing?" Montalvo asked, his gaze on Megan.

"Why, she'll tell you she's listening. She hears voices, you know."

SEVEN

OKAY, THERE WAS NO USE putting it off, Megan thought. She had promised Venable and she had to keep that promise. Perhaps she'd get lucky and wouldn't hear anything.

She could see Eve Duncan sitting with Montalvo on the slope. Poor woman. What hell she had gone through when her daughter had turned up missing. What hell she was going through now. She wished she could do something to help her.

She couldn't worry about Eve now. She had to lower the block and let the voices in.

If there were voices.

Please let there be no voices.

She closed her eyes, tried to relax and open her mind.

Nothing.

The sound of the river, the birds waking at the dawn, the breeze blowing through the trees.

No voices.

If Bobby Joe had been here, he had not been hurt or frightened.

Or was she keeping him out because she was frightened?

She tried again.

Screams.

Bobby Joe. Bobby Joe. Bobby Joe.

Not here. Close. Very close.

No. Stay out. I can't bear it. Hurts.

Agony.

She tried to close him out, but she couldn't.

Where? Where are you?

Screams.

Where are you?

Screams, striking her heart, striking her soul.

She curled up in a ball as Bobby Joe's pain overwhelmed her.

Maybe in a moment she'd be able to get control. He wasn't here. Close. But not here.

Where?

"WHAT'S WRONG WITH HER?" Eve jumped to her feet. "She looks like she's—" She ran down the slope. She might be stupid to be so panicked. It could be an act. But there was something agonized about the way Megan was lying there. Hell, it could be a stroke or a heart attack.

Montalvo was there before her. "She's conscious."

Eve fell to her knees. "Megan. Tell me what's wrong. Where do you hurt?"

"Not me." Megan opened her eyes. "Bobby . . . Joe." She drew a shaky breath. "Give . . . me . . . a minute. I'm trying to close him out. I might be able . . . It didn't happen here."

Eve sat back on her heels. "Don't *do* this, Megan. Don't lie about—"

"Not lying." Tears were running down Megan's cheeks. "Hurts. I couldn't . . . lie."

Eve wanted to hold her in comfort. She

wanted to shake her. "You stay with her, Montalvo. I'm going to call the sheriff and get him down here." She stood up and walked away from them. She dialed the sheriff. "You should be here."

"What's happening?"

"I don't know." It was the truth. She was so torn and bewildered that she couldn't think clearly. No matter how she tried to deny it, there was no doubt in Eve's mind that Megan Blair believed she had heard Bobby Joe. "She thinks there's something . . . Maybe she's nuts and having delusions. Just come down and talk to her."

She drew a deep breath, turned, and went back to Montalvo and Megan. Megan was sitting up and Montalvo had pulled her into the circle of his arm. She was pale and her lips were set and tight.

Montalvo glanced up at Eve as she was coming toward them. "She's not good. She's shaking like a leaf in a windstorm."

"I'll be all right," Megan said. "I was able to close out the voices." She quickly straightened away from Montalvo. "Thank you. I shouldn't have let you do it, but I needed someone. I think it will be all right."

"You're very welcome," Montalvo said. "And I have no idea what you're talking about, but I'm sure all will be well."

"There's nothing sure about anything in this world." Megan's eyes lifted to watch the sheriff coming toward her. "I have to find Bobby Joe. It's going to hurt me. I don't know what will happen, what I'll do. Sheriff Dodsworth is a nice man, but he might do something he thinks will help me that wouldn't be . . . smart. Will you come with me?"

Montalvo nodded. "But I don't believe you're capable of hurting our strapping sheriff. You were weak as a kitten a few moments ago. Will this be worse?"

She moistened her lips. "Much worse." Her gaze shifted to Eve. "I'll understand if you want to stay here. Just thinking about the little boy will hurt you, and you believe nothing will come of it."

Eve stared at her. She was right, the thought of the suffering and death of a child was almost unbearable. But she could see it was unbearable to Megan too. "Give it up. You're just imagining all this."

Megan shook her head. "I have to find him now. It's not that I promised Venable.

Whoever killed him didn't want him found. I'm not going to let him get what he wants." She gave Eve a ghost of a smile. "You should understand that. You've spent years identifying lost children." She got to her feet. "But I've got to do it now. I don't know if I'll have the courage later."

"And where are we going?" Montalvo asked.

"East." She looked out at the woods. "He was with him here, but the voices were only a whisper. There was no fear. He led him deeper into the woods."

"Those woods had to have been searched. Couldn't he have moved the body?"

"Yes, but I don't think he did."

"Why?" Eve asked.

"It was part of the pain." Megan swallowed. "And I can't talk about it right now." She started forward to meet the sheriff.

Eve watched her as she talked to the sheriff. Megan's back was very straight, her shoulders squared, but there was still an air of fragile vulnerability about her.

"Are you going?" Montalvo asked her.

She should stay here. The entire scenario had not gone as she had thought it would. She had started out as resentful and completely disbelieving, and somehow she had been swept up into bewilderment and pity. Of course, Megan would find nothing in those woods. But if she thought she did, would she collapse as she had here by the river?

And if she did, Eve suddenly knew she wanted to be there to help her through it.

She started walking toward where Megan and the sheriff were talking. "Yes, I'm going."

"WE'VE GONE OVER TWO MILES," the sheriff said. "Are you sure were going in the right direction, Dr. Blair?"

"I'm sure." Megan increased her pace. She was getting near. Even through the block she could hear the echoes. "It's not far."

Mama, hurts.

No!

She could feel tears stinging her eyes. If it was this bad now, what would it be like when she lifted the block?

She went another two hundred yards before she heard the shriek of agony.

Please. Hurts. Please.

Bastard. Stop doing it to him. Stop.

But she couldn't place where the voice was coming from. She braced herself and lowered the block.

Another shriek.

Hot. Burning. Please.

Mama, make him stop.

Megan fell to her knees. "Here. He's burning . . . The acid." She couldn't see. She couldn't breathe through the sobs. "Help him. Somebody help him."

Eve was beside her, trying to draw her into her arms.

"No." She fought to get free. "Don't touch me. Not now."

Make him stop!

I can't, Bobby Joe. I can't make him stop.

She pitched forward in a dead faint.

"HOW IS SHE?" MONTALVO ASKED when Eve answered the phone in her room at the hotel. "Still unconscious?"

"Yes, it's been four hours now. The doctor said that she should be okay, but I don't like this. Are you still with the sheriff?"

"Yes. He called in a forensic team and we've been digging. If the boy is buried here, Kistle went deep."

"She could be wrong."

"Yes." He paused. "Somehow I don't think so."

Neither did Eve. "Call me if you find anything."

"Have you talked to Quinn?"

"I reached his voice mail. He's probably still in the forest." But he had to know by now. Everyone at the command center at Clayborne Forest must have known after the sheriff called for the forensic team. "I asked him to call me."

"I'll go back to digging. We have to go very slow because of the possibility of disturbing existing evidence." He paused. "It's all a very curious business, isn't it? I've always been a complete realist. But it makes one wonder." He hung up.

Yes, it made one wonder, Eve thought, as she moved across the room to the bed where Megan Blair was lying. Watching Megan in those woods had shaken her.

She had always tried to convince herself that the visits from her Bonnie were dreams because she couldn't bear the thought that she was unstable enough to believe in spirits. Like Montalvo, she was a realist. Only desperation had led her to try those psychics years ago, and she had been bitterly disappointed.

Perhaps Megan Blair would also be a disappointment. Eve admired her courage and endurance, but that didn't mean that she wasn't a nutcase. Schizophrenics sometimes heard voices too.

But what if Bobby Joe was found where she had led them? What was Eve to believe then? Coincidence? Truth? The first would be a scramble for rationalization. Truth would be an admission that she had to realize that reality was not what she thought it to be.

She sat down in the chair beside the bed and leaned back to wait until Megan woke.

MEGAN OPENED HER EYES an hour later.

"How do you feel?" Eve asked. "Would you like some water?"

"Please." She looked around her. "Where am I?"

"My hotel room." She helped her sit up in bed and poured her a glass of water from the carafe on the nightstand. "I thought you'd feel better than going to a hospital. I had a doctor to see you. He said he thought you'd be okay and to call him if you didn't wake in eight hours." She glanced at her watch. "You just made it. I'd say that was one hell of a case of shock."

"It . . . hurt." She took a drink of the water. "I was afraid I would do that. It happened before. I thought about it later and I think it may be a kind of hibernating to heal, or maybe I just can't take it and have to go away."

"You were in agony."

Megan smiled faintly. "Are you sure I wasn't pretending?"

Eve nodded slowly. "You weren't putting on a show. If you were, you're a complete masochist. I've never seen anyone in that much pain."

"It was Bobby Joe," Megan said simply. "It's not only the echoes of sound, it's the echoes of emotion."

"God in heaven," Eve said. "And the little boy was dying?"

"Kistle was very slow. It took a long time," she said unevenly. "You don't want me to talk about this."

No, she didn't. But she had to ask one more thing. "You said he was burning, the acid. What did you mean?"

"Kistle had a large vat of acid he'd buried ahead of time in the ground. Bobby Joe could see it bubbling. Kistle had tied him down and was dripping the acid on him." Megan finished the rest of the water. "Feel sick? Me too. I told you that you didn't want to hear it."

Eve did feel sick with horror. She could visualize that monster with that poor little boy. "I had to hear that part. I had to be sure." She leaned back in the chair and closed her eyes. "Montalvo called ten minutes ago. They uncovered a large covered metal vat. When they took off the lid, they found a child's bones floating in acid. It's just a skeleton, so they can't determine if it's Bobby Joe. They'll have to check DNA."

"It is Bobby Joe."

"I know." Eve opened her eyes. "I think I knew when Montalvo told me. Could you tell if it was Kistle who killed him?"

"Not by name. He was a stranger to Bobby Joe." Megan shook her head. "You knew about the acid, yet you had to test me. Why? Why should it matter to you?"

"Because I was wrong, and if I was wrong, I have to understand this. May I ask you questions?"

"I don't talk about it." Megan studied her. "It really means something to you, doesn't it? It's not just curiosity."

"No, it's not just curiosity. I don't quite know what it is yet. But I have to know what happened out there."

Megan was silent a moment. "Very well, but I may not know all the answers. I'm new at this."

"Not as new as I am." Eve got to her feet. "But I'm not going to interrogate you right now. I'll let you get up and take a shower. I'll call room service for you. What would you like to eat?"

"Nothing. Coffee." She shook her head. "No, I know I have to eat something. A chicken sandwich." She swung her legs to the ground. "And I have to call my uncle. I promised I'd call him when it was over. He'll be worried about me."

"I can see why." She watched as Megan

got slowly to her feet. She was still obviously shaky, but a little of that wonderful vitality Eve had noticed when she'd first seen her had returned. "How do you feel?"

"Drained. Terribly sad." She headed for the bathroom. "Afraid of the nightmares about Bobby Joe I may have for the rest of my life. Angry at the bastard who did that to him. That's how I feel." The door closed behind her.

Nightmares of Bobby Joe. Eve might have nightmares just from hearing about the way he died. What would it be like for Megan, who had experienced the full horror of that death? She could imagine that agony.

Because Eve had also had her share of nightmares over the years.

Her cell phone rang. Joe.

She picked up the phone. "You've heard about Bobby Joe."

"Yes, my phone was turned off while I was in the woods, but the sheriff called me a few minutes ago. It would have been better if I'd heard it from you," he said curtly. "Before the fact."

"He was killing those men, Joe. It had to stop. The FBI can help."

"I know why you did it. You couldn't stand not being in on the action and you knew what I'd think about a harebrained scheme like this. I don't like the way you did it. And I don't understand how the hell Montalvo talked you into this psychic bullshit."

"She found the little boy, Joe."

"You actually believe that she did it?"

"Yes, you should have been there."

"Hell, yes, I should have been with you, but not to watch a phony psychic pull the wool over your eyes."

It was no use arguing. She would have had the same response before she'd met Megan Blair. "And Montalvo didn't bring her, Venable sent her."

"Because Montalvo made a deal with him."

"Probably. It doesn't matter. If we have enough competent men searching, we may catch Kistle before he kills anyone else."

"And Kistle may decide that it's too dangerous, leave the forest, and take off somewhere else. Right now we know where he is."

"They're watching the roads around the forest."

"We're not going to agree about this,

Eve. And I'm too pissed to argue with you. I've been in those damn woods for ten hours and I'm cold and wet and tired. I'll say something I don't want to say."

"Say it."

He hung up.

She pressed the disconnect. She had known Joe would be angry and she couldn't have been more right. She didn't know if it was principally because of Montalvo or the fact that a psychic had been involved. He'd been with her during those episodes after Bonnie's disappearance and seen what she'd gone through. He must think she was nuts to let herself in for that disappointment again. She couldn't blame him. She had gone to that river with the same attitude Joe had just shown her. And what did she believe now? She just didn't know.

She went to the phone on the end table to call room service for Megan.

THE ROOM SERVICE ORDER arrived a few minutes before Megan came out of the bedroom. She was carrying her duffel and medical bag and appeared tired but composed.

"You look better," Eve said as she poured her a cup of coffee. "Did you call your uncle?"

She nodded. "He chewed me out. He said I should have called him before this."

"Did you tell him you were unconscious?"

"No, I skirted that. Phillip would have been on the next plane here." She took the coffee and sat down on the couch. "I told him it took longer than I hoped it would." She made a face. "That was certainly true."

"He's seen you do things like that?"

"No, but his wife was a Listener before she died and he knows what it can do to you."

Eve frowned. "What are you talking about?"

"Never mind. I can see it's hard for you to understand any of this." She rubbed her temple. "It's hard for me to understand. I just have to accept it."

"How can you accept it? It nearly tore you to pieces."

"I can block it most of the time. I didn't

block Bobby Joe. I let him in." She took a drink of coffee. "And I don't usually run around letting myself in for this kind of punishment. I made a deal with Venable." Her lips twisted. "Did you think I'd given up medicine to go to crime sites? No way. I couldn't take it."

"You're still practicing medicine?"

She looked away. "Not at the moment. I have some things to work out."

"What?"

"I told you, I'm new at this." She reached for her sandwich. "A few months ago I had no reason to be bitter like you, but I was definitely a disbeliever. Then a few things happened that changed all that. I had to accept that I was a Listener or that I was crazy as a loon. I preferred the former."

"I can see how you would." Eve looked down into her coffee. "Do you see . . . ghosts?"

"Lord, no." She went still, her eyes narrowed on Eve's face. "Do you?"

"Of course not." Eve lifted her cup to her lips. "I just thought it might be a package deal with you. Do you know anyone who does?"

"I don't have a wide acquaintance with

any other psychics, but I don't know anyone who sees ghosts." She finished her
sandwich. "Is that all?"

Eve nodded. "Thank you."

"But you still don't know if you believe
me, do you?"

Eve didn't answer for a moment, trying
to piece together the exact truth. Megan
had been open with her and she had to
be open in return. "What you did was very
impressive. But it's out of my realm of
comprehension. I don't know if I want to
believe in those echoes, that they exist
but that most of us can't hear them. It's
disturbing. Life is difficult enough without
worrying about things that go bump in the
night."

"Yet you deal with them every time you
do a reconstruction," Megan said. "I read
an article once about you that said your
similarity ratio was astonishing, almost
unbelievable. Instinct? Or something
else?"

It was strange that Megan had sensed
how she felt when she was working on
her reconstructions. "Maybe a little of
both. But you can say that about any cre-
ative endeavor, can't you?"

"But you don't create; you actually bring back the reality." Megan paused. "I remember when I first heard about you a few years ago, I thought how difficult that must be. I admire you." She got to her feet. "And that's the only reason I've been sitting here trying to explain something I find nearly as bewildering as you do. Now I'm going to go downstairs, get a taxi, and go to the airport. I want to go home."

Eve stood up. "I have a rental car. I'll take you."

Megan shook her head. "People know who you are. I don't want anyone connecting me to you or this case. Venable promised me there would be no media leaks, but I'm not taking any chances."

"Montalvo said that the sheriff had given out the story that the boy was found through an anonymous tip."

"Which was probably not so much to keep his word as to save himself from embarrassment. He was polite but very uneasy about having a psychic on the case." She extended her hand. "Thank you for taking care of me. I hope what I did will help you get that son of a bitch."

Eve shook her hand. "I do too. I don't

think just saying thank you is sufficient for what you went through. I'll let you know when we get him."

"Do that." She picked up her duffel and started for the door. "Good-bye. Good luck."

"Wait."

Megan looked back at her.

"You shook my hand. You didn't want to do it at the river. Then you were worried about having Montalvo touch you. Later you said to me, 'Don't touch me. Not now.'" She frowned. "Why?"

Megan opened the door. "I was very upset. I don't like to touch people when I'm upset."

"You're a doctor. You have to touch people and there must be occasions when you're upset. Does it have anything to do with this being a Listener?"

"No, not with being a Listener. Q and A is over, Eve." She closed the door behind her.

She shouldn't have pushed her, Eve thought. Megan had answered more questions than she wanted to answer. She had a right to shut her out. Yet Eve had felt an odd compulsion to know more.

Yes, compulsion was the word. Stronger than curiosity, more intense than fascination.

Well, Megan wasn't about to tell her any more and Eve had to forget about it. She had to get on the phone with Montalvo and see if they'd been able to get the FBI to come back to Clayborne Forest.

EIGHT

"**CASSIDY WILL BE BACK** tomorrow morning," Montalvo told her. "He'll be kicking and screaming, but it's difficult to refuse a case involving a murdered child. The media would have a field day. Attacks on children arouse a community to fever pitch. My bet is that he'll bring a truckload of agents and trackers to get this business over with in a hurry."

"Let's hope he does."

"How is our medium doing?"

"Gone. She didn't want to risk being connected with the case."

"She's not like the psychics you were previously exposed to, is she?"

"No, she's nothing like that."

"It was a weird experience. I didn't know whether to believe her or not. When we had to dig so deep to get to that vat, I thought we'd been taken in. But there it was. Did you talk to Quinn?"

"Yes. He thinks she's a phony."

"And he was mad as hell."

"Yes, but I'm not talking about Joe to you, Montalvo."

"Right, I'll back away."

"What are you going to do now?"

"Go back to the forest and try to find our man."

"He's not a man, he's an animal. What he did to that little boy . . ."

"Then I go after the beast. But I'm having trouble keeping Miguel on the sidelines. It would help if you'd let him do something for you to keep him out of trouble."

"I've got work to do. I can't babysit Miguel." She had a sudden memory of the young man's bandaged hands. "Okay, I'll think of something."

"It would be a kindness. Good-bye, Eve."

After she hung up she moved across the room to the reconstruction of Carrie. In another day if she concentrated she might finish her. Heaven knows, she needed to concentrate on something to keep her mind off what Kistle had done to Bobby Joe. The horror had been with her all day. She couldn't ignore it, but perhaps she could submerge herself and it might fade to the back of her mind.

Yet even while she was working on Carrie, it wouldn't leave her alone. Carrie had been found buried in that shallow grave in Kentucky. If Megan went to that spot, would she hear Carrie's voice and that of her murderer? Would she be able to identify the person who had done this? Megan had not been able to tell them the name of the man who killed Bobby Joe because the boy had not known him. But would that be the same in every case? Surely the victim would sometimes know the killer.

Yet bringing Megan into a case would not save a life and it could do serious damage to her if she was frequently exposed to that degree of punishment. She shivered as she remembered the look on Megan's face before she had collapsed.

No one with any humanity would ask that of her.

Good heavens, she was debating this with herself as if she had already made the decision to believe in Megan's gift.

Because, admit it, she had made that decision. She wasn't sure she understood what was happening, but she did believe that Megan had not cheated or lied when she had led them to find that little boy. And that meant that she could—

The phone on the end table rang and she wiped her hands on an alcohol towelette before picking it up. Joe? God, she hoped it was Joe.

"How are you, Eve? Did they tell you about your presents?"

She went rigid with shock. Kistle. "They told me. Did you think that I was going to get upset because you killed those men? I didn't even know them."

He chuckled. "And you're trying to keep me from doing it again. Oh, yes, you did get upset. I knew you would. You have a tender heart and you respect life. You don't know that most of those guys here in the forest are just bugs to be stepped on."

"You're still in Clayborne Forest?"

"Why not? I'm king here. They can't touch me."

"They'll get you. The FBI will be all over those woods tomorrow. Why don't you give up?"

"Give up? Why? They'll never get me and I'm still enjoying myself."

"How are you able to call me?"

"I still have my phone, but at the moment I'm using Sheriff Jedroth's again. It's the last time. It's so easy to trace a cell these days if it's not protected. If they try to trace the sheriff's phone they'll find it at the bottom of the bog. From now on I'll have to change phones with every kill. I had to think for a moment where to call you, but the Brown Hotel is the best hotel in this little burg and they wouldn't put you up anywhere else."

So he had just decided to call her out of the blue. He was on the run and the cocky bastard had to show her it meant nothing to him. "You must have gotten to know Bloomburg very well."

"I make sure I do. I can never tell when it might come in handy. By the way, I saw your Joe Quinn day before yesterday. I was considering handing you his head, but I decided to keep to my original plan and just give you an easy kill."

A chill went through her. "You're lying."

"No, I'd lie if it suited me, but there's no reason to lie. I recognized him immediately. I followed your life very closely for a long time after Bonnie."

"Why?"

"You were so pathetic. It amused me. And then you became this hotshot forensic sculptor and it made me angry. You meddled and you shouldn't have interfered. You became a threat. I take great care in disposing of my kills so that no one will ever find them."

"Like in that vat of acid where you put Bobby Joe?"

There was a silence. "There's no way you found him. You'll never find him. I planned it all out and I was very careful."

"Evidently you're not as clever as you thought."

"They couldn't have just stumbled over the place where I buried him. I was too careful. I've never had a body recovered."

"Is it bothering you? I'm glad."

"If I believed you it might. I'm proud of my disposals. It takes intelligence and care to keep a kill secret. Fame and glory are tempting, but I don't need them. I know what I've done, how I've fooled them all."

"No? Then why do you sound bitter? Perhaps you'll realize that it's all falling apart. Things aren't working out for you, are they? All these years you've had it your way, but everything's changed. You killed that sheriff and had to go on the run. You've had to go to earth like a weasel. And we did find Bobby Joe, you bastard. Tomorrow or the next day, we'll find you."

"You're beginning to annoy me, Eve." He paused. "But when I think about it, you're right: my present ill fortune is due entirely to you. You started it and evidently you're trying to make sure I remain uncomfortable. But I don't mind because it's something fresh and different in a world of sameness. But I do mind you unearthing that little boy. I had him all settled. Now when I think about him he won't be in that vat any longer."

"I wish we could throw you in that vat with him."

"How cruel. When it's so very painful."

Anger seared through her. "You'll never do it again, Kistle."

"But I will. The vat is such a clean and anonymous method of disposal." He added softly, "Do you want to know how I got rid of Bonnie?"

She started to shake. "No, I wouldn't believe you."

"It wasn't the vat. That's a fairly recent solution."

"Where is she?"

"Far away. You'll never find her."

"You thought that about Bobby Joe."

"That's true. Perhaps you might be able to find her if I gave you enough clues. I'll have to think about it. I might find it very entertaining. But to make it worth my while you'd have to be actively involved, none of this sitting on the sidelines."

"Tell me where she is."

"Are you begging me? Then you mustn't sound so demanding."

"I'm not begging you." She tried to control her temper. "And I have no proof you killed my daughter. Tell me something that you couldn't find out from the newspapers."

"I don't have to do that." He was silent.

"But maybe I will anyway. She had a favorite little song. It was something about wishing on a star. I made her sing it over and over to me. Towards the end she was crying so hard I couldn't make out the words."

Bonnie cuddling close to Eve. "Can we go out on the porch tonight and sing the song about the wishing star, Mama?"

The shock and pain were so intense she couldn't think for a minute. "You son of a bitch. That may not have been in the police reports, but there were so many sob stories written about Bonnie that it could have been in one of them."

"But you're not sure, are you? I'm going to hang up now. I hear someone in the brush behind me. Quinn? No, of course not, I wouldn't hear him. He's too good. Just one of the local searchers. Shall I circle around and take him out?"

"No!"

"I think I will. Good-bye, Eve." He hung up.

Would he do it? He might have been bluffing because he was annoyed with her.

That could also be the reason he had begun to talk about Bonnie. It was the only surefire way that he could upset her.

If he wasn't bluffing, she could do nothing about it. As he had said, she was sitting on the sidelines.

And Joe was in the thick of the game. If what Kistle had said was true, he'd been close to killing Joe. It was probably a boast. Joe was too good to become prey to that monster.

But she had to call Joe and tell him about Kistle's call. She couldn't think of anything that would help them, but they could go over the nuances and that might make them more familiar with Kistle himself. She began to dial Joe's cell.

PHILLIP MET MEGAN AS SHE came up the escalator at the airport.

"You didn't have to meet me." She gave him a quick hug. "Stop frowning. I'm fine, Phillip."

"You look like hell." He pushed her back and his gaze raked her face. "What did they do to you?"

"I did it to myself. I had a choice and I

made it." She started for the exit. "It wasn't easy."

He took her duffel and medical bag and fell into step with her. "Was the little boy murdered?"

She nodded. "And tortured."

"God in heaven, why didn't you back away?"

"It was too late. Bobby Joe had me. I couldn't leave him until it was over." She looked away from him. "Do you mind if we don't talk about it, Phillip?"

"No." He smiled gently. "How about the two of us going home and letting me fix you a hot chocolate? Then we'll watch that new Robin Williams DVD."

"Sounds good." Hot chocolate was Phillip's remedy for almost everything. Hot chocolate, understanding, and love. Lord, she was glad she had him. "I told you on the phone that Eve Duncan was there. She was kind to me, Phillip. I liked her." She made a face. "Though she didn't like me much in the beginning. She thought I was a phony and she didn't try to hide it. She's one tough cookie."

"So I've heard. Did she make it difficult for you?"

"At first. It didn't matter. I was too upset to care."

"Dammit, you were doing them a favor."

"Stop being so protective. She was almost as tense as I was. She thinks Kistle may be the one who killed her daughter. I can see how she'd be impatient with some so-called psychic coming on the scene. Later it was okay. Though she did ask me a lot of questions."

"Did you answer them?"

"Most of them. But I ducked the one about why I hadn't wanted to touch anyone. I was surprised she remembered that, after everything else that went on."

"Damn, I forgot that being that upset might be a trigger."

"I didn't. I can't forget it. It's with me all the time now." She shook her head. "But I think it was all right. I tried to be careful."

"Well, it's all over now." Phillip opened the car door for her. "You won't have to see any of them again."

"Yes, it's over." She got into the car. She hoped she sounded convincing. She kept remembering Eve's face as she'd sat there asking her questions. She'd been deeply intent and yet curiously receptive to everything Megan had told her. Megan had said good-bye to her when she'd walked out of that hotel room, but she had a feeling it was not a final farewell. She hadn't told Phillip the truth.

It wasn't over.

"HE KNEW ABOUT BONNIE'S song, Joe," Eve said when she'd finished telling him about Kistle's call. "I told him he could have read about it somewhere, but it's such a little thing."

"I'll call the office and have them go back and check all the news stories written about Bonnie. It will take a while to go through them. If he was as obsessed as Montalvo said, then it could be in an out-of-town newspaper."

"And do you think Kistle was bluffing? Do you think he was going to kill that man he heard in the bushes behind him?"

"Who the hell knows?" Joe said. "I'd say he was bluffing, but there's no telling. And there are so many men here that there would be no way to know which one he's targeting. I can't go and find him."

"Then we just have to wait and see." Her hands tightened on the telephone. "I hate it, Joe. I'm tired of sitting here and waiting. I want to *do* something." She paused. "He wants me there. That's why he called me. He's getting bored with long-distance harassment."

Joe cursed. "I knew that was coming. No. Hell, no. If he wants you there, all the reason for you stay where you are."

"You wanted me to stay in Atlanta, now you want me to stay here at the hotel. You're smothering me in the name of safety. Kistle is my business, Joe. If he wants me in that forest, then my being there will make it easier to trap him."

"And easier for him to kill you," he said harshly. "I'm not letting him put a stake through your heart. You'll get in the way. You got what you wanted. By morning Cassidy will have this place crawling with agents. Now let them do their work. Let me do my work."

She didn't speak for a moment. "I'll wait a little while, if he hasn't killed another man. But not long, Joe. He wants me, and, by God, I want him." She hung up.

CASSIDY ARRIVED AT THE command site at five-thirty the next morning. He was obviously not pleased. He came immediately over to where Joe was standing. "Let's get this over with. I've sent a forensic team to the grave site and I have agents coming in from Atlanta and Chicago. They should be here by noon. What areas have you already searched?"

Joe shook his head. "He's moving around. You're not going to be able to zero in on him that way."

"Have you brought in dogs?"

"The second day. No luck. He killed squirrels and spread false blood trails. They were completely distracted."

"I'm bringing in the trackers from North Carolina we used for the Rudolph operation."

"Good." Joe rubbed the back of his neck. God, he was tired. "But they didn't find Rudolph, did they?"

Cassidy immediately bristled. "That was an impossible mission. Knock it off, Quinn."

"No offense. I'm just telling you that you

may run into the same problems." He looked Cassidy in the eye. "And I think you know that, or you wouldn't have had the good sense to go back to St. Louis. Now you're stuck with us, but you'd better realize that it's not going to be a slam dunk." He turned and headed for his car. "Now I'm going to go get a shower and some breakfast and at least four hours' sleep. Dodsworth is a good man and you'll find that Deputy Pete Shaw is smart and eager to learn. Don't step on his toes. Call me if you need me."

As he got into the car, he saw Montalvo coming out of the forest. He looked wet and dirty and as tired as Joe was feeling. He had passed him coming and going in the last few days. Needless to say, they hadn't exchanged more than a curt nod of recognition. But today Joe was feeling a sort of odd kinship with him after talking to Cassidy. Montalvo knew the difficulties and frustration of chasing that bastard, and whatever other emotions he felt toward Montalvo, the man knew what he was doing in that forest. He had as good a chance as Joe at snagging Kistle.

And if he did, Joe would take Kistle

away from him. There was no way he was going to let the authorities take over Kistle until he got some answers from him.

He looked back at the forest that was still shadowed with night. Are you there, Kistle? Are you sitting there watching us run around trying to find you? Enjoy it. It's not going to go on for much longer.

NEW BLOOD, KISTLE THOUGHT, as he watched the man in camouflage garb kneel to check which way the blades of grass were bending. An experienced tracker, and he was traveling with another tracker who was about a hundred yards north. They would find nothing, but their presence made things more difficult. The woods had been teeming with searchers all day and night. At first he'd regarded it as an escalation of the challenge, but it was beginning to annoy him. These men were like Quinn, they knew what they were doing. They were hobbling him and taking the joy out of the night.

And they were stopping him from going after Quinn. If he couldn't have Eve Duncan, then Quinn was the obvious next choice. Quinn had been relentless and he would never stop. It would be smart to take him out and accomplish the dual purpose of hurting Eve and ridding himself of a threat.

But how could he do that when he was being kept busy just surviving?

No, it was time he thought about the alternate plan. Things were not going his way at the moment. He had been furious that Eve had managed to find Bobby Joe. It had hurt his pride and made him want to strike out hard and deep. It was bad enough that he was unable to take credit for the splendor of his kills. Now his skill at concealment was in question. But he must handle any response very efficiently and with style. He mustn't let anyone think he was desperate or afraid.

He looked up at the night sky. It was a full moon and he could feel the excitement start to build inside him. It was almost like the time when he was a boy and he had pretended that the full moon transformed him into a werewolf. He could feel the strength flow into his muscles and his heart was beginning to beat harder.

He was ready.

EVE'S PHONE RANG AT THREE-THIRTY in the morning.

"He's killed another man," Joe said baldly. "Sometime tonight. Cassidy just found him. It was one of his trackers."

Eve stiffened as the shock ran through her. "A note?"

"Yes, I don't know what it said yet. I've just notified the forensic boys and now I'll be on my way to him as soon as I hang up."

"No. Meet me at the command site. I'm going with you."

"Is there any way I can talk you out of it?"

"No." She swung her legs to the floor and stood up. "I'm on my way. I should be there in twenty minutes." She hung up.

Another dead man with another note. Dammit, would it never stop?

Miguel was waiting for her in the hall when she came out of the hotel room five minutes later. "Your car or mine?"

"Who called you? Joe?"

"No, Montalvo. But Quinn evidently told him to do it. He didn't like you driving to the forest in the middle of the night alone. Neither did Montalvo."

"You mean they actually agreed on something?"

Miguel smiled. "They are more alike than they would like to admit, but they always agree on keeping you safe. Me too. My car or yours?"

"Mine. You shouldn't even be driving with those hands."

"It's not easy. I feel like a polar bear trying to knit."

"And you still want to go hunting in the forest with Montalvo?"

"I would not be knitting if I were chasing down Kistle." He punched the elevator button and then flinched with pain. "Ouch. But I'm becoming hopeful. I've been ordered to watch over you and you're edging closer and closer to Kistle. That means I'm closer."

"I'm glad someone is happy about it."

"Not happy. Just looking on the positive side. Montalvo and Quinn both want to give you Kistle. Wouldn't it be amusing if I did it instead?" He chuckled. "I wonder if I could do it. Montalvo would probably want to break my neck."

"This isn't some kind of contest, Miguel. A man died tonight."

His smile faded. "And I'm truly sorry. But it's natural for men to compete against each other. We've been doing it since the cave days. Why else do we have wars? Wars are competition, no matter what the politicians call them. All those searchers in the forest who are going after Kistle are instinctively vying with each other to be the one to get him."

"Miguel, I don't want a discourse on why men believe this kind of horror is a game."

He nodded understandingly. "I'll shut up. I didn't mean to upset you." He followed her into the elevator and then shook his head and frowned as he faced the elevator panel. "I'm strong as an ox, smart as a fox, and I'd fight like a tiger to protect you. But would you please press the button for the lobby? Buttons are hard for me right now."

THE COMMAND SITE WAS BRIGHTLY lit and a medical examiner's SUV was parked beside the road when Miguel and Eve arrived.

Joe strode over to the car and opened

the door. "Okay, you're here. Let's get on the move."

"Excuse me, Eve," Miguel said. "I believe Quinn considers me *de trop* now." He jumped out of the car. "I'll go try to find Montalvo."

Eve got out of the car. It was the first time she'd been here and the bustle and number of searchers amazed her. "It's like a military camp."

"They liked their sheriff in this town," Joe said. "And with every death more volunteers poured into the area. More doesn't necessarily mean better. It's hard to keep track of everyone. I think it's out of control, but it's not my show. The town is up in arms and the interim sheriff is trying to satisfy them." He took her arm and led her toward the woods. "And now we've got the FBI to stumble over and Cassidy is going like a steamroller."

"I still think it was right to bring them in."

"Except that he killed one of the trackers Cassidy brought in, to thumb his nose at us." Joe shrugged. "But it doesn't make much difference. A kill is a kill to him. It would have been someone."

"I'm not sure. His pride was hurt because we found Bobby Joe. He had to make the kill different. He had to make certain that we knew he was superior, that we couldn't stop him."

He gave her a glance. "You're talking as if you know him."

"I'm on my way. He wants me to—" She stiffened as they came out of the brush into a small clearing. There were several people milling about, but she barely noticed them. Her gaze went immediately to the man dressed in camouflage who was propped against a pine tree. He was staring straight ahead, blue eyes wide open. She could barely see the note staked through his heart, for the blood covering his chest.

"Steady," Joe said quietly. "You wanted to see him. It's not pretty, is it?"

"I didn't expect it to be." It seemed terrible referring to this man who had been alive only hours ago as "it." "What's his name?"

"Ellis."

She moved forward. "And who is that red-haired man kneeling in front of him?"

"Cassidy."

"He's looking at the note." And so was

she, trying desperately to make out the words on the bloodstained note.

Cassidy looked up as Eve and Joe approached. "You're Eve Duncan? I was going to come to the hotel and talk to you. Why the hell is he doing this?"

"Back off. I've told you what connection he has with Eve," Joe said. "There's no reason to bother her."

Eve shuddered as she looked at the dead man. "The note. Can you make out what it says? Is it the same?"

Cassidy shook his head. "It's longer than the others. But it's still addressed to you."

"What does it say?"

His gaze went back to the note. "Look for yourself."

She was looking, staring, making out word by word until she had the entire message.

Go home, Eve, Bonnie's waiting.

She flinched back. "My God."

Joe's arm slid around her in support. "Will you get away from here now? Have you had enough?"

She nodded numbly. "I'll go." She turned and started back through the woods.

Joe was silent for a moment. "It's just

his way of putting a stake through your heart, Eve. Don't let him do it."

"Only partly," she said. "By killing that man he was taunting the searchers, but he was also sending me a message. He's gone. He's left the forest, Joe."

His gaze narrowed on her face. "Why do you think that?"

"He told me to go home. He's luring me away with the one bait he knows I can't resist. And he's impatient and doesn't want to have to wait until all of these searchers decide that he's no longer here. He wanted to tell me that if I go home he'll be waiting for me."

"It's possible," he said slowly.

"No, it's more than possible. He's telling me to go home to Atlanta where Bonnie was taken. He's teasing me with the idea that he might lead me to where he buried her."

"He'll never do it."

"Not if he can help it. But I told you what he said about giving me clues about where to find her. He could have decided to open a new game. But if he's left this forest, then we may never find him if he disappears as he's done in the past. We know more about him now and he's going to be even more careful. This may be our only chance."

"A chance to have him butcher you."

"A chance to bring Bonnie home."

"What if he decides it's not safe to leave the forest with all the guards around the perimeter?"

"You told me once you thought he'd be able to break through."

He started to curse. "You're going to do it, aren't you?"

"Why even ask? You know I will." She opened the door of the car. "I'm going home, Joe."

NINE

"SHE'S LEAVING," MIGUEL TOLD Montalvo when he reached him on the phone. "She's heading for the airport. Quinn is with her."

"Of course he is," Montalvo said. "He wouldn't let her go into the lion's den alone."

"You think Kistle's gone?"

"If he wanted to go. You could, I could. And I'd bet he wanted out. It was getting too tight for fun. He couldn't spread his wings and swoop like an eagle. And he couldn't get near Eve. The notes were the only way to contact her and there couldn't be much satisfaction if he couldn't see her, hear her."

"Are you staying around to make sure?"

"Eve is sure. I trust her instincts. I'll talk to Cassidy and give him a heads-up that Kistle may have flown the coop. He won't give up the search until he makes sure, but that's his prerogative. I'll meet you at the airport in an hour."

EVE AND JOE ARRIVED AT THE lake cottage at sunset. The sun was casting a scarlet mirror image on the lake. Beautiful, Eve thought wearily. It was good to see beauty when she had come from such ugliness.

Joe parked the car in front of the cottage and jumped out. "Stay here a minute." He took the porch steps two at a time and disappeared inside the cottage. He came out a few minutes later. "It's secure." He opened the car door for her. "Go inside and lock the doors. You know where the pistol is. I'll go and pick up Toby from Jane's friend. I should be back in twenty minutes."

"I don't think Kistle would be that obvious," Eve said as she climbed the steps.

She was already feeling a sense of peace and contentment. It was like being in the tranquil center of a hurricane. It seemed impossible that anything bad could happen here, where she'd been happy for so many years. "There's nothing subtle or clever about breaking into a house. I'll rummage through the freezer and see what I can find us to eat."

"Do that." Joe started the car turned and went back down the road.

She went inside and locked the door before taking Carrie over to the easel and setting her up. One more night and she should be finished with the reconstruction. "Sorry, Carrie," she murmured. "It's not that you're not important to me. It's been a hell of a few days."

That was an understatement. Horror and death and ugliness had stalked her from the moment she had taken the call from Kistle that first night.

Forget it. She was home. She needed to take a little time to get her breath and heal.

Megan had talked about healing. Something about hibernating and—

But she didn't want to think about Megan either. To remember Megan was to remember those moments when she had been caught up in that other horror. To remember Megan was to be pulled into wondering about questions she'd avoided for all these years.

She headed for the kitchen. She was sure there was some lasagna in the freezer. Joe liked lasagna. She'd make some garlic bread and they'd eat and talk and maybe the tension between them would ease.

Lord, she hoped it would ease.

MONTALVO CALLED AS SHE WAS putting the bread in the oven.

She hesitated. She didn't want to talk to Montalvo right now. She wanted to keep the fragile serenity she had felt at this homecoming. But if she didn't talk to him now she'd have to talk to him later. She punched the button. "What do you want, Montalvo?"

"Many things. But at the moment I only want to tell you that you did the right thing by coming home. You looked frayed the last time I saw you and you value your home. You'll feel better there."

"Everyone values their home."

"Providing they have one. It takes more than four walls." He changed the subject. "I just wanted to call and tell you that I'm here in Atlanta if you need me. I'm at the Plaza and you have my cell number."

"I won't need you."

"You can never tell. If you don't want to see me, Miguel would be glad to stand in my place."

"You'd let him?"

"If I had to do it. Not willingly. But I have an uneasy feeling that you may need someone."

"I have Joe."

"Who is beyond compare. Call me if you need me." He hung up.

Dammit, she'd known he would manage to disturb her. He had been low-key and said nothing intimate or controversial and yet she was still uneasy.

She turned away from the stove and took down plates from the cabinet. Why did an offer from Montalvo to keep her safe make her feel just the opposite?

Get over it. He was an expert manipulator and those words had probably been carefully calculated.

"Smells good." Joe was on the porch

and opened the door to let Toby into the house. The retriever tore immediately over to Eve licked her hand and then went over to his bowl and stared at her accusingly.

"Did Patty feed him?"

"I forgot to ask."

"Bad mistake." She sighed. "Give him some dog food while I dish up the lasagna."

"Right." Joe went to the dog food canister. "Though we could call Patty."

"I don't feel like calling his bluff tonight. Let him be happy." She wished making everyone happy would be that simple. People were a hell of a lot more complicated than dogs. "Was he good at Patty's?"

"Probably not. She doesn't care. She's besotted with the dog and spoils him rotten." He set the table. "We should probably board him."

"Yeah, sure." Joe was as crazy about Toby as the rest of the world was. He'd hire an army of dog-sitters before he'd board him. "And Jane would take a contract out on us. After all, he's her dog."

"He likes us a little too." Joe got the garlic bread and put it on a plate. "We're family, and that makes a difference."

Home and now family. The basic concepts seemed to be popping up in everyone's mind tonight. And Joe was being casual, almost normal, she noticed with relief. It was as if being here in a familiar place was taking the edge off, soothing him, as it had her. She set the lasagna on the table and sat down. "Yes, it makes a big difference."

He didn't look at her as he dished her up a portion of lasagna. "I never really had a family before you and Jane. My parents were always off on a yachting trip or skiing somewhere or other. Not that I had anything to complain about. I had food and good schools and that's a hell of a lot more than you had growing up." He lifted his gaze to stare into her eyes. "I just wanted you to know that I value every day we've been together as a family. Whatever happens between us, I want you to believe that."

"I believe it." She reached across the table to cover his hand with her own. "Likewise." She squeezed his hand and then picked up her fork. "And it's going to go on forever."

"I'll be happy for one day at a time," Joe said. "Because I can't promise you I'll feel any different about Bonnie. I've watched you suffering for too long. And in the end that could break us, not Montalvo."

She could feel the shadows returning, chilling her. "Shut up, Joe." She handed him a piece of garlic bread. "I don't want to talk about Kistle, Montalvo, or Bonnie. I just want to have a good dinner and then go to bed. Can't we put everything else on hold?"

He was silent a moment and then a slow smile lit his face. "Only if you eat a piece of this bread too. I refuse to be the only one in bed reeking of garlic."

JOE WAS SLEEPING.

Eve rolled over on her back to stare into the darkness. She wanted to go to sleep too, but it wasn't going to happen. Perhaps because she desperately wanted to continue on with the same warm, loving mood that had been present all evening. The conversation had been casual but affectionate, the sex had been hot yet heartbreakingly tender. Joe had held her for an hour before he'd drifted off to sleep.

Would it be the same in the morning? Probably not. Life would intrude and peace would vanish. She couldn't lie here brooding about it. She'd get up and get a glass of water and then maybe work on Carrie for a while.

She gently brushed her lips across Joe's shoulder and carefully got out of bed. She pulled on her robe and glided toward the door.

Toby was sleeping on the couch in the living room. He always jumped up there when they weren't around to keep him from it. He lifted his head, wagged his tail, and yawned.

"No, it's not morning." Eve got her glass of water. "And you have no business up there." She glanced at Carrie, then went out on the porch. Toby jumped down, followed her, and settled down on the top step. "But I'm not going to yell at you. I'm feeling mellow tonight." She stroked the retriever's head. "You were a big part in giving us a good evening. But don't think you can do it tomorrow."

He cuddled closer and licked her arm.

She should probably go back inside. Joe wouldn't like her being out on the porch without him. But as she'd told him, she didn't believe that Kistle would stalk her here. It might be unreasonable, but she felt as if she would be able to sense him if he was close to her. Unreasonable? There had been nothing reasonable about anything that had happened to her since Kistle had entered her life. There had only been darkness and threats and death.

And he was still out there, waiting to do it again.

"HE'S NOT GOING TO WAIT long, Mama."

She turned to see Bonnie sitting on the porch swing with one leg tucked beneath the other. "I know, baby. But that may be a good thing. It may be over soon."

She frowned. "I hope it will. Joe is so sad. I used to think you were the only sad one, but Joe is hurting too. I wish I could help him."

"You can't help him. You're the problem. He said he wished you'd never been born."

"Because he loves you. Don't be angry with him."

"I'm not angry. I'm sad. Because he can't love you the way I do." Eve smiled faintly. "Of course, I suppose you could always pay him a visit and let him get to know you."

"You're joking." She shook her head. "But I wish I could, Mama. I don't think it works that way. You're the only one who can see me."

"Because I'm the one who's nuts?"

"Because you open yourself to me. I can feel your mind open and saying welcome. It's like someone rolling out the red carpet at one of those Academy Awards ceremonies."

"Oh, yes, I'd spread the red carpet, strike up the band, and give you any gold statue I had on hand."

"Would you? It sounds like a party."

"The very best party." She looked down at Toby, who was lying with his head on her knee. "If you're a ghost, why isn't Toby barking and cowering? Aren't they supposed to be afraid of spirits?"

"That's a myth. Besides, Toby knows me by now. He'd be silly to be scared of me."

"He's pretty silly most of the time anyway. He thinks he's still a puppy."

"Isn't that wonderful?"

"I guess it is." She looked down at Toby. "Childhood is a special magic time. Every minute should be enjoyed."

"You're thinking about Bobby Joe."

"Yes, his childhood didn't last much longer than yours, baby."

"It was bad for him?"

"Very bad. Don't you know?"

She shook her head. "I know he's happy and not hurting anymore."

She cleared her throat. "You're saying that because that's the way I want it to be."

"Am I?"

"And because I'd rather you be a ghost than a figment of my imagination."

"Then why do you fight me?"

"Because I have to do it. It's the sane thing to do." She smiled. "And because I ran into an authority on the subject lately who told me she'd never met a ghost."

"Oh, the lady with the box."

Eve frowned. "Box? Oh, you mean Megan's medical bag."

"No." Bonnie set the swing to moving gently. "The other box. She doesn't like it, but it belongs to her. She has a good heart, but she can hurt you, Mama. Stay away from her."

"I have no intention of seeing her again."

Bonnie shook her head. "Mama . . ."

"I just asked her a few questions."

"Don't let her hurt you," Bonnie said. "Don't let her hurt me."

"Why should she be able to—"

"Look at Toby. He's wagging his tail. He hears Joe coming."

She glanced down and saw that Toby's head was lifted and he was staring at the screen door. "Bonnie, what did you mean about—"

Bonnie was no longer sitting on the porch swing.

"WHAT ARE YOU DOING out here?"

Joe had opened the screen porch and was gazing at her with a frown.

"Just getting a breath of air." She got to her feet. "I couldn't go to sleep."

"Why didn't you wake me? Or didn't you want the company?"

"I wanted the company. I was just trying to be considerate. You haven't gotten much sleep in the past few days."

"Neither has Kistle."

"I'm sure he's tucked in somewhere taking care of that." She laid her head on his chest. "I'm worried about you, not him."

His hand cupped her throat and he gently rubbed the fine hairs at her nape. "I'm glad I rank above a slimeball like him. Does that mean you'll come back to bed and keep me company?"

She started toward the door. "Good idea." She wanted to stay close and hold him for as long as she could. "I don't want to do anything else." She linked her hand with his. She wished they could always be linked together, with nothing and no one between them. She avoided looking at the swing where Bonnie had been sitting. Feeling as he did about Bonnie, there was no way she could tell him about her visits. To him it would be yet another sign of the damage done to her by

Bonnie, not only an emotional but a mental wound.

No wound now. Only love, Joe. She only brings me love . . .

"SHE'S AT THE LAKE COTTAGE," Miguel said as he came into the hotel suite. "No protection but Quinn. Do you want me to stake the place out?"

"No, Quinn would know and probably break your neck. She's safe with him." Montalvo moved over to the window and looked down at the almost-empty street below. "For the time being. Kistle wouldn't have been able to just jump on a plane as we did. He'll have to make his way down here and set his plans in motion."

"But you think he'll definitely come after Eve?"

"Oh, yes. I believe it's been sort of a game to him from the beginning. He'd already had a fixation on her because of Bonnie and it amused him to make that first contact. But then she began to trip him, get in his way. Then, when we found Bobby Joe, it really bothered him. Now his ego demands that he show her how superior he is, how he can manipulate and hurt her." He paused. "And eventually kill her."

Miguel sighed. "I don't like this standing back and watching and waiting. It's boring. I liked it much better in Colombia where you were in control. I think you did too."

Montalvo shrugged. "Sometimes it's necessary to play a waiting game." But he should have realized that Miguel knew him well enough to see the impatience that was beginning to gnaw at him. He was accustomed to being the one to plan and take action and Eve's reliance on Joe Quinn completely blocked him. His time would come, it always did, but he might have to make an opportunity, as he had when he'd contacted Venable.

"You're thinking about it. Good. You don't like to be bored either. She's an unusual woman, but is she worth it to you?"

Montalvo turned to look at him. "That's none of your business, Miguel."

"Of course it is. You saved my life, that means you belong to me. I must take care of you."

"I believe your reasoning is screwed."

"Whatever." He grinned. "But the fact remains that is a truth to me. I take it you're not going to answer me?"

"I made a promise. I would still go after Kistle no matter who I made it to."

"And?"

He shook his head resignedly. "Yes, she's worth it, you persistent bastard." He headed for his bedroom. "Tomorrow morning I want you to go and look up Murdock, the man who gave us the information about Kistle. He's supposed to still be here in the city. I want to know every little thing he might remember about Kistle. Where he went, what he talked about besides Bonnie."

"It's a long time ago. Years."

"Make him remember. Kistle's proved he likes to go back to old haunts. He returned to Detroit even though he'd made a kill there. If he did kill Bonnie, then he might have disposed of the body in a familiar place. Or he might want Eve to believe he buried her in one of those places. Either way, we'll be ahead of the game if we can check it out."

"What method should I use? Force? Intimidation? Bribery?"

"Just get the information." He glanced

back over his shoulder as he opened the door. "And don't damage those hands."

"That means trickery or bribery. No problem. I'm excellent at the first and I'm truly superb at giving away your money."

"I've noticed you have that talent," Montalvo said dryly. "Try not to beggar me. I still have your final operation to pay for."

ATLANTA HAD GOTTEN BIGGER and even more congested since he'd left, Kistle thought distastefully. He hated this traffic. All those bastards flying by him, when he had to keep steady and within the speed limit. He couldn't afford to be stopped, even though this car he'd stolen from a farm outside Chattanooga wouldn't be reported missing for some time. He'd ditched the car he'd stolen in Illinois in a junkyard near the farm and he'd needed wheels and money and a new cell phone. He'd hidden the bodies of the farmer and his wife well enough so that anyone dropping by the farmhouse would just think they were off on a trip.

Another truck zoomed by him in the right lane. Damn, he hated this concrete jail of a city. He wanted to be back in the woods, where he ruled supreme.

Be patient. It wouldn't be long now and he'd be outside the city and ready to roll. He had money and had picked up the special equipment and supplies he needed. But his primary advantage was his own ingenuity.

You're waiting for me, aren't you, Eve?

Just a little longer and I'll come for you.

EVE LOOKED UP FROM PACKING Carrie in a carefully padded box when Joe came into the cottage from taking a call on the porch. "What did you find out from the sheriff?"

"Surprise. Cassidy thinks that Kistle has left Clayborne Forest. If he can wrap up the forensic reports on Bobby Joe, he's planning on going back to St. Louis tomorrow." He went to the refrigerator and took out the pitcher of iced tea. "The deputies and volunteers still haven't given up. They'll probably be in that damn forest for the next six months."

"Why does Cassidy think he's gone?"

"A car was stolen from a Wal-Mart parking lot in a town about thirty miles from Bloomburg. The man suspected of stealing it was seen by one of the greeters and meets Kistle's description. It was abandoned outside Chattanooga." He paused. "And so far we haven't been able to find any story about Bonnie that mentioned her favorite song. But there's still a lot of articles to check."

I made her sing it over and over.

It could still have been a lie. Don't think about it.

Joe's gaze went to the reconstruction. "You finished her?"

"Last night." She took the glass of tea he offered her. "FedEx will pick her up in a few hours."

"And her hometown police can start publicizing and checking comparisons."

She nodded as she dropped down on the couch. "I'm glad it's done. It took longer than it should have."

"You were a little distracted. It's not as if your Carrie is in a hurry."

"I know. I'm the one in a hurry. I want her brought home." She took a sip of tea. "She's a pretty little girl, Japanese descent."

"That should make it easier?"

"It's never easy. On a cold case the police want the identities and suspects served up to them on a platter. Otherwise it's not worth their time. Have they gotten the DNA report on Bobby Joe?"

He nodded. "It's confirmed. I suppose you want to call Megan Blair and tell her?"

She thought about it and then shook her head. "She doesn't have any doubts that it was Bobby Joe. She asked me to call her when we caught Kistle." She paused. "I know you don't want to hear it, but she may be the real thing. How else could she find that little boy?"

"You're right, I don't want to hear it," Joe said flatly. "And I'm sure Cassidy is scrambling to find out how she did it. I'd start out checking the possibility of a connection with Kistle. Then I'd go to the manufacturer of the vat where they found Bobby Joe and see what I could find out there. Or maybe she's been quietly interviewing townspeople and found a witness or a lead of some sort."

Eve shook her head. "I believe her."

"Eve." She could see him trying to subdue his impatience. "Don't let yourself do that. She'll prey on you. She's just cleverer than those other crooks you ran across."

"I believe her," she repeated. "But I won't try to convince you. It's not important now." She picked up the FedEx box. "It's a pretty day. I'm going to go out on the porch and wait for FedEx."

He nodded. "I'll take Toby for a walk. I'm restless."

She could see the nervous energy charging him. Joe would always rather dive into trouble than wait for it to happen. It wasn't that way with her this time. She would rather enjoy these rare moments of peace before the storm. Right now she could sense the dark clouds coming toward her and they'd be here soon enough.

She went out on the porch and settled on the swing, watching Joe as he trotted with Toby down the lake path. In the late afternoon sunlight Joe looked strong and powerful and completely in control. So different than a few months ago in Colombia when he'd been wounded and was fighting just to get out of bed.

Her phone rang and she pulled it out of her pocket. Jane.

"I'm fine, Jane," she said when she answered. "The sun is shining and I'm sitting at home on the porch and watching Joe walk Toby."

"And where is Kistle?"

"Not here."

"Dammit, they should catch that bastard." She sighed. "Am I being a worrywart?"

"Yes, but it's very becoming. How is Paris?"

"Beautiful and full of itself. It's not as easy to get things done over here." She paused. "I could let my agent do all the diplomatic work for the show and come back home. They wouldn't miss me."

"They'd miss you. You can be diplomatic when you want to be."

"Well, I've already antagonized the gallery owner. He wanted to put all the paintings on sale even though I'd put a reserve on one of them."

"Which one?"

"*Guilt.* The one Montalvo liked." She paused. "Where is Montalvo?"

"I have no idea. He called me yesterday when I arrived and told me he was in Atlanta at the Plaza, but I haven't heard from him since."

"I imagine he'll be in touch." She hesitated again. "I know you want to keep him at a distance, but I'm glad he's there, Eve. Whatever else Montalvo may be, he impressed me as a man you could count on in a pinch."

"Yes, he knows what he's doing." She changed the subject. "We're fine here. Nothing is happening. Your show is in three days. Stick it out and then come flying to my rescue if you feel you have to do it."

"You'll call me if you— No, I'll have to call you. You won't want to worry me. I'll phone you tomorrow. 'Bye, Eve."

"Good-bye, Jane." She was smiling as she hung up. She wouldn't be surprised if Jane appeared on the doorstep tomorrow in spite of the show. Which meant Eve would have to persuade her to turn around and go back. Not an easy task with someone as stubborn as Jane.

The FedEx truck was coming up the road and she picked up the package and went to meet it.

Good-bye, Carrie. I hope I helped you. I hope they bring you home.

TEN

SHE WAS CLIMBING THE PORCH steps when her cell phone rang again.

"Who is Montalvo?"

She went still. "Kistle?"

"Who is Montalvo and why does your Jane feel safer that he's with you?"

Her heart started to pound and her gaze darted around her. "How did you know what Jane—"

"I decided I needed to be closer to you. There's such wonderful equipment available these days to encourage intimacy."

"You have a machine to let you listen in on my phone conversations?"

"Who is Montalvo?"

"Never mind him." Her gaze searched the woods. "You must be nearby if you can tune in on my phone."

"Not that near. Ask Quinn. I don't need to have you within touching distance yet. That's for later. I'm anticipating it."

"You're crazy. It's not going to happen."

"Then why did you accept my invitation? You knew why I told you to go home."

"You said . . . Bonnie."

"And Bonnie is the magic word, isn't it?"

"You meant me to think that you'd lead me to Bonnie."

"Then I'll have to do it, won't I? I have to keep my word." He paused. "But is bringing your little girl's body home worth your life? That's the question. It will be interesting to find out."

"Tell me where she is," she said unevenly.

"In time. But first we have to come to an agreement. Clayborne Forest was entertaining, but it began to annoy me toward the end. No police. No FBI. The moment I see any signs of the law I'm gone and your chance of getting Bonnie back is zilch. Do you understand?"

"Where is Bonnie?"

"Of course, you can bring Quinn. He's been on my preferred list from the beginning. And who is Montalvo?"

He wasn't going to give up. "A friend."

"Who can keep you safe? Now I wonder who would be able to . . . Ah, I think I know. There was another man in that forest who was woods-savvy besides your Joe Quinn. I had to use all my wits to avoid him a few times. He was very stimulating." He was silent a moment. "But I really don't want you to be kept safe, Eve. I want you to feel vulnerable. I may have to seriously target this Montalvo. You know, I've already begun to miss the little communications I've been sending you. I'm sure they had a wonderfully powerful effect."

"A stake through the heart of an innocent man would have a powerful effect on anyone, you bastard."

"*Tsk-tsk.* You mustn't be insulting. I can appreciate your attitude, but I'm the one in control and you have to be polite."

"You're not in control."

"Of course I am. Now, here's the way it's going to be. In a few days I'll give you the approximate location of where to find your Bonnie. You go after her and if you find Bonnie and I don't manage to kill you, then you win the game."

"And how do I know that Bonnie is where you say she'll be?"

"Oh, you don't. I may decide to make a few dry runs before I tell you the right location."

"While you get to take potshots at me on the chance that you've told me the truth. That's ridiculous."

"No, it's the prerogative of the one in control. I'm sure Quinn is certain he's capable of protecting you from me. He might even be able to do it. Take it or leave it."

"I'll have to think about it."

"By all means, just sit twiddling your thumbs in your cottage as you did in that hotel room in Bloomburg. In the meantime I'll be composing the next note I'm going to send you. Let's see, his name is Montalvo . . ."

He hung up the phone.

Her heart was beating hard, fast, and her hand was shaking as she pressed the button. Kistle would do it, she thought. He would kill Montalvo just to prove he could.

He wasn't really worried about Montalvo as a threat. His ego was too great to admit anyone was a danger to him.

It was stupid to worry about Montalvo. No one was better at taking care of himself. But, dammit, how could she not worry when the danger to him came from helping her?

She had to see Joe. She had to tell him about the call from Kistle. He had said he wasn't close, but Joe would know if that could be true.

She jumped to her feet and ran down the steps. Joe and Toby were on their way back, but she couldn't wait. She started down the path toward him.

"YOU TELL HIM NO," JOE SAID flatly. "You sit tight and let him come to you."

"Is it true? Could he monitor my call from a good distance away or is he right on top of us?"

"He could do it with a high-tech scanner."

"He doesn't have my cell number."

"He doesn't have to zero in on a number. He can do a general scan until he locates the phone he wants. But he probably does have your number now after he monitored you."

"Shit."

"I can get a block put on the phones by tomorrow."

"Good. Do it."

"But we can't take a chance he's telling the truth about keeping his distance. I'll call in some security boys to make sure the cottage is guarded. And I'll check out the woods myself."

"Okay," she said absently. Then she quickly shook her head. "No, he'd regard a security team in the same light as the police. He said no police."

"Too bad. We'll do what we have to do to keep you alive. He's not in control unless we give him the reins."

"You're wrong," she said quietly. "He's in control because he has something I want more than anything."

"For God's sake, Eve," he said through his teeth. "We're not even sure he's the one who killed Bonnie."

"There's a damn good chance. You think so too."

"Not enough to risk your neck." He was

staring at her expression. "I can't believe it. You're going to play the bastard's game."

"Maybe. I don't know. I have to think about it."

"No, you stay here."

"Listen to me, Joe." She turned to face him. "One thing that son of a bitch said was true. I can't sit on my duff and wait for things to happen. This is really my fight and I have to be involved as more than a rooting section. I didn't want to be in the way in Clayborne Forest, but maybe if I'd been on the scene, he'd have gone after me instead of those deputies and we'd have been able to catch him."

"And maybe you'd have been the one with the stake in your heart."

She shook her head. "He doesn't want to kill me immediately or he wouldn't have set up this elaborate baiting. He wants to be entertained."

"And you're going to let him torture you to amuse him."

"No, but I want Bonnie. I'm willing to take a chance to get her." She looked away from him. "But it should be my risk, not yours. I don't have the right to ask that of you."

"You're closing me out?"

"I don't want to be responsible for—"

"Screw it," he said harshly. "Do you think I'd let you go up against him alone? I may think you're nuts, but I couldn't do that."

"You've been with me all the way, but I thought . . ." Lord, this was difficult. "It's too hard for you now. You told me how you feel about Bonnie. I don't want you doing anything you're going to regret."

"I don't have any choice. I'd regret it more if I let him kill you. Go in the house." He strode away from her. "I'll check out the woods."

She watched helplessly as he disappeared into the woods. He was angry and frustrated and the bridge they had been building over the breach between them had collapsed. Damn Kistle. Damn her own obsession that was going to pull Joe into danger again.

Okay, she knew she had to do it and Joe refused to be left behind. It was going to happen. Now, how could she make it any more likely that they'd come out of this alive?

JOE DIDN'T COME BACK UNTIL dark and then he went immediately to the bedroom and took a shower.

"No sign of him?" she asked when he came into the living room.

"No," he said curtly. "You were right. He's not ready to play yet."

"There's stew in the refrigerator. Are you hungry?"

"No, I'll eat later." He went out on the porch.

She hesitated before following him. The tension was back and what she was going to say to him wasn't going to make him any more pleased. There was no use putting it off. He'd be pissed no matter when she told him.

She opened the screen door and went out on the porch. "I need to talk to you, Joe. I've been thinking."

He turned to face her. "Tell me you've changed your mind."

She shook her head and drew a deep breath. "I'm going to call Montalvo."

He stiffened. "What the hell."

"Kistle won't permit any help from the police or FBI, but I don't think he'd consider Montalvo as official. He'll only think of him as a friend of mine who might get in the way."

"My, my, that's exactly how I think of him."

"Dammit, Joe. We need help. Kistle's going to be waiting for us."

"Not Montalvo."

"Yes, Montalvo. I told you that Kistle was planning on targeting him. If he comes here to us, then he'll be safer, and if he goes with us to find Bonnie, we'll be safer. It makes sense."

"Not to me." His lips twisted. "But then you might be the winner no matter which one of us was killed by that bastard."

She flinched. "I didn't deserve that, Joe."

"Maybe not," he said. "I'm not thinking too clearly right now."

Because he was too hurt and angry to even try to understand what she was doing. "It's the best solution to a bad problem. I'm going to call him, Joe."

"Go ahead." He turned away from her. "But you should warn him that there's a better chance for death by friendly fire than in most wars."

"I'LL BE THERE IN TWO HOURS," Montalvo said. "Though I believe I'm a little insulted that you'd think I need protecting. If you think Kistle may be trying to dispose of me, it might be better for me to stay put and let him try."

"For God's sake, stop being macho. I'm sick of you and Joe thinking of this as some sort of cat-and-mouse game. And now Kistle is trying to set up his own game and it's scaring me to death. I know you won't go away and there's strength in numbers."

"What does Quinn say?"

"What do you think? Something about friendly fire."

He chuckled. "With Quinn the fire would definitely not be friendly. I'd come just to annoy him."

"And then I'd feel like shooting you myself. Don't make this difficult for me or I'll deal with Kistle on my own. I'd rather do that anyway. I'm tired of watching other people risk their lives because I'm choosing to let Kistle lead me down the garden path because of Bonnie."

"You forget that I did that to you. I used Bonnie to make you risk your life when I first met you. Turnabout is fair play. But I wouldn't expect a garden path. I'd say it will be full of thorns." He went on crisply, "But I'll try to restrain myself from antagonizing Quinn unduly. And I won't stay at your cottage. Miguel and I will camp out in your woods until you hear from Kistle. That way I can keep an eye on you." He added, "And you can keep an eye on me. Won't that be cozy?"

She ignored the question. "Kistle may object to Miguel."

"He appears fairly innocuous. He's young and boyish and he has two bandaged hands. Kistle will think he can pick him off at will. And I don't want him targeting Miguel because I'm out of his immediate reach. I want him with me."

He was right, Eve thought. Kistle would strike out at whatever victim he could if cheated of the one he wanted. "I'm sure Miguel will like that. He's been aching to go after Kistle since the beginning. I'll see you in a few hours." She hung up and went back out on the porch, where Joe was sitting on the swing with Toby at his feet. "He'll be here tonight. He's bringing Miguel and he's going to camp out in the woods."

"Good. I can't say I'd enjoy having him underfoot." He looked out at the woods. "At least he'll be of some use protecting you if he's out there."

She sat down in the swing beside him. "Everyone wants to protect me and I'm the one causing all this. Change your mind, Joe. I'm neither stupid nor helpless. Let me do this alone."

"No way." He looked away from her. "Let me do it alone."

"No way. I'm done with hiding away and waiting. Kistle wants me out on the firing line and that's where I want to be."

"Then we're at an impasse."

It seemed to Eve as if they'd been living in that state for months. "I guess we are." She reached out and tentatively touched his hand. "Does that mean you don't want to hold me? That's not what it means to me."

"No." His arm slid around her shoulders and drew her to him. "I'd want to hold you if you were going to lead me down to hell. Because if that's where you were, that's where I'd want to be."

She put her head on his shoulder. "Sometimes I think that's where I have been leading you," she said unsteadily. The moment was filled with love and poignant sadness and she wanted to hold him, touch him, and protect him. "And anytime you want to turn back, I'll understand."

"I'm not going anywhere." He was still staring out at the lake. "And I'll work with Montalvo because, when I'm not pissed off, I can see how he might help to keep you alive."

"I wasn't sure you'd be willing to do that."

"I knew every minute I was in Clayborne Forest that I was fighting against time. I was sure you'd dive in as soon as you couldn't stand it any longer. Do I want to break Montalvo's neck every time I see him? Hell, yes. But I can't afford indulging my feelings toward him right now. My focus has to be totally on you. And I'd put up with a Saddam Hussein or a Satan if he could help."

"No friendly fire?"

"Maybe later. I'm not promising anything." He reached for his phone. "But right now I'm going to call Jane and try to keep her on the other side of the Atlantic. I don't want her caught up in this hell ride."

"How are you going to do that?"

"How do you think? Make up a whopper of a lie."

THE CALL FROM KISTLE CAME an hour later. "Really, Eve. You're spoiling all my fun. I was counting on a more dramatic death for Montalvo than the rest of you. It was going to be like the riveting prologue to the main novel. Now he'll just be one of the crowd."

"You were listening in on my phone conversation."

"Yes. Are you surprised?"

"No, I thought there was a good chance. You knew I'd warn him."

"I didn't realize I'd drive you to tuck him under your wing. But I did learn something of value. Quinn and Montalvo are at odds. That may mean I can divide and conquer."

"Don't count on it."

"I never count on anything. That's why I'm so good in the wild. There are certain patterns that never change, but almost everything else is unstable."

"Including you."

"Including me. I'm sending you a present tomorrow. I think it will serve to keep the adrenaline flowing. Good night, Eve."

She turned to Joe sitting on the couch beside her. "He's still scanning my phone. He knew about the call to Montalvo. I think he's accepted his coming here."

"The block will be on by morning. What else?"

"He's sending me a present tomorrow." She shuddered. "He was practically salivating. I kept thinking of those men with a stake in their hearts. He wants to scare me."

"So what's new?" Joe turned away. "I saw two cars' headlights coming up the road before I came in from the porch. It's probably Montalvo. I'm going down to meet him."

She started to follow him and then stopped. It would be better if she let him go alone. She wasn't going to be able to play referee forever. They were grown men and they'd have to work it out for themselves.

She went to the door and watched him stride down the path toward the place on the other side of the lake where the cars had parked.

A very sensible decision but, dammit, she wanted to be down there with them instead of waiting here like some nitwit lady in a tower.

MONTALVO AND MIGUEL HAD already built a fire and were unpacking their gear by the time Joe reached their camp.

"Ah, Quinn, I was expecting you," Montalvo said. "Perhaps not quite this soon, but I had the foresight to bring an extra coffee from Starbucks for you in case you came before I had time to make a pot." He handed him the large Starbucks cup and turned to Miguel. "Stop unpacking, Miguel. Don't be rude. We have a guest."

He probably expected Joe to toss the coffee in his face. Instead, Joe took off the lid and lifted the cup to his lips. "None for Eve?"

"It would be smart of her to let us go at it face-to-face." He leaned against the car and took a drink of his coffee. "And Eve is very, very smart. She's probably gnawing her fingernails because she wants to run down and handle this meeting herself, but she let you go alone."

And Montalvo knew her well enough to be able to predict that response. Joe smothered the flare of anger the thought brought him. Keep cool. "That's right." He lifted his cup to his lips. "But as you said, she's very smart. She knows I'm not going to break your neck . . . yet."

"May I go back to unpacking?" Miguel asked. "Violent discussions upset me."

"No, stay. I'm going to need you." Montalvo smiled. "But, I assure you, not to protect me. Drink your coffee and be quiet. Go on, Quinn."

"I'm just here to say that we're going to work together on this. This isn't going to be another Clayborne Forest. No working alone, no competition. That suited me too. But this is different. Eve is going to be right in the middle of it. She's not going to be at risk because you want to make points with her."

Montalvo's smile faded. "I didn't expect this. I expected anger, perhaps an attempt to shut me out. Not this."

"I'm angry. I *will* shut you out. But that's not what's important right now." He took another drink of coffee, threw the rest of it on the ground, and crushed the coffee cup in his hand. "And if your ego demands you try to operate on your own, I'll crush you like I did that cup."

Miguel gave a low whistle. "I really think the tent needs to be put up."

Montalvo didn't look away from Joe. "Relax, Miguel, nothing is going to happen. When I was a boy like you, I might have acted precipitously and gone for the jugular, but I have a tendency to think before I leap these days." He finished his coffee. "And I do have a certain amount of ego, but I control it, Quinn. It doesn't control me. I happen to agree with you in this case, so I'll ignore your warning and chalk it up to concern for Eve."

"How kind," Joe said sarcastically.

"It is, isn't it?" Montalvo turned to Miguel. "Lay out those maps on the ground beside the fire."

"Right away." Miguel quickly reached into a box in the car and drew out several maps. "Anything for a diversion." He spread two of the maps on the ground. "I brought boxes of books and magazines about the possible sites where we might find Kistle. And I bought three sets of maps. I can give you one set, Quinn."

"And why am I supposed to want these maps?" Joe asked.

"Because according to Murdock, the informant who told us about Kistle and Bonnie, these were the areas where Kistle liked to go hunting. He talked about them all the time." Montalvo pointed to the first map. "Chattahoochee Oconee National Forest." He pointed to the second. "Okefenokee Swamp. The first place is fairly close, about two hours away. The second is in south Georgia. My bet is that he's going to lead Eve to one of those places."

"Maybe both of them," Joe said. "I've been to Chattahoochee National Forest. It could be a nightmare. Rough terrain, bluffs, streams."

"How well do you know it?" Montalvo asked.

"Pretty well. Several years ago I followed a lead that Bonnie was buried there. We didn't come up with anything." His lips twisted. "But that doesn't mean she's not there. We couldn't search every inch of that acreage and we had no coordinates."

"What about the swamp?"

Joe shook his head. "Never been there."

"Swamps are a good place to dispose of bodies."

"You speak from personal experience?"

"Very personal." Montalvo looked down at the map. "And, no, I haven't tossed any enemies into the swamp. We had to retrieve my wife from a swamp. She was murdered and thrown away like so much refuse."

"I don't think Kistle would take a chance on a body being retrieved. He's too careful. Of course, he could lie just to bring Eve to him."

"He could pick another place entirely," Miguel said. "But these were the only grounds where he mentioned hunting. It makes sense, if he was going to bury a body, that he'd have it planned out ahead of time, as he did with Bobby Joe."

Joe nodded. "He was younger then, but the basic MO was probably the same."

Montalvo nodded. "That's what I thought. That means we have to learn these places as well as Kistle."

"No way," Joe said. "We've got a chance with the national forest since I've been there, but none of us knows anything about the swamp."

"I'm going down there tonight," Miguel said. "I've paid lots of Montalvo's money to a park ranger who will take me through it and reveal all its secrets."

"Optimistic."

"I'm good in the jungle, even better in a swamp. You would have seen for yourself if the colonel had let me go into Clayborne Forest." He held up his hands. "But I've told him the park ranger will do all the work and keep my bandages pristine clean."

"He'd better," Montalvo said grimly. He looked at Joe. "I was going to go to the national forest, but it would be a waste of time if you know it well."

Joe's lips lifted in a sardonic smile. "You'd follow my lead?"

"You wouldn't lead Eve astray," Montalvo said softly. "And I'll have to be close to her if I'm to protect her." He got to his feet. "Give him his maps, Miguel. I'll start to put up the tent."

Joe took the maps Miguel handed him and stood up. "I'll let you know when Eve hears from Kistle."

He wheeled and started up the path toward the cottage.

MIGUEL STOOD WATCHING QUINN for a moment. "I didn't think you would let him talk to you like that. It's not like you, Colonel."

Montalvo shrugged. "I'm sorry to disappoint you. Do you think I'm afraid of him?"

Miguel shook his head. "No, but I don't understand."

Montalvo drove the tent pegs into the ground before he spoke again. "I would have handled the situation in exactly the same way that he did. It's hard to condemn a man who does that." Montalvo remembered saying something to Eve about them being mirror images of each other. Strange. Now he was seeing his reflection in Joe Quinn.

He dismissed the thought. "As soon as we get the tent up, I want you to get something to eat and sleep a few hours. I want you to be at Okefenokee by daybreak."

KISTLE'S PACKAGE WAS DELIVERED by UPS late the next afternoon. It was the size of a shirt box and wrapped in brown paper.

Joe brought it up to the porch. "It's very light. Do you want me to open it?"

"No, I'll do it." Eve stared at the box for a moment before taking it. It wasn't going to bite her. Or maybe it would. She wouldn't put it past Kistle to put a tarantula in the box.

Nevertheless, she had to open it.

She tore off the brown paper and opened the white box.

A child's blue hair ribbon.

She felt sick.

"Is it Bonnie's?" Joe asked.

That had been her first thought. But Eve had seldom put ribbons in Bonnie's hair because she had too many curls. When she did, the ribbons were always yellow. Bonnie loved yellow. She said it reminded her of the sun. "No, it's not Bonnie's." She touched it gingerly. On closer inspection she could see traces of brown stain on the satin. Dirt?

Or blood?

"There's an envelope." Joe took it out of the box and opened it. "Two pictures." He handed her one taken somewhere outdoors. There was a pine tree and close to it was a huge rock. Then he handed her the second one.

"Oh, God."

It was a picture of a little girl with shiny brown hair tied back with a blue ribbon.

Eve's gaze flew up to Joe's face. "He's still doing it. It's Clayborne Forest all over again. He's still doing it."

"Easy. We don't know that yet. He didn't send us a body part. He sent us a ribbon."

"With blood on it. That stain has got to be blood."

Joe was checking the envelope. "There's a piece of paper here." Joe pulled it out and glanced at it before handing it to Eve. "He evidently wants to drag this out."

Watch the news tonight, Eve. Her name is Laura Ann.

"The evening news," she repeated. "What time is it?"

"Three-thirty. Channel two has news starting at five."

She looked at the other picture, of the pine and rock. "And what the hell is this?"

"A clue?"

"Where he buried Bonnie?" She shuddered. "Or where he buried that little girl, Laura Ann?"

"We'll have to wait and see." Joe headed for the kitchen. "In the meantime I'll make a pot of coffee. You're pale as a tombstone. You can use it. Hell, I can use it."

Pale as a tombstone.

Only Bonnie had never had a tombstone. She was lost, and so might be this other little girl.

Watch the news. Five o'clock. It was going to seem like forever.

ELEVEN

NINE-YEAR-OLD LAURA ANN Simmons was the first story on the news. She had not shown up at home the day before and her mother, Nina Simmons, had at first thought her ex-husband might have picked her up at school. He had denied it when she managed to contact him. Laura Ann was still missing and the police were now considering foul play.

"Foul," Eve repeated. "Oh, yes, no one could be fouler than Kistle." She felt sick as she looked at the photo of the little girl on the television. She was small for her age and had long, dark brown hair held back by a ribbon. Her blue eyes were wide and bright and her eager smile lit the screen with warmth. "Can you find out anything more from the department, Joe?"

"I can try." Joe pulled out his cell phone. "But it sounds like the investigation is just beginning. We probably don't know much."

"Wait." She looked at the blue ribbon in the box sitting on the couch. "Don't tell them about this yet. There may be a chance that—"

"I wasn't going to tell them anything. One way or another Kistle is going to use that little girl. Until we know how, I don't want to rock the boat." The precinct answered and he started talking and went out on the porch.

She looked at the snapshot of Laura Simmons. The little girl wasn't smiling, but she didn't look frightened either. Maybe the picture was taken before she realized she had something to fear from the man taking her picture.

Her cell phone rang. She looked down and saw the ID. John Spacek. She wasn't surprised that it was Kistle when she picked up. She had been expecting him.

"Who is John Spacek? How did you get his phone?"

"The usual manner. He and his wife won't need it any longer. Did you see the news?"

"Have you hurt her?"

"Laura Ann? Not yet. I've been too busy making plans to welcome you."

"Let her go. This is between you and me. There's no reason to involve a child."

"There's every reason. It will add spice to the pot. For you, the prize of a dead girl's bones would be enough. But what about Quinn and Montalvo? I'm sure keeping Laura Ann alive would be more of an incentive."

"We don't even know if she's alive now."

Joe had come back into the house and stopped short at the door as he saw her expression.

"She's alive," Kistle said.

"Let me talk to her."

"Not yet. I'll do that when I think you need encouraging. Besides, she's sleeping now. I had to keep her quiet. But I'm moving her out in a few hours and it won't matter if she screams."

Eve's hand tightened on the phone. "Send her home."

"No. Laura Ann will be near Bonnie's resting place. If you find one, you find the other. If I win and you die, then Laura Ann dies. And though you'll no longer care if her body goes back to her parents for proper burial, I'll guarantee that will not be the case. They'll never find her. Just as they've never found Bonnie."

"Why involve her at all? She'll just get in your way. Let her go."

"Oh, I'll never let her go. That's part of the game. The only way that she's going to stay alive is if you take her away from me. Now for the rules. You've got two days to find Bonnie and Laura Ann. I sent you a clue. Use it." He hung up.

"Is she alive?" Joe asked as he watched her press the disconnect.

"I don't know. He says she is. He wouldn't let me talk to her. He said she was unconscious."

"He's using her as bait?"

Eve nodded. "He thought it might be a stronger motivation for you and Montalvo. He wasn't sure I'd care. For God's sake, what does he think I am? Of course I care." She drew a deep, shaky breath. "We have two days. Laura Ann is near where Bonnie is buried. We have to find Bonnie to find Laura Ann." She looked down at the picture of the pine tree and massive boulder. "And I guess this is our so-called clue." She got to her feet. "Dammit, it could be anywhere."

"But the chances are it will be either Chattahoochee National Forest or Oke-fenokee Swamp. He'll have figured out who must have tipped us off about him and will know we know about his old haunts."

"And what are we supposed to do? Flip a coin?"

"It may end up by us doing that." Joe took the photo and headed for the door. "But I'm banking on Kistle leaving us a lit-tle stronger clue. I'm going down to Mon-talvo's camp and look through those books Miguel unearthed. You start pack-ing and call Patty and ask her to take Toby again. If we've only got two days, we'd better make tonight count."

"Wait."

He looked back over his shoulder.

"I want to go see Laura Ann's mother.

Can you arrange it so that no one knows about it?"

"It will be difficult as hell. Her telephone lines will be monitored in case there's a ransom demand."

"Can you do it?"

"It would be smarter not to try, Eve."

"I don't care. I know what that woman is going through. Any information is better than none at all. She needs to know someone is doing something to help Laura Ann, that there's a chance of getting her back."

"Not the greatest chance." He lifted his hand as she opened her mouth to speak. "Okay, I'll set it up. I'll go over to her house and ask the captain if I can question her alone. Nina Simmons lives in a rental house in Marietta, right outside the Atlanta city limits. You follow me and I'll try to bring her outside and away from everyone else."

She nodded. "Thanks, Joe. I only want a few minutes."

"If she gets hysterical it may be a few minutes too long." He opened the screen door. "But we'll deal with that if it happens. You're right; she deserves any comfort we can give her. You're not the only one who remembers how those first days when Bonnie was missing tore you apart."

THE SUN WAS LOW IN THE SKY when Eve saw Joe and Nina Simmons walk out of the house on Meadow Place Drive and down the porch steps. Laura Ann's mother was a pretty woman in her thirties with brown hair cut in a breezy style and the same blue eyes as her daughter. Those eyes were swollen from weeping and she looked totally devastated.

Eve got out of her car and waited on the corner as Joe walked with her down the street toward her. Now that she was here, she felt helpless. She didn't know enough to give comfort.

But she could give hope.

Joe stopped and let Laura Ann's mother go the last few yards alone.

"Nina Simmons?" She stepped forward and took the other woman's hand. "I'm Eve Duncan. I won't keep you long. I just wanted to—"

"I know who you are," Nina Simmons said jerkily. "The detective told me. He said that you were looking for my daughter. He said you might have a chance of finding Laura Ann."

"We'll find her." Lord, she hoped she was telling the truth. "But you won't be able to tell anyone we may have a lead on her. It would be—it wouldn't be good."

"You mean he might kill her," she said baldly. "Have you talked to her?"

"Not yet."

"Then you don't know she's alive."

"I think the chances are that she's alive."

"But you don't *know*." Her voice broke. "You don't know anything. You're like all the rest."

"I know we'll find her. We won't stop until we do."

"You've *got* to find her. You don't know how special she is. She's had to fight all her life just to stay alive. She had two heart operations before she was four and she came out of them like a champ." Tears were running down her cheeks. "She had a mother who couldn't be with her because she had to work twelve hours a day to keep food on the table and a father who didn't think that Laura Ann was worth sticking around for when the going got tough. Yet she never complained and she just keeps getting brighter and stronger every day of her life." Her voice became fierce. "So don't you dare let that monster do anything to her."

Eve wanted to reach out and touch her, comfort her, but she could see how frail the balance was that kept Laura Ann's mother's composure intact. "We'll bring her back to you. I think that I'll be able to talk to her soon. Is there anything that you'd like me to tell her?"

"Tell her—I love her. I'm proud of her. I know she'll come home to me." She turned on her heel. "Now get out of here and go find my daughter." She strode past Joe down the street and into the house.

Eve was barely aware when Joe took her elbow and nudged her gently back toward her car. "She's hurting so," she whispered. "Did I help at all, Joe?"

"You did what you could," Joe said quietly. "She'll get through it. She's tough."

"Yes." But being strong didn't stop the panic and pain. Seeing Nina Simmons had brought back all the agony of the time when she had lost Bonnie. She opened her car door. "Now let's get busy and see if we can keep that promise I made her. I'll meet you back at Montalvo's camp."

"IT COULD BE EITHER THE swamp or Chattahoochee National Forest." Montalvo opened a coffee-table book on the national forest and started quickly going through it. "Dammit, this is the third book we've gone through and there's nothing like that rock."

Joe tossed a boating travelogue on the swamp aside and picked up another book. "It's got to be here. If we don't get close, it won't be any fun for Kistle."

"Try the brochures you pick up in the lobby of hotels." Eve stood in the doorway of the tent. "He doesn't really want to fool us. He'll want to make this part easy for us. What's easier than one of those tourist brochures?"

"Good idea." Montalvo reached for a pile of brochures at the bottom of the case. He raked Eve with a searching glance as he pulled them out. "How are you doing?"

"I'll be better after we find where Kistle's set up his trap." Eve knelt beside them and started going through the brochures. "Good

God, Miguel has everything here from Okefenokee to Stone Mountain."

"He believes in overkill," Montalvo said.

"So does Kistle." She systematically
started to go through the brochures, carefully opening each one and scanning the
inside pages.

It was five minutes later that Joe found
it. "Chattahoochee National Forest." He
threw the brochure down and pointed to
the photo inside. "The bastard picked an
all-American family to go with it."

The photo was of a mother, father, and
little girl, all in hiking gear, climbing the hill
where the rock and pine tree were clearly
in evidence. The little girl's face was closest to the camera and she looked wonderfully happy and vibrantly alive. It was
not Laura Ann, of course, but the choice
of the little girl did what it was meant to
do. It reminded them of life that could be
so easily taken away.

"Where was it taken?" Eve asked. "It's
not a landmark."

"That would be too easy." Joe got to his
feet. "I'll call the precinct and get them to
get me a telephone number for the people
who did this brochure. In the meantime,

let's hit the road. We can reach the national forest in a couple hours."

"It will be dark by then." Eve moved toward the SUV. The twilight was already beginning to fade from gold to purple. "How are we going to make our way through that forest? We've got flashlights, but that's rough territory and we don't know where we're going."

"Quinn should know where he's going as soon as he gets a location," Montalvo said. "He told me he'd spent some time there."

"Yes, he did." Eve remembered those weeks Joe and the searchers had been in that forest all those years ago looking for Bonnie's grave. She recalled the tiredness and frustration and finally the despair. That had almost destroyed their relationship.

Now it was starting all over again.

"GOOD. YOU'RE WAKING UP. WHAT a sleepyhead you are, Laura Ann. That little bit of chloroform shouldn't have kept you out this long."

Laura Ann felt a jolt of terror. It was him, the man who'd said he was Daddy's friend and then stuffed that handkerchief over her mouth. "I want to go home. You let me leave right now or I'll tell the police you did this to me."

"My, we have a fighter. Do you know I've always found that little girls are much tougher fighters than little boys? And I have a vast experience with both." He checked the ropes binding her wrists. "I believe it has something to do with survival of the species."

"My mother said I was a seven-month baby and that I wouldn't have lived if I hadn't wanted to do it." She glared at him. "Now you let me loose and let me go home. My mom is going to be worried about me."

"And so she should be." He stroked her throat. "Because whether you live or not is not up to you this time, little girl."

She felt her heart beating hard beneath his hand. He meant he was going to hurt her. Mom had told her about dirty men who wanted to hurt kids.

"There, now, that's what I like to see." He was staring at her face. "What wide eyes you have, Laura Ann. How scared are you? I can make you very scared. Do you want to beg me not to hurt you?"

She was scared. She wanted to run away, but she couldn't move. She hated him. She hated him.

"Tell me," he said softly.

She opened her mouth to beg him, to promise to do anything he asked, but she hated him too much.

She spit in his face.

"Bitch." His hand tightened on her throat until everything went red, then dark.

Then he let her go and was wiping his face with a handkerchief. "What a pleasure you're going to be, Laura Ann. I can hardly wait. But I have to be patient because I need you to talk to another bitch." He picked her up and threw her in the back of his car. "And then we'll see how tough you are."

She didn't feel tough. Her throat hurt and she was as scared as he wanted her to be. She could feel the tears run down her cheeks. She wanted Mama to come and get her. But Mama had said that the two of them were on their own after Daddy left and Laura Ann had to be able to help take care of herself. Maybe this was one of the times when Mama couldn't help her.

Maybe she'd have to get away from him all by herself.

THE PRECINCT CALLED JOE back as they were entering the Chattahoochee National Forest. He listened for a moment. "Right." He hung up. "It's about four miles from here near a bluff overlooking a stream. There's supposed to be a path leading around the bluff, and the rock is on the backside. They said the path is so covered by brush that it's almost indiscernible."

"Do you remember the area?" Montalvo asked.

Joe nodded. "I went over that stream a dozen times when I was on the search, but I never went south of the bluff. I never knew there was a path. I sure didn't see it. We can go by car as far as the stream, but then we'll have to go by foot around the bluff."

They reached the stream fifteen minutes later and got out to look up at the bluff. It was huge and Eve shivered as she looked up at it. "Anyone on top of that monstrosity would have a great shot, wouldn't he?"

"Yes." Montolvo moved forward. "And that's why I'll climb up and take a look before you and Quinn start the path around the bluff."

"And what's to keep him from picking you off?" Eve asked. "Don't do it."

He smiled back at her. "Don't worry. I'm good at this. Give me fifteen minutes. Put your phone on vibrate, Quinn. I'll call and hang up and call again if it's safe." He disappeared into the shrubbery.

Eve muttered an oath. "Dammit, he shouldn't have gone."

"You couldn't have stopped him. What a wonderful grandstand." Joe drew her back into the shrubbery. "He'll enjoy every minute of it."

"Unless he gets killed."

"Yes, unless he gets killed. That would put a crimp in his show."

She was edgy as hell and Joe wasn't helping. "Don't be an ass."

He didn't speak for a moment and then he said, "You're right. I was jealous. I want to be the one on that damn bluff and I'm down here on the ground looking up. I always seem to be stuck with that role when Montalvo's around."

"Because you want to make sure I'm safe, and I'm no good at climbing bluffs. I'd say that's pretty much of a star role." Her gaze went to the shrubbery jutting out of the bluff where Montalvo had disappeared. "I don't see him any longer."

"He's three-quarters up the bluff. That branch on the southern ledge moved a little as he went past it. He should be at the top in a few minutes."

Her eyes strained to see Montalvo in the darkness, but she couldn't make out anything. It was incredible to her that Joe could see what was happening.

"There he is." Joe's phone had vibrated until it went to voice mail. Then it began to vibrate again. "No one's on the bluff." Joe turned and started down the path. "Stay behind me. Let me check the path out as we go."

She hurried to keep up with him. The shrubbery was almost growing over the path, hanging over her, all around her, and she felt suffocated, as if she were caught in a verdant trap. Kistle could be anywhere in that growth. So close she would never see him.

"I'd hear him," Joe called softly back to her. "And if I didn't smell him, I'd sense him."

She had felt that she'd sense Kistle when she was at the lake cottage, but this was different. She was disoriented and her heart was beating so hard she couldn't hear anything but that pounding.

"There's a break in the foliage just ahead," Joe said. "I think we've made it around the bluff."

"Good." Her pace instinctively quickened until she was just behind him. "Going back I might just try my luck on the bluff." Then she was out in the open and could draw a deep breath.

"Stay here a minute," Joe said. "You're out of rifle range if he's in that pine grove. And I can't see anywhere else he'd be able to take cover."

Neither could Eve. She tensed as she saw the huge rock and behind it a little grove of pines. Other than those features it was all open area. "How are we going to get to the grove without being seen?"

His gaze was raking the bluff. "We

don't. There's Montalvo." He raised a hand and made a sweeping motion at the grove. "He's angling in on the other side of the grove and checking it out. In the meantime, we move around outside firing range and keep Kistle distracted, if that's where he is." He moved along the edge of the shrubbery bordering the clearing. "Come on."

She followed him but couldn't keep her eyes from the pine grove. Was that where Bonnie was buried? Was that where Kistle was keeping Laura Ann? Was that where Kistle was waiting with his rifle to kill all of them?

"VERY SMART," KISTLE MURMURED. "Don't you think so, Laura Ann? Isn't it fun to watch them at play? Oh, that's right, I had to gag you again. But I'm sure you agree with me."

He couldn't see Montalvo, but he had probably gone over the bluff and was in the grove. He was glad he hadn't killed Montalvo off before the game actually began. It was exciting to deal with two such interesting opponents. He could feel his anticipation mounting more by the moment.

"Come closer," he whispered. "Just a little closer . . ."

MONTALVO CAME OUT OF THE grove twenty minutes later and motioned to them. He met them halfway across the clearing a few yards from the boulder. "No Kistle."

"You're sure?" Eve asked. "There's no other place for him to hide."

"He's not there. The grove isn't that big and I'm no amateur," Montalvo said. "He's not on the ground. He's not in the trees. He not there."

She braced herself. "Then I want to go into the grove and look around."

"If Bonnie's buried there, you wouldn't be able to tell," Joe said. "Too much time has passed."

"But not for Laura Ann," Eve said. "If he's killed her, the earth would be freshly turned. And he said Laura Ann would be near Bonnie."

Montalvo nodded and turned on his flashlight. "That's true. Okay. We'll take a look."

"You take a look. I'll stay here. Kistle could be behind us on that trail." Joe's gaze lifted past the boulder to the top of the bluff. "Or he could be coming over the bluff as you did, Montalvo."

"Eve?" Montalvo asked.

"I want to make sure there's no grave in those woods," Eve said. "I can't believe he would have brought us here if he hadn't set up a way to hurt me in some way." She started for the pines. "If the grove's that small, it shouldn't take long, Joe."

Joe didn't answer and she looked back over her shoulder. He was staring intently up at the top of the boulder. Or was he looking beyond it to the bluff?

"Joe? Do you see something?"

"I thought I saw a sort of glittering on the top of that boulder." He started to take a step closer and then stopped. "Holy shit!" He dove to the ground and started rolling. "Get down! It's a camera, and that means he may have—"

Montalvo jerked Eve to the ground. "Booby trap!"

The earth erupted and the boulder exploded.

Rock flew in all directions.

Eve buried her head in her arms. She could feel sharp bits of rock stinging her arms like shrapnel.

Joe. Joe had been much closer to the boulder than either she or Montalvo.

She lifted her head to see Joe lying crumpled across the clearing.

"No!" She jumped to her feet and tore across the clearing. "Joe . . ."

He didn't move.

She fell to her knees beside him.

"Don't move him." Montalvo was beside her. "That was a hell of a blast. We don't know what it did to him."

"He's bleeding." The blood was trickling from a cut on Joe's temple.

Montalvo handed her his handkerchief. "So are you."

"We've got to get help for him." She started dabbing at the cut. "This isn't too deep, but it may not be—"

Joe opened his eyes. "Are you . . . hurt?"

Relief poured through her. "No, but I thought you might be. How do you feel? Can you move your arms and legs?"

He tested one limb after another. "No breakage." He sat up. "I'm sore as hell. I feel as if someone punched me in the back."

"I was nowhere near you," Montalvo murmured. "It must have been the blast." He looked at the boulder and gave a low whistle. "Kistle must have packed a truckload of explosives under that boulder. There's not much left."

"And there wouldn't have been much left of us if Kistle had pressed the detonator a few minutes earlier," Joe said. "He waited until you'd moved a little away from the boulder, Eve. He didn't care if I caught the blast, but he's obviously saving you for something more interesting to him."

"There was a camera on that boulder?"

He nodded. "Probably with a detonator programmed into it. That way he got to enjoy watching us try to catch him and still was able to cause mayhem." He slowly got to his feet. He waved Eve away when she tried to help. "I've got to do it myself. I have to make sure I don't have any damage a hot bath won't cure."

She clenched her hands at her sides as she watched him, but she didn't touch him.

"Okay." He turned to her. "I'm all right. Let's go check out the grove and then go home. I have a hunch you'll be hearing from Kistle soon."

"We could check out the grove later," Eve said. "Why don't we leave now?"

He shook his head. "You'd worry about there being a grave in those pines. Even though this was more than likely a setup, it would be in the back of your mind." He shrugged. "And I believe it's safe enough. I don't think Kistle is going to be anywhere near here or he wouldn't have set up that camera."

"I don't either," Montalvo said. "But you could wait here while we check out those woods. You look like hell."

"Three will do it faster. We'll split up." He met Montalvo's gaze. "And I do feel like hell right now. But I'll get better and I won't let it stop me. Nothing is going to stop me from getting Kistle." He strode toward the pine grove. "Let's get this over with."

KISTLE STARTED THE CAR. "Did you hear the blast, Laura Ann? I did that. I pressed a button and I shook the earth." He drove down the rock road toward the highway leading out of the national park. "And I probably blew up Quinn to meet his maker. Have you ever seen a dead man?

Before this is over I may be able to show you a few." He glanced over his shoulder and looked down at her on the floor of the car. "I heard a sound behind that gag. Are you crying, Laura Ann?" He shook his head. "No, I see your eyes glittering in the darkness. You're staring at me with such anger and hatred. You know, I'm not accustomed to that from children." He turned back to the road as he put on speed. "Children are usually very frightened. It's what makes the experience so exquisite. And I was counting on wringing Eve's heart when she spoke to you. Oh, well, we have little time. Maybe if I tell you what I'm planning you'll give me the right response."

TWELVE

MONTALVO DROVE WITH THEM up to the front door of the lake cottage.

"Are you coming in?" Eve asked as she got out of the SUV. "I'll make coffee." She made a face. "Or maybe you'd prefer a drink. I'm going to make one for Joe and give it to him while he's in the bath."

Montalvo shook his head. "Not right now. I'm going to go back to my camp and call Miguel and see what's happening with him." He took the steps two at a time. "But first I thought I'd check out the cottage."

"I can do it," Joe said. "Go on."

"It will go quicker for me. You're a bit stiff." Montalvo turned to Eve. "Keys?"

Eve tossed him the keys. "I don't believe Kistle is going to come after us here. He wants to lure us onto his turf."

"Neither do I. But I don't assume anything." He disappeared into the house.

"Neither do I." Joe started up the porch steps. "And it doesn't hurt to be safe, Eve. By all means, put the bastard to work."

"I'm glad you're not objecting to a little help."

"I'm the one who took the hit, let Montalvo take up some of the slack. He wanted to be involved? We're going to let him be involved up to his eyebrows."

Montalvo came out of the cottage and gave the keys back to Eve. "All secure. I'll check outside the house in case Kistle had some extra explosives he wanted to put to use." He ran down the steps. "Call me if you need me. Otherwise I'll be in touch after we all get a few hours' sleep."

"Right." Joe opened the screen door. "But phone me when you get Miguel's report on Okefenokee."

Montalvo didn't answer. He'd already gone around the side of the cottage.

Eve followed Joe into the house. "Oke-fenokee?"

"Kistle's led us down the garden path at the national forest. He may send us back there. But I'm betting on the swamp." He headed for the bathroom. "I think Chatta-hoochee was a false trail, a decoy. He was saving the real thing for Okefenokee."

"We'll see as soon as he calls me." She took off her jacket. "Can I get you any-thing?"

"That drink you promised." He glanced over his shoulder, stiffening. "For God's sake, your arms look like pincushions. Why didn't you tell me you were hurt?"

"I'm not." She glanced at her arms. He was right, both her forearms and wrists were riddled with cuts from the flying rocks. "It's nothing."

"Well, forget the drink and clean them up. All we need is for you to get blood poi-soning."

"I can do both. Get into that bath." She went to the sink in the kitchen and got down antiseptic and bandages from the cabinet. Clean up, stick on some Band-Aids, and she'd be fine.

Joe would be fine too, thank God.

Her hand was starting to shake. Probably shock starting to set in. They had been so busy since the blast that she had not fully realized how close Joe had come to death. Now it was hitting full force. She had almost lost him.

She leaned her head against the cabinet. Joe had almost lost his life, and it brought home to her how empty her own life would be without him.

"Okay, Eve?" Joe called from the bathroom.

"Fine. I told you it was nothing." She drew a deep breath and got down a glass and the whiskey bottle from the cabinet. "I'll be right in."

She poured his drink. Stop shaking, dammit. Don't let Joe see how upset you are. She couldn't fall apart when she was the one who had brought them all into this. They had been blundering around, keeping to Kistle's rules, letting him call all the shots, hoping against hope that they could see through the lies.

And Joe had almost died.

It couldn't go on, not like this. Something had to change.

EVE'S CELL RANG AT 4:35 in the morning.

She didn't look at the ID. She didn't want to know if Kistle had taken another victim to get his cell phone. She knew who it was. So did Joe, who rose up on one elbow to watch her take the call.

"Are you terribly bereaved, Eve?" Kistle asked. "How long had you been with Quinn?"

"A long time. And I'm still with him. You screwed up, Kistle. That blast didn't get any of us."

"No? I suppose it was my mistake. I was so interested in watching you all creep around trying to find me that I waited a little too long to press the detonator. Laura Ann and I found it very entertaining."

"She's still alive?"

"Yes, and very annoying. She stares at me with those big blue eyes and it makes me want to put them out. She's too stupid to know enough to be afraid of me."

"And now you can tell her you've made another mistake and you didn't kill anyone with those explosives." No, she mustn't taunt him with anything connected with Laura Ann. The little girl's position was too precarious. "And perhaps she is scared and doesn't want to show it."

"The little bitch spat in my face."

Eve felt a surge of fierce satisfaction. "Let her go, Kistle, she's more trouble than she's worth."

"I agree. That's why I've been considering dispensing with her."

"No!"

"See, I believe it would bother you. That's why I have to keep her alive as a carrot to lead you on."

"How do I know she's still alive?"

"I'll let her speak a few words to you later. Now let's go on to Act Two. Okefenokee Swamp. You'll find what you want on one of the lands there."

"Lands?"

"That's what they call the islands in the swamp. I'll put a picture of Bonnie's island on the bulletin board of the visitors' bureau."

"Same tune, Kistle. Why should I let you lead me into a trap when you lied before?"

"Obsession?"

"That won't be enough for Joe or Montalvo."

"Laura Ann?"

She couldn't deny that would draw them on a possible wild-goose chase. "It's not enough. Not after you almost blew us all to kingdom come. Give me some proof that Act Two isn't just going to lead to Act Three if you don't kill us."

He was silent a moment. "This is a two-act play, Eve. I don't have to give you proof, but you'll not find that island barren soil. It was a perfect place to hide a body. And I may decide to hide yours there as well."

"Let me talk to Laura Ann."

"Of course, I promised you, didn't I? Come along, little bitch, speak up."

A few seconds passed and then a wisp of a child's voice. "Hello."

Relief poured through Eve. At least Kistle had told the truth about Laura Ann. "Listen, baby, my name is Eve and we're going to come and get you. But you're with a very bad man and you mustn't make him angry. Try not to talk to him at all."

"He doesn't like that either. Will you tell my mama that I'm sorry? She told me not to get in a car with a stranger, but he told me he was Daddy's friend. I wanted to see my daddy. I thought maybe he wanted to see me too."

"I'll tell her." Her eyes were suddenly stinging. "I'm sure she'll understand. She gave me a message for you. She said to tell you that she loves you and is very proud of you. She'll see you soon."

"Enough." Kistle was back on the phone. "I'll let you talk to her again when you reach the swamp. The clock is ticking, Eve." He hung up.

She slowly pressed the disconnect.

"What did he say?" Joe asked.

"You were right. It's an island in the Okefenokee. We're to check the bulletin board at the visitors' bureau. Laura Ann is still alive." She swung her feet to the floor and got out of bed. "Call Montalvo and tell him, will you? We're going to need all the information Miguel gathered about the swamp."

"What if this is another blind alley?"

"That's what I asked him," she said jerkily as she headed for the bathroom. "He said this was the final act and I wouldn't find barren soil on that island."

"And you believe the son of a bitch?"

"Yes. This time I believe him. I think that island's somebody's burial ground." She closed the bathroom door behind her. Take a shower, get dressed, and use that time to think. She had already decided that they couldn't go blindly into Kistle's traps, that something had to change.

Dear God, and she had known all along what that change had to be. She had just refused to admit it to herself. But she couldn't ignore it any longer.

The clock was ticking.

THE RESIDENCE WAS A PLEASANT little house in Morningside with a wide front porch and pots of ferns hanging from the arches.

"This is crazy, Eve," Joe said harshly. "I know you're desperate, but this isn't going to do anyone any good."

"You're right, I'm desperate. I want insurance." She got out of the SUV. "You almost died at Chattahoochee. I don't want to have to go into that swamp blind." She nodded at Montalvo, who had just pulled up behind them, then she turned and walked up the path to the front door. It was barely six in the morning and the house was still dark. They were probably asleep. Should she wait before she—

The clock is ticking.

She rang the doorbell.

No answer.

She rang it again.

A small, thin man opened the door. His hair was mussed and he wore a red robe. "Yes?"

"I have to see Megan Blair. I'm Eve Duncan. You must be her Uncle Phillip?"

He nodded. "Megan's still sleeping. Can you come back later?"

"No, I have to see her now. Will you wake her?"

He stiffened. "I'm not sure I should. It took her three days to recover from—"

"It's okay, Phillip." Megan was coming down the hall. She wore only a Falcons T-shirt and red furry scuffs, but she was definitely wide awake. "She wouldn't have

come at this hour unless it was important."

"Important for her," he said. "Maybe a
problem for you." He shrugged. "I'll make
some coffee. Go into the sunroom."

Megan nodded and moved down the
hall. "Though there's not much sun in
the sunroom at six in the morning." She
opened the French doors. "Sit down." She
curled up on a shabby green-and-white-
print cushioned couch. "And I don't think
you'd notice anyway."

Eve's gaze went around the small room
as she sat down in a rattan chair. As
Megan had said, the room was dim and
shadowed. "This is nice. Comfortable."

"We like it." She met Eve's gaze. "But
you didn't come here to compliment our
interior decorating, did you? They haven't
caught Kistle yet?"

"No, he's moved out of Clayborne Forest. He's here in this area. You saw the
news story about Laura Ann Simmons?"

Megan stiffened. "He's got her?"

"But she's still alive. I talked to her on
the phone only a few hours ago. He's using her as bait to draw me into the trap."

"Where?"

"Okefenokee Swamp. He gave me two days, but I've already wasted too much time on a wild-goose chase."

"And why come to me?"

"I think you know."

She nodded slowly. "But I wouldn't be any good to you. Unless he's already killed her."

"You said you hear these voices in places that echo tragedy or high distress. For God's sake, what Laura Ann is feeling must be the highest distress. She must be scared out of her mind." She paused. "And he said I'd find Laura Ann in the same place he'd used as a burial spot. Bonnie must be there."

"He could be lying."

"Yes, but I don't think he is. Not this time." She moistened her lips. "But he'll try to trick us. I know it. We need you."

Megan said nothing. She just looked at her.

"I know what I'm asking. I know what you went through in Bloomburg."

"No, you don't," Megan said curtly. "You don't know anything."

"Maybe not," Eve said. "But I'm asking it anyway. Will you come with us?"

She was silent a moment and then said wearily, "Hell, I was going to tell you no when you came to me."

"You knew I'd come? I didn't know myself until this morning."

Megan's lips twisted. "Oh, I don't have any gift for precognition. But I have a friend, Renata, who can judge cause and effect with wonderful accuracy. I don't have her talent, but it didn't take much analyzing to realize what your next step would be." She added, "And you're lying to yourself if you think you weren't planning this all along. If it hadn't been for Laura Ann and Kistle, you'd still have come to get me to help you find Bonnie. You couldn't help yourself."

Eve stared at her a moment as her words sank home. Dear God, it was true. It had been there beneath the surface and she had not admitted it to herself. "I was fighting it. I didn't want to do it. I know how it will hurt you."

"When you started to believe me about Bobby Joe, it was only a matter of time before you'd want me to find your Bonnie."

Megan shook her head. "It's wrong. I shouldn't do it, Eve. Not only for my sake but for yours. You know she must have died horribly. Do you really want me to bring that all back to you?"

"I want to bring her body home."

"Not like this. Find her in any other way. You don't want to know how she died. You don't want to see me going through it with her."

Eve could feel the blood drain from her face at the thought. "No, I don't want that."

"It will happen. I can't control it."

Eve shuddered. "I have to bring her home, Megan."

Megan gazed at her helplessly. "Eve, find another way."

"It's not only Bonnie, it's Laura Ann now. There's no other way for Laura Ann. And Joe was nearly killed when we walked into one of Kistle's traps last night. I can't let that happen again. Come with us, Megan."

"Leave her alone." Phillip Blair stood in the doorway carrying a tray with a carafe and cups. "She helped you before. That's enough."

"You don't understand Mr. Blair," Eve said. "It's an emergency. We need—"

"And what about what she needs?" Phillip asked harshly. "She can't go on like this. This damn Listening isn't her only problem and she can't cope with—"

"I can cope with it." Megan got to her feet. "But I don't want to do it if I can think of any other way. Just give me a minute and let me pull myself together. I'll be back in . . ." She left the room.

"Don't *do* this to her," Phillip said to Eve. "You must have seen what finding Bobby Joe did to Megan. When she comes back, I want you to tell her that you've changed your mind. I've heard about your daughter and I'm sorry for you. But she's dead and Megan's alive. I'm not going to let you put her through that hell again."

"I don't want to hurt her. I don't want to hurt anyone. But I don't see how I can—"

"Then work at it, find a solution that doesn't concern—"

"I have to do it, Phillip," Megan said quietly from the doorway. "God knows I don't want to be pulled into this again, but I don't have a choice. Did Eve tell you that Kistle has that little girl we saw on the news?"

Phillip muttered a curse beneath his breath. "Shit."

Eve let out her breath in a sigh of relief. "Thank you, Megan. I was afraid you'd—"

"Wait a minute." Megan held up her hand. "I just want you to know I'm going into that swamp to get Laura Ann Simmons out and that's all. If I hear any other voices, I may or may not tell you about them. I'm the one who is going to be in control. This isn't for you or your Bonnie." She wearily shook her head. "Because I have a feeling that me finding your daughter would be the worst possible thing for you." She got to her feet. "I'll get dressed and pack a bag." She turned to Phillip. "The little girl is alive, Phillip. I have to try to help keep her that way."

"Okay, okay. I know you're caught." He scowled. "Take a cup of coffee into your room and drink it while you're packing." He set the tray on the glass coffee table. "I'll pack my bag and meet you in the hall in ten minutes."

"You're not going, Phillip," Megan said. "I have to go into the swamp and I won't let you go with me."

"Then I'll check into a hotel and wait until you come out." He glanced at Eve. "And you'd better take care of her. I don't want her hurt again." He strode out of the room.

"I'll take my own car and drive down with Phillip," Megan said as she rose to her feet. "He's obviously going with us. There's no use arguing with him. Phillip can be very stubborn."

"He cares for you," Eve said. "And he's not at all pleased with me. Who can blame him?" She rose to her feet. "Joe is waiting in the car and Montalvo is coming too. We'll wait outside for you." She hesitated. "I should tell you that Joe may not be . . . friendly. He was with me years ago when we were dealing with those psychics. He won't believe you can help."

"Smart man." Megan poured her coffee and carried it out of the sunroom. "I don't know whether I believe I can help either."

PHILLIP MET MEGAN IN THE hall and took her duffel. "I don't suppose I can talk you out of this."

"I wish you could." She opened the door. "I was all set to turn her down if she came knocking on my door. My heart ached for her, but I know it will be a mistake for all of us. But I can't turn away from Laura Ann. I wasn't able to help Bobby Joe, but I have a chance of saving her." She braced herself as she saw the man sitting beside Eve Duncan in the SUV. "Get in the car, Phillip. I'll be right with you. I have to talk to Joe Quinn."

Quinn's gaze was cool and his face without expression as he watched her walking toward them.

"Joe," Eve said. "This is Dr. Megan Blair."

Quinn inclined his head. "I'm not going to pretend that I want you to come along," he said curtly. "Or that I think you can offer any help. And since you'll probably end up either dead or getting in our way, I'd suggest you change your mind and go back to reading tea leaves."

"I told you what to expect, Megan." Eve grimaced. "I just didn't expect Joe to be quite so rude. I apologize."

"I don't care if he's rude." She stared him in the eye. "But if we have to put up with each other, I wanted to lay all the cards on the table before we start out. I don't want to go with you. I have to do it. I don't give a damn what you think of me.

I'd probably think the same thing if I were in your shoes. Voices and the dead reliving their last moments? It's nuts. But it's true and I have to live with it. And now you have to live with it too. All you have to do is take me into that swamp and pay attention to what I say. It's up to you if you act on it. Then you bring me out and you never have to see me again."

Joe's smiled sardonically. "Not quite all. I understand you have a habit of dramatically casting yourself down in a faint. I'll probably have to carry you out on my back."

"No," Megan said sharply. "You don't touch me. No matter what happens in that swamp, none of you touches me." She turned to Eve. "That's a deal-breaker, Eve."

Eve nodded. "I understand." She made a face. "No, I don't understand, but I'll go along with whatever you say. I owe you."

"Yes, you do." Megan turned and started toward her car, where Phillip waited. "I'll get Phillip settled in a hotel at Waycross, Georgia. That's on the outskirts of the Okefenokee. He usually likes to stay at Best Westerns. If I can't book him there, I'll call and let you know. It should take us about five hours to get down there. Where do we go from there?"

"The visitors' bureau. Kistle said he would let me talk to Laura Ann again when we reached the swamp, but that will be later. He said he'd fasten a photo on the bulletin board in the visitors' bureau. We'll meet Montalvo's friend, Miguel, there. He should have some information for us about the swamp."

"We could use it." Megan got into her car. "I've never been tempted to go sightseeing in a swamp. Snakes and alligators don't appeal to me."

JOE WATCHED MEGAN BACK OUT of the driveway. "She's smart. She didn't try to persuade me that she was something she's not. I can see how the contrast between her and those other crooks we ran into would tip the scales for you."

"You mean blind me?" Eve shook her head. "As you said, she's smart. I didn't lie to her about what she'd have to face in that swamp. Neither did you. She'd have to be crazy to go along with us just to run a con."

"So maybe she's a little nuts." Joe started the car. "And neither you nor she can expect me to listen to her when we get into that swamp."

"You don't have to listen to her. But I will, Joe." She looked straight ahead. "I'll be listening very closely."

A TALL YOUNG MAN DRESSED in khakis and boots straightened away from the wall of the Best Western when Megan and Phillip drew up to the registration area. His dark, Hispanic good looks reminded Megan vaguely of Antonio Banderas. His hands were bandaged, but his smile was bright. "You must be Megan Blair. I'm Miguel Vicente. Montalvo called and told me to meet you all here." He grimaced as he looked down at his bandages. "And since Montalvo says you have trouble with the civility of shaking hands, we'll get along fine. I'm having problems in that area right now myself." He looked at Phillip. "How do you do, sir? It's a pleasure to meet you, Mr. Blair."

"Phillip." Her uncle got out of the car. "I'll check in, Megan. I imagine you're going to want to discuss matters without me being in the way,"

"You're never in the way, Phillip," Megan said.

He gave her a glance over his shoulder. "Then why aren't I going with you into that swamp?" He didn't wait for an answer but went into the hotel.

Miguel gave a low whistle. "Do I detect a hint of indignation?"

Megan got out of the car. "He's very protective."

"And so he should be. After the time I've spent in the Okefenokee, I'd say you're going to need it." He smiled. "But don't worry. Since Eve wants you there I will guard you." He tilted his head. "Or maybe you should guard me. Can you keep the swamp devils away? Montalvo says you have very peculiar ways."

"Sorry, you're on your own," Megan said. "I have enough trouble warding off my own devils. I thought you were going to meet us at the visitors' bureau."

"You seem to have changed the scenario. Montalvo told me to check the bulletin board and bring anything I found here." He raised his head as a car drove into the parking lot. "There's Montalvo now."

And it was followed by the SUV driven by Eve and Joe Quinn, Megan noticed.

"You're tensing," Miguel said softly. "If you're this on edge with the people on your side, what will you be when Kistle appears on the scene?"

"Not everyone is on my side," Megan said. "Joe Quinn would just as soon I drowned in that swamp, and Montalvo doesn't care about anyone but Eve."

"How perceptive of you. But he does care about me, so perhaps he might spare a little concern for you." He turned and strolled over to Montalvo's car as he drew up beside them. "Here I am, Colonel. I'm brimming with information and eager to give it up." He nodded to Eve as she got out of her car. "Montalvo told me that you'd brought in help from the twilight zone. I approve. She's quite wonderful. I may be in love."

"You said that about Jane," Eve said.

"But she deserted me."

"Who can blame her?" Quinn said. "She has a good head on her shoulders. What kind of information?"

"There's a coffee shop inside the hotel." Miguel turned and headed for the front entrance. "I need a table to spread out my map."

"Did you stop by the visitors' bureau?" Montalvo called after him.

"Of course." He disappeared into the hotel.

Eve fell into step with Megan. "Miguel isn't as shallow as he seems. You can trust him."

"I hope I won't have to trust him," Megan said. They were a strange and diverse group, she thought uneasily. And the vibrations between them were far from friendly. The only person she could trust was Eve, but she didn't know how far. Not because of any lack of honor but because in the end there was only one thing of utmost importance to her. Bonnie overshadowed everything else. "How did Miguel hurt his hands?"

"One of Montalvo's enemies nailed him to a cross."

"God in heaven." She looked at Montalvo. "I'm not sure I'd want to be on your list of friends."

"I don't blame you," Montalvo said. "But

Miguel has no sense of caution. It didn't make any difference to him at all. Let's get inside and see what he has for us."

"I have to go see my uncle before I join you." Megan turned to Joe Quinn. "He's not going to be happy staying here twiddling his thumbs."

"So?"

"So I love him and don't want him unhappy. There's no way I want to take him into the swamp, but I want you to find him a job that will be safe but make him feel he's helping."

"Safe? Then let him stay here."

It was the kind of cooperation she would have expected from him. "Okay, safer."

He shrugged. "He can stay at the boat launch and be on hand to call in the police and direct them if we phone him. Will he be satisfied with that?"

"Probably not. But it's better than nothing." She went into the hotel to find Phillip.

THIRTEEN

MIGUEL SPREAD HIS MAP ON the polished oak table in the coffee shop. "This is the map I purchased from my guide, Bubba Garfield, with a great deal of Montalvo's money. He made it himself and he assured me that it was the finest one I could get."

"Like BlackJack Calahan sold you the finest bottle of wine in Bloomburg?" Eve asked.

"That's a bitter blow." Miguel grimaced. "But this is different. I know about maps. And I made sure Bubba was a little intimidated by me. The swamp is approximately seven hundred square miles and is thirty-eight miles long and twenty-five miles at its widest. It's principally a wildlife refuge, but that wouldn't have bothered Kistle. He would probably have enjoyed breaking the rules. There are seventy islands that are greater than twenty acres." He pointed to the green spots in the middle of the swamp. "These are the islands they call lands. There are twenty-two that have names. But there are smaller ones that are considered too unimportant to deserve recognizing on a map. Bubba indicated those with an X." He pulled a photo out of his jacket pocket and put it in front of Eve. "This is the photo that was on the bulletin board."

It was a color photo of an almost barren island, with the only vegetation being a stand of swamp oaks and pond cypresses. Floating in the tea-colored waters of the swamp surrounding it were thousands of water lilies.

"Is there anything unusual about this island?" Joe asked.

Miguel shook his head. "Except maybe the way the lilies are growing in that T shape in the water."

"Are we sure this photo is the one Kistle left?" Montalvo asked.

"Oh, yes." He reached in his pocket and drew out a yellow Post-it note. "This was taped to it."

A child's blue satin hair ribbon.

Eve touched it gingerly. "Another one?" She tried to ignore the horror she felt staring at it. "This can't belong to her. He must have bought it at Target."

"It got his message across." Megan was gazing compulsively at the ribbon. "That's all he wanted to do."

"Why don't you touch it?" Joe asked. "Maybe it will tell you something."

"Leave her alone, Joe," Eve said.

Megan deliberately reached out and touched the ribbon. "It tells me that Kistle is a son of a bitch and that you're one cynical bastard. Back off."

Joe smiled. "What a shallow observation. You'll have to do better than that."

"I'll work on it." Her gaze shifted to Miguel. "What else? Can you ask this Bubba if he can remember any island that has that kind of floating foliage surrounding it?"

He nodded. "I'll get right on it." He

looked at Montalvo. "This can be ugly. There are trees all over the place where a man could climb and be waiting for anyone passing in a boat below. Providing he doesn't object to cohabiting with coral snakes and other nasty, slimy creatures."

"I don't believe Kistle would care," Eve said. "He'd feel right at home with them. But where would he be able to stash Laura Ann?"

"That's the question," Joe said. "On this island? What about it, Dr. Blair? Do you have any thoughts on the subject?"

"I won't know until we get there. Maybe not then." She looked him in the eye. "No promises. When do we leave?"

"Dark. It will be safer." Joe turned to Miguel. "In the meantime, I want to go with you to see this Bubba Garfield and then go into the swamp and get the feel of it. Montalvo, you bring Eve, Megan, and Phillip Blair. I'll meet you at the dock at seven."

Miguel looked at Montalvo. "Colonel?"

Montalvo thought about it and then nodded slowly. "Go ahead. I don't need to get the feel of that swamp. One swamp is pretty much like another, and I practically lived in one while I was searching for my wife."

"I'm glad to have your permission." Joe got to his feet. "You've rented the motor-boats, Miguel?"

Miguel nodded. "At the dock at the north entrance."

Joe headed for the door. "I'll see you at seven, Eve. Come on, Miguel."

Eve checked her watch after Joe and Miguel had left the coffee shop. "It's two thirty-five." It seemed a long time until seven. She turned to Megan. "What are you going to do?"

"Go have late lunch with Phillip. Then go to his room and try to rest." She finished her coffee and stood up. "And then try to keep myself from getting back in my car and heading back to Atlanta."

"You won't do that," Eve said.

"No, I probably won't." She moved toward the door. "Though your Joe Quinn is making it seem like Mecca right now." She glanced over her shoulder. "If you need a place to crash for a few hours, come up to Phillip's room."

"Thank you." Eve watched her leave before saying to Montalvo, "She's being more tolerant than I would. After all, I invited her and Joe is giving her a hard time."

"So did you. Quinn had to stand by and watch those other psychic publicity-seekers tear you apart. It must have been rough on him too. He's only trying to protect you by poking holes in her so-called powers."

"You're defending him. Does that mean you think he's right? You were there, Montalvo. You helped dig up that little boy."

"Is he right? I don't know. It was a weird thing that seemed to be happening to her. I don't know how she knew the boy was buried there." He shrugged. "And I've seen some strange things happen in the jungle. Did I really see them or did I only dream them?"

She looked away from him. "Dream? About what?"

"Comrades who had died beside me. My wife, Nalia. As a sane realist, I prefer to think they were dreams." He took a drink of his coffee. "The dreams of Nalia ended when I put her to rest. Maybe that's all she wanted. I miss those dreams."

"I can see how you would."

She could feel his gaze on her face. "Look at me, Eve."

She forced herself to meet his gaze.

"You too?" he asked softly.

She wouldn't talk to him about dreams of Bonnie if she couldn't talk about them to Joe. "I'm glad if you think your wife is at peace now."

He nodded. "But I'm not at peace. I'm alive and I have to find a life again."

"Well, you can't take mine. I have Joe."

He was silent a moment. "And does your Joe have 'dreams' of Bonnie?"

"How could he? He never knew her."

"Yet he's lived with you for a long time. It must seem as if he does."

She shook her head. "Someone told me once that's not the way it works. Your mind has to be totally open to be able to accept anything that . . . unusual."

"Really? Now who told you that?"

Bonnie.

She shrugged. "I don't remember."

"Megan? It would seem the kind of thing with which she'd be familiar."

"I don't remember."

"And what would trigger that openness?

Sorrow? Desperation? Or maybe a psychic sensitivity like Megan's?"

"I don't want to talk about this any longer, Montalvo."

"I know. But it's interesting to find another bridge that we've gone over together. We seem to find new ones all the time, don't we?"

Yes, they did, and it was the last thing she wanted. "The only sensitivity we have to be concerned with is Megan's ability as a Listener." She finished her coffee and set down the cup. "And you're not even sure that she has that talent."

"I'm willing to be convinced. Quinn is not." He smiled. "Can't you see how compatible we are?"

"No. And I won't talk about it any longer."

"You should talk about it. Oh, not to give me any advantage. But I believe you've allowed yourself to feel a little guilty about feeling something for me." His smile faded. "We're trained to believe we should cling to one person only. Yet there are so many people who pass in and out of our lives. Good people, worthy people, interesting people. Most of them stay for a little while and then move on. Some of them find a

place with us and, if we let them, they en-
rich us. Don't close yourself off from the
rest of the world, Eve. If you find someone
who can make you understand a little
more, laugh every now and then, give you
a new experience, then never feel guilty.
You'll just have more to give back to those
who are closest to you."

She didn't speak for a moment. "Good
heavens, a philosopher. I wouldn't have
thought it of you, Montalvo."

"I do think occasionally." He was smiling
again. "I truly believe what I said, but I understand why Quinn is trying to keep you
to himself. I'd do the same. Philosophy is
all very well, but men tend to lean closer
to the Neanderthal than Aristotle."

"And your philosophy also leans closer
to polygamy than monogamy," she said
dryly.

"Not really. I wasn't talking about sex. But
it would be a miracle if you went through life
and didn't find someone besides Quinn
who attracted you. Maybe for only a moment or an hour. It's a natural chemical reaction and nothing to be ashamed of. Life is
all a matter of choice. You have your code
and you decide what to take and what to

give. And the only way to lose is to close yourself away and ignore."

She couldn't look away from him. The moment was too intimate, dammit. She had thought she knew him well, but she was learning more every moment. He said they were alike, but he was a thousand times more open and accepting than she was. Perhaps she would not have withdrawn if Bonnie had lived, but her life was closed and she did ignore almost everything but her work. What would it be like to open her world and reach out to touch and feel and experience?

She stood up. "I've already made my choice. It's Joe. And I'm an old-fashioned monogamist. Therefore, any reaching out would have to include him. I'll see you later, Montalvo."

"Don't run away." He stood up and threw some bills on the table. "If you're uncomfortable, I'll talk about anything you like. It's a long time until we have to go into that swamp. You don't want to be alone and neither do I." He took her elbow. "Let's go for a walk and see if we can find a souvenir store."

He had turned off that charismatic intimacy as if it had never existed. Relief surged through her. He was right. She wanted the time to pass like lightning, and company would help. "Why a souvenir store?"

"I want to buy a T-shirt with an alligator on it for Miguel. It may remind him to keep his hands out of that swamp water tonight."

THE SUN WAS GOING DOWN and casting a weird golden light over the swamp as Montalvo, Eve, Megan, and Phillip walked from their car down to the dock.

Megan shivered. "It looks like something from a macabre fantasy movie."

"Swamps can be beautiful," Montalvo said. "But, yes, they're always eerie."

"Dammit, I don't want to stay on this blasted dock," Phillip said. "I want to be in that boat with you, Megan. You might need me."

"I always need you," Megan said gently. "But I can't let you go, Phillip."

"It will be safer if I'm the one closest to you. You know that's true."

Eve frowned, puzzled. "What are you talking about?"

Megan didn't answer her. "No, Phillip, it will be okay. I've told them how it has to be." Megan smiled. "Now stay here and hold down the fort. Will you do that for me?"

"I seem to have no choice," Phillip said. "It's a mistake, Megan."

"I know. The whole thing is a mistake. None of us have a choice." She looked at Eve. "When is Kistle going to call you?"

"I don't know. It could be anytime now." She saw Joe and Miguel standing beside two motorboats near the end of the dock. Joe was looking down at a map and she could sense the intensity that radiated from him. "Let's hope Bubba was able to supply some information about that island."

Then Joe looked up and she unconsciously stiffened. Intensity? Oh, yes. She had thought she had seen his reckless intensity at Clayborne Forest, but this was even a cut above. He was in warrior mode.

"Did you find out anything?" she asked.

"Not much." Joe pointed to an area in the south. "Miguel's guide said that he vaguely remembers a water lily bed resembling that kind of T-shape near an island about here. But there's an island to the north that had a grove of cypresses that resembles the one in the photo. So we might as well flip a coin." He shrugged. "But the clue is probably bogus anyway. We all know he's leading us into a trap. It's just pointing us in the direction where he's waiting." He glanced at Megan. "So finding a grave where she might hear her voices isn't that important. He may not even be near there."

"And then he might," Eve said. "And if he's planning on killing Laura Ann, then he might take her to the same place where he took other kills. He's very careful, very thorough. Look at all the preparations he made for disposing of Bobby Joe. He's familiar with that particular area and he probably hasn't had time to scope out any other places in this godforsaken place. He's been moving fast since he left Clayborne Forest."

He shrugged. "I was just trying to eliminate a useless member of our little party."

"Thank you," Megan said sarcastically. "I appreciate your concern."

"And I'm probably more useless than Megan will be," Eve said. "Except I'm the bait and that may have value." She looked out over the tea-colored water at the trees that were wreathed now in a bloodred glow from the setting sun. He was in there somewhere. He was waiting. She could *feel* him.

Call me, bastard.

Let me know that little girl is alive.

"ARE YOU ENJOYING THE BOAT ride, Laura Ann?" Kistle asked as he dipped his oar into the water. "It's beginning to get dark. See all the shadows. That cypress tree looks like a monster, doesn't it? With its roots spreading like an octopus beneath the water." He felt the excitement building as he looked around him. It had been a long time since he'd been to this swamp. What pleasure he had experienced here. The fear, the blood, the power . . . "There are all kinds of monsters here. There's an alligator hiding near that island waiting to be fed. Perhaps I'll decide to feed you to him."

Laura Ann tried to keep from sobbing. He always smiled when she cried. He liked it.

"You see how the water is moving, shivering? Some say that's the peat masses on the floor of the swamp trembling. But I know better. Even the water knows about the monsters."

She wouldn't look at the water. She was afraid she'd see what he wanted her to see. She stared straight at him.

"I'm getting tired of you not talking to me. There's no one around now, so I'm going to take your gag off. If you scream, I'll throw you off the boat and let the monsters have you." He leaned forward and cut the ropes binding her wrists and then ripped the tape off her mouth. "Did that hurt? An alligator's teeth can rip and hurt much more."

Her mouth was swollen and stinging. Don't let him know. "Didn't hurt," she said defiantly. "And I don't think there are any monsters in this swamp. You're a liar."

"Yes, I am," he said. "And you're very smart to realize it. I'd only throw you to the alligators as a last resort. Because I'm the only real monster in this place and I want to spend a long time ripping and tearing at you."

Don't cry. Don't cry. "The police will get you and burn you up in one of those electric chairs. Or that lady will come and help me."

"Eve. Yes, she'll come and try to help you." He took out his phone. "And it's about time I called her and told her how safe and happy you are. I'm sure she'll want to speak to you. But, little bitch that you are, you aren't going to reflect the mood I wanted to show her." He dialed quickly. "Here I am, Eve. I was just telling Laura Ann about the monsters that live here in the swamp. She thinks you're the knight who can come and slay them. I'm waiting for you to come and try." He listened for a moment and then handed the phone to Laura Ann. "Like you, she thinks I'm liar. Talk to her."

"Hello."

"Listen, baby, I know you're in a scary place, but try not to be afraid of it. He's the one you have to be afraid of," Eve said. "I don't know how long it's going to be before we find you, but we will do it."

"He says he wants to hurt me."

"And that means he needs time to do it. You'll be safe for a little while. But if you find any way, get away from him. He's worse than anything in that swamp, Laura Ann. We'll find you."

"He's a bad man," she said fiercely. "I wish I could push him off the boat and let the alligators eat him."

Kistle took the phone away from her. "Charming, isn't she? She's going to be a real pleasure. Now I have to take her to Bonnie's haven. I'm sure that your little girl is lonely, aren't you?" He hung up. "What a vicious little girl you are." He picked up the paddle again. "You've been a real disappointment to me, but I'm sure that will change."

Get away from him.

He's worse than the swamp.

He hadn't tied her up again. Maybe she'd get a chance soon.

But she could see a black alligator slide away from the island and into the water.

Don't cry.

"SHE'S STILL ALIVE." EVE hung up the phone. "But I think the only thing that's keeping him from killing her is that she's annoying him. He's not used to defiance and it's infuriating him. He wants to break her slowly."

"As he did Bobby Joe." Megan's lips tightened. "You were right, he's worse than anything else she'd face in that swamp."

"Except drowning, quicksand, snakes, and alligators," Miguel enumerated. "She's only a little girl, Eve."

"What was I supposed to tell her?" Eve asked fiercely. "If we corner him, he'll kill her. There's no question about that. Even if we get too close, he might do it. She's safer anywhere than with him."

"You did the right thing," Joe said. "Shut up, Miguel." He moved toward the boat. "Let's get moving. Eve, you and Megan come with me. Montalvo, you and Miguel take the other boat. I'll head north and you head south to the other spot Garfield indicated. Call if you see anything that looks like that island. Okay?"

"I'm glad you asked for assent," Montalvo said dryly. "I was beginning to get a little pissed at all those orders." He turned and headed for the other boat. "But it's intelligent to split up. If you get into trouble, call me."

Megan gave Phillip a quick hug. "I'll be back before you know it," she whispered. "It will be fine, Phillip."

"The hell it will. Take care of yourself." Phillip looked at Joe and said coldly, "And you take care of her. I don't give a damn if you believe her or not. She's risking more than any of you by going after Kistle. She deserves your support."

"She'll get it," Joe said curtly. "As long as she doesn't get in my way." He jumped in the boat. "Let's get going. I want to make a little headway before we lose daylight entirely."

THEY WERE ONLY A FEW MILES into the swamp when full darkness fell.

The blackness was smothering. It was like being buried alive. No, even though she was blind, she could still use her other senses. The sounds and smell of the swamp were all around her. Night-bird calls, the rustling of snakes, the smell of decayed vegetation. Eve struggled for breath, her heart beating hard. "Should we turn on the flashlights?"

"Only if you want to be a target." Joe pitched them goggles. "Infrared night glasses. There's a full moon and we'll only need them while we're under this canopy of trees. Put them on. If you see something, tell me."

Eve handed a pair of goggles to Megan and put on a pair herself. "Are we almost there?"

"Close. Maybe a mile or two. Negotiating these waterways is slow going. In a few minutes I'm going to cut the motor and use the paddle."

Because it would be quieter, Eve thought, and Kistle would not hear them coming. "He'll probably have night glasses too, won't he?"

"Yes. He'll have all the equipment that will give him an advantage."

Even with the glasses it was still dark, but she could see the creatures of the night as red phantom shadows. That was almost as frightening as the stygian blackness.

She suddenly realized that Megan had not spoken for a long time and turned to look at her. "How are you doing?"

"I've done better." Her voice was uneven. She tapped the glasses. "These help."

Joe glanced back at her. "No psychic vibrations? I'm disappointed. I could use a little help right now."

"So could I." She gazed at him. "This isn't a good place. It reminds me of a cave near where I grew up. Too much has happened here. I'm having trouble keeping the voices away."

"Voices?" Eve whispered.

"Nothing to do with Kistle. At least, I don't think so." Megan looked down at the water. "A man drowned about a mile back. He had a heart attack and fell off the boat. His wife was with him and she jumped in after him and tried to revive him, but it was too late. His name was Ray Ebert. She kept screaming over and over. 'Ray Ebert, you breathe. Do you hear me? Ray, you come back to me.'" She looked back at Joe. "Of course, you probably think I had time this afternoon at the motel to research tragedies at the swamp."

"It's possible."

"Think what you like. I don't care." She shivered as an alligator slid down into the water from a sandbar they were passing. "I never thought much about alligators before tonight. A teenager lost his leg to one near here. His buddy dared him to go into the water and he did. The alligator was under the lily pads not five yards away."

"He didn't die?" Eve asked.

"Not here." Megan's lips tightened. "So maybe I will be able to hear Laura Ann if she's scared enough. God, I hope so."

Joe stared at her thoughtfully, but for once there was no sarcasm forthcoming. He turned off the motor and picked up a paddle. "So do we all."

"AH, HERE WE ARE, LAURA ANN." Kistle moored the boat behind a pond cypress and jumped out onto firm ground. "Come along. We have places to go, people to see. Isn't that from Dr. Seuss? Children love him, don't they? Well, answer me. I don't like to be ignored."

"Dr. Seuss is for kids," Laura Ann said. "I gave all my Dr. Seuss books to my little cousin last year."

"How kind. But there are parts of his books that I enjoy. What about the one about the empty pants? Wouldn't that strike terror in a little child's heart?"

"No. It was silly."

"How brave you are." He knelt on the ground and pulled her down beside him. "Now look over there. Do you see all those trees and bushes that seem to be growing out of the water across the way?"

"Yes."

"Behind all those trees is an island like this one. No one can tell it's there. It's my own secret place. I can stand on the bank over there and see everything that happens on this island and no one can see me. Do you know why I'm telling you all this?"

"I don't care," she said defiantly.

"I think you'll care. Because on one of these islands you're going to die. You'll have to guess which one. Perhaps you're kneeling on it right now. It's hard for children to realize the horror of death. How can I bring it home to you . . . ? Do you miss your mama? You'll never see her again."

Mama!

"I think that got through to you, bitch," he murmured. "Are you afraid at last?"

She had always been afraid. "Someone will come and get me."

"I'm going to let them try." He got to his feet. "I'm leaving you here. You can scream if you like. It will just draw them to you."

Hope surged through her. "You're going away?"

"Only for a little while." He smiled. "I'll be back. I wouldn't miss playing with you. It may be the highlight of my year." He gave her a flashlight. "Here, a light to keep you company and show Eve the way to you. Be sure to keep it on." He headed back to the boat. "Don't move too close to the water. I've seen a few alligators basking in the sun on this bank. I wouldn't want to waste you."

Laura Ann watched him paddle away until he disappeared into the darkness.

She was alone.

He was gone.

And Eve would be here soon to get her. She had promised. All she had to do was sit here and wait. She turned on the flashlight.

FOURTEEN

THE FLASHLIGHT BURNED BRIGHT in the darkness.

Kistle could see Laura Ann huddled close to the light as if it were a fire to warm her and keep her safe.

He stroked the paddle through the water. Kistle Island was just across the water, as he'd told the child. It had no real name, so he had given it his own. He landed, hid the boat in the swamp shrubs, and unpacked his weapons. He felt exhilaration soar through him as he stepped onto the island.

They should be here soon, but he still had time to savor this homecoming. Sweet memories of power and total subjugation. He had been king here. He *was* king here. Life and death made him master, and that never changed.

He cast another glance at the light burning on the other island.

Bring them to you, Laura Ann.

Make them flutter like moths to your flame.

"IT'S NOT THE SAME." MONTALVO glanced at the island and then down at the photo. He clicked off the flashlight. "This one is a wild-goose chase."

"So what do we do? Check out the rest of the area?" Miguel asked.

Montalvo thought about it. They were already here and that would be the practical course to follow.

Yet every instinct was telling him to go north in the direction Quinn had taken.

To hell with being practical.

THE BEAM FROM THE FLASHLIGHT was like the night-light in her bedroom at home, Laura Ann thought. They both made her feel safe. Only the one at home was Tinker Bell and there were no fairies here. No one to tell you to believe. Only scary trees and slithering sounds in the darkness.

And that man Kistle who had left her here to wait for Eve. Would Eve bring the police with her? She hoped she would and they would catch Kistle and put him in jail for a hundred years.

But he had said he would come back and hurt her. So why would he give her the flashlight and leave her?

She didn't want to think about that. He had done it and she had the flashlight and soon Eve would come for her.

But if she had the flashlight it must be bad for her, bad for Eve, or Kistle would never have given it to her. He only wanted to do bad things.

Get away from him.

But he wasn't here now. She was safe. He'd be back.

Get away from him.

No, she had her little pool of light here. There were bad creatures out there in the darkness. Maybe not monsters, but things that could hurt her.

She had to stay here in the light.

"WAIT." EVE SEARCHED THE darkness ahead. "I thought I saw something."

"What?" Joe asked.

"Light."

"Where? I don't see anything."

"It was just a glimpse through the trees. Up ahead and to the right. I'd swear it was . . . maybe I was wrong." She glanced at Megan. "Did you see a light?"

Megan didn't answer. Her body was tense, strained. Her gaze was fixed straight ahead and her face gleamed pale in the darkness.

"What is it?" Eve couldn't look away from the horror she saw in Megan's expression.

"I don't know," Megan whispered. "Oh, God, I don't know."

THEY WERE COMING!

A surge of fierce joy tore through Kistle as he saw the boat in the distance. Three in the boat. Quinn, Eve, and who else? It didn't matter. First he'd take out Quinn, and then he'd be able to lure Eve. He positioned himself more comfortably on the high cypress branch that allowed him a clear vision of both the other island and the water leading to it. He sighted and drew a bead on Quinn's figure in the front of the boat. Too far yet for even a good shot. He could afford to wait. Laura Ann's light would draw them right into his line of fire. As soon as they got close enough, they'd use binoculars and see the little bitch hovering over that light, all alone and waiting to be rescued. Quinn wouldn't swallow that Kistle released her, but he'd still have to come and investigate. He gave a glance back at the other island. Quinn should be putting on speed because they'd be able to see—

No light.

What the shit? Where was the flashlight? Where was the little bitch?

He raised his binoculars. No light. No Laura Ann.

Dammit, not *now*. Quinn was on his way and he needed to keep him focused and distracted.

Where the fuck was the kid?

THE WATER WASN'T COLD, BUT Laura Ann's teeth were chattering. It was dark and she couldn't see what was in the water with her. Alligators. Kistle had said the alligators would tear and hurt her. She wanted to be back on the island with the flashlight where she could see. Maybe she should have stayed there.

But if Kistle wanted her there, then it was the wrong place to be. Wrong for her and wrong for Eve. She could swim, she could climb. If she could get to one of those huge cypress trees growing out of the swamp water, then maybe she'd be able to climb up and hide.

Monsters.

The waters are trembling.

Alligators.

The tears were pouring down her cheeks as she started to swim toward the trees a short distance away. She didn't have to hide them; she didn't have to be brave. He wasn't here. It didn't matter if she cried now.

MEGAN BENT DOUBLE AS THE pain hit her. She couldn't stand it. But she had to stand it. She couldn't get away from the voices.

Don't hurt me. Don't hurt me. Don't hurt me.

I'll be good.

Let me see my Mama.

Shrieks.

Don't do it again.

Stop him.

I can't do it. Too late. Too late.

So many . . .

Nora Jean. Cambry. Paul. Letitia. Eric. Danielle. Monty. Natal—

"Megan," Eve whispered. "What's happening?"

"Too strong," Megan sobbed. "Too many. I can't close them out. So much pain. Lonely. Hurting. Mama. They want their mothers. They want to go home. Why won't he stop? I can't *help* them."

"Them?" Eve asked. "Bonnie?"

"I don't know. There are too many voices. I can't . . . separate. Names, but not all. Not all."

"What the hell is happening?" Joe was looking back at Megan. "This isn't the time for playact—" He stopped as he saw her expression. "My God."

"Too many," Eve echoed. "Not just one grave?"

Megan shook her head. "Dozens. I don't know . . . Too many." She was shaking. "And I can't close them out. I don't want to close them out. They need— But it hurts. It hurts."

"Laura Ann?" Eve asked.

"I can't—I don't think so. I might not be able to tell the difference."

Mama!

Sobbing.

You shouldn't do that to me.

Please, can I go home? I'll be good.

Shock. Pain. Shock. Death.

"Megan." Eve's hand was gripping her own. "We need you. Where are the voices coming from?"

Where? They were surrounding Megan, filling the world. But Eve needed her. Laura Ann needed her. She might still be alive.

"Where?" Eve repeated.

Megan made an effort to pull herself together. She jerked away from Eve's grip and tried to get the voices to stop.

Let me alone. Just for a moment. I want to help you, but I can't do it. Help me. Help Laura Ann.

She drew a deep breath and pointed to

the left. "There. There's an island behind all those trees and swamp shrubs."

Eve shook her head. "There's an island on the right. That's about where I saw the light."

Megan shook her head. "On the left. They're all there . . . the children. Every one of them."

"You're sure the light was on the island on the right, Eve?" Joe asked. "That island looks like the same one that's in the photo."

He wasn't going to believe her, Megan thought in despair.

Eve nodded. "I'm certain I saw—"

"I don't care where you saw a light," Megan said fiercely. "That's not his island. That's not his damn burial ground. It's there, across the way, hidden somewhere in that mass of trees and foliage."

"There's no hint of any island there," Joe said. "It's just a bank of dense trees and plant life. We're supposed to trust you that it's there and try to find it?"

Screams.

Help me, Mama.

Hold on. Keep the voices at bay.

"His island is there," she said. "I hear him talking about it to one of the children. Danielle . . . He loves it. He says her blood is going to soak into—"

"Shut up." Joe's gaze was on Eve. "She shouldn't hear—"

"No one should hear it," Megan said. "But I do, and I didn't come here to suffer through this hell without it meaning something." She stared him in the eye and her voice was vibrating with passion. "You listen to me, Joe Quinn. I can only say this once because I don't know how long I'm going to be able to stand this. I can't hold them off. As God is my witness, there is an island that's a burial ground in those trees. If there was a light on the other island, it was a trap. You expected a trap, didn't you? Well, there it is." Her voice broke. "Now you go and find Kistle and those children so that we can get the hell out of here."

He didn't speak for a moment. "Only one child, Megan. Laura Ann."

She shook her head. "So many children. They all want to go home," she whispered. "Believe me, Joe, so many children."

"Joe," Eve said.

He was still searching Megan's expression. He slowly nodded. "The light could have been a trap." He was taking off his boots as he spoke. "If it was, Kistle had to have a vantage point to spring it. That island's pretty barren and there's no place to hide. So there's only one other thing I have to swallow as truth, and it's sticking in my throat." He handed Eve his rifle and his Magnum before fastening on the belt holding his machete and the water-proofed holster holding his .38. "But I'm going to force it down."

"What are you going to do?" Eve asked.

"I'm going to swim past that jungle of foliage and see if I can find an island." He smiled recklessly as he took off his shirt and threw it on the bottom of the boat. "And, if I do, I'm going to go hunting."

"And you expect me to stay here and let you go alone?" Eve asked. "No way. Tell me what to do to help."

"Not a damn thing until I see if there's an island there." He slipped out of the boat and into the water. "Other than that, stay out of Kistle's way so that he can't use you as a hostage against me." He started swimming in the direction of the bank of trees. "And take care of Megan. She looks as if she's—take care of her."

Eve muttered a curse beneath her breath as she turned to Megan. "He couldn't wait to go on his damn hunt. Why can't he see that I—" She stopped. "Good God. You look as if you've turned to stone. Can I do anything for you?"

Megan wished she was stone. Then she wouldn't be able to hear the voices that wouldn't be silenced. "You can kill the bastard," she said hoarsely. "Then you can get me away from here before I fall apart." She drew a long, shaky breath. "Just find Laura Ann and let's go back to the dock."

"To find Laura Ann I have to go after Joe," Eve said. "That means I'll have to row the boat to the island. Can you take it?"

The closer to the island, the louder and more persistent would be the voices. "I don't know." She closed her eyes. "I don't have a choice, do I?"

"I wish I could say that you do," Eve said. "You don't have to set foot on the island. You can stay in the boat. Will that help?"

"Probably not." Megan opened her eyes. "But I'm the one who decided to go with you to this hellhole. I have to go through with it. What's next?"

"I'll phone Montalvo and tell him to get here and help. Then I'll wait until I'm sure Joe isn't coming back, that there really is an island hidden in those shrubs. Then I'll go after him."

"The island is there." Megan could hear her words slurring as she tried to speak through the fog of voices. "How strange, that your Joe believed me and you're the one who's not certain."

But maybe Eve didn't want to recognize the horror on that island. Not if Bonnie was a part of it.

Bonnie, are you there?

EVE'S PHONE RANG AS SHE was dialing Montalvo.

"How did you know about my island, Eve?" Kistle asked. "I was planning to show it to you personally, but I'm afraid you're going to invade my space. I saw Quinn slip into the water and head this way. I was going to go down to the bank to meet him, but he's disappeared. Do you suppose an alligator got him? No, I'd bet on him over an alligator. That means he's managed to slip onshore. I wonder where he is . . ."

"Behind you every step of the way," Eve said. "I want to talk to Laura Ann."

"I'm afraid you can't do that. The game has commenced and she's no longer a viable pawn."

"Is she dead?"

"I'm not certain. Perhaps."

"You have to know, you bastard."

"I'm not lying. The little bitch spoiled my nice scenario and took off. She was supposed to lead you right under my rifle and she blew it. I gave her a flashlight and left her on that other island to wait for you. Now, what kid is going to leave dry land and a cozy light to run into a swamp? I even warned her about the alligators that are waiting to eat little girls on the north end of the island." His voice turned vicious. "I hope they've decided to have her for dinner."

Eve felt a sinking sensation as she remembered the light that had disappeared from one moment to the next. She had been the one to tell Laura Ann to run if she got the chance. When she had realized she was bait for the trap, the little girl had evidently taken her opportunity to escape, even though she must have felt safe for the first time since her nightmare had begun. "I'd bet on her over an alligator too," she said unevenly. "She beat you, Kistle."

"Only temporarily. If the alligators didn't get her, then I'll be able to take my time finding her. When are you coming for your Bonnie, Eve? Quinn is going to try to put himself between us. Are you going to let that happen?"

"No."

"I didn't think you would. We've both been waiting too long. Come to me. I'll find you. Now I have to get on the move. Quinn will be on the hunt." He hung up.

Eve pressed the disconnect. "Joe reached the island. Kistle hasn't caught him yet."

Megan didn't answer and Eve wasn't even sure she had heard her. She was enveloped in her own nightmare.

Eve dialed Montalvo. When he answered, she filled him in on what was happening.

"Stay where you are," Montalvo said.

"I'm not five minutes away from your location. Wait for me."

"I can't wait," she said. "Find Laura Ann. She's alone out there somewhere." She hung up and picked up the paddle. Joe had been able to swim to the island, but how was she going to get through those palmettos in this boat?

Stop worrying and just do it.

LAURA ANN GRIPPED THE CYPRESS desperately, but it did no good. She slipped back into the water with a splash.

Had Kistle heard it? Had he come back to get her? He had said he would.

She listened.

No sound. Only the birds.

And the slithering of a snake.

Snake can't hurt me. Snake can't hurt me.

She tried frantically to climb the tree again.

She slipped. The bark of the tree was slick with water, moss, and peat.

Her heart was beating so hard with panic she couldn't breathe.

Try again. Get out of the water.

She caught a glimpse of movement on the bank. Something low, something dark.

Something big.

EVE JUMPED OUT OF THE BOAT and tied it to a thin pine tree near the edge of the bank. She had found a cove where she could dock, but it offered little concealment. Joe had left his rifle and Magnum. Which weapon to take with her? The rifle. It had a night scope and she'd be moving in and out of the darkness of the trees. She grabbed it and said to Megan, "I know I said you wouldn't have to step onshore, but I'd feel better if you'd hide in the bushes until I come back. I don't like to leave you here alone."

"Not alone." Megan's voice was stilted. "Not alone. Get . . . him. Kill him. Don't let him ever . . . do it again."

Eve felt a chill run through her. Megan could barely talk and her body language was tortured. What had Eve done to her by bringing her here?

And what was Kistle doing to all of them?

She had to ask one more question.

"Do you know where those children are buried?"

"North."

"I'll be back as soon as I can."

Megan didn't answer as Eve moved into the palmetto shrubs.

Where was she going? She was no hunter.

Come to me. I'll find you, Kistle had told her.

And Kistle was a hunter. He'd have no trouble tracking her, finding her.

All she had to do was find a place to wait for him to do it.

Her gaze went to the north side of the island.

Oh, yes, and that's where I'm going to wait for you.

That's where we'll all be waiting for you, Kistle.

MIGUEL CUT THE MOTOR. "There it is."

Montalvo nodded. This island obviously was the one in the photo. And to the left was the bank of trees and shrubs that Eve had said hid Kistle's island.

"We go after the child?" Miguel asked.

"You go after the child." He pulled off his boots and shirt, slipped his phone into his waterproof belt, and went into the water. "I go after Kistle."

NO GRAVES.

Eve stopped as she came out of the brush when she reached the north end of the island. A level mossy glade stretched before her and it gave an almost manicured appearance at odds with the wild chaos of the swamp.

No graves.

Unreasoning relief soared through her. Maybe Megan had been wrong. Maybe there was only one grave and it was on some other part of the island. What did Eve really know about Megan's ability or inability? It was all beyond understanding and belief anyway. She had just accepted because she wanted answers and she—

There was a large wooden box lying on the ground across the glade. It had been placed on a bed of branches in a place of visible prominence.

So that she would see it. So that she

would know that he wanted her to look at it, touch it.

Dread iced through her. She didn't want to go near it.

It didn't matter what she wanted. The box was drawing her like a magnet. She had to see what was inside; she had to lift the lid.

The moss was moist and resilient beneath her shoes as she slowly crossed the glade toward the box.

She dropped to her knees in front of it. It was an old, brass-bound coffer, and the wood was stained by frequent handling. Why had Kistle used this box so often?

Oh, God, she was afraid she knew the answer.

She braced herself and lifted the lid.

Hair ribbons, toys, strands of silky hair bound by rubber bands, fingernails. It was full to overflowing, and some items were labeled with names, some were not. She lifted a strand of curly black hair and stared blindly down at the neatly written tag. *Letitia*.

She felt sick. She dropped the strand back into the box. She didn't want to touch the poor horrible remains of those children.

But she was going to do it. Because she had to see if one of those pitiful thatches of hair was red and curly and was labeled *Bonnie.*

"Ah, you've found it. You've been very quick. I didn't expect you to stumble on my memory box for hours. I'm very proud of it. It's unique."

She lifted her head to see Kistle standing several yards away, his rifle cradled casually in his arm. There could be no mistake. The same gray-brown hair, the same features as in the photo Montalvo had shown her. But he was taller, more powerfully built than she had thought. All that power and strength devoted to the subjugation of helpless children. Anger flared through her. "It's not unique. Memory boxes are common with serial killers. You probably saw it on TV and copied it."

"Now, that was vicious. I pride myself on my originality. But I forgive you because you're probably shaken by looking at my little trophies."

"Trophies?" Her voice was shaking. "A trophy is given for some great victory. These are children. They're helpless. What kind of man would you have to be to think of kids as being worthy of fighting at all? You're weak and stupid to believe—"

"I think I'm beginning to get annoyed with you," Kistle interrupted. "I was anticipating a much more satisfying meeting. I've allowed myself to be distracted from playing cat and mouse with Quinn to come and see you. You could be more entertaining." He smiled maliciously. "Have you found the Bonnie trophy yet?"

She went rigid. "No."

"There are some more personal mementos at the bottom of the box. They're blackened, withered, but still recognizable as body parts."

Don't scream. Don't lunge at him. "Are you telling me that one of them belongs to Bonnie?"

"I could tell you that." He tilted his head. "It would take you a long time to verify it. No, I don't believe I'll lie to you. You're not going to live long enough for me to stretch out the pain." He smiled. "But you don't care about whether you live or die, do you? You haven't even looked at the rifle on the ground beside you."

"I care. I wouldn't let you take that away from me."

"You care more about whether Quinn dies, whether Jane MacGuire dies, even whether Laura Ann dies. I think your fear of your own death ended when you lost Bonnie."

"Is there a trophy in this box from Bonnie?"

He stared at her a moment and then shook his head. "But that doesn't mean anything. Bonnie was my inspiration. Maybe I didn't want to class her with the rest."

"Where are the graves?"

"Why, you're kneeling on one right now." He smiled. "If I remember correctly, that should be Nora Jean's grave."

Eve stiffened and slowly looked down at the moss-covered earth. Then she stared around the mossy glade. When she had first caught sight of the glade it had appeared level, but from where she knelt now she could see that it had slight, gentle swellings like the waves of an ocean. Dear God, were all those swellings graves?

"Though it's hard to recall exact locations. It became very crowded here. Though I did label the little darlings' bodies just as I did my trophies. A stake through the heart." He gestured around the glade. "You can hardly take a step without desecrating a grave. I was going to have to really branch out for Laura Ann." He nodded. "And you, Eve. You deserve a place of honor here."

She ignored the threat. "Where did you bury Bonnie?"

"I can't remember. I'll have to think about it."

"Dammit, where did you—" There was something in his expression, just a flicker, but she stiffened as a thought suddenly occurred to her. "Maybe you didn't kill my daughter. Maybe this was all a big lie. Maybe you're just a copycat after all."

His smile faded. "I don't have to lie about kills. Dig up this graveyard and you'll see."

"Show me her grave."

"Do you actually think I didn't kill her?"

"Your friend Murdock said you were obsessed with all the news stories about Bonnie. He said your attitude was weird. Feverish and bitter. Why bitter? Jealousy?"

"You don't know what you're talking about!"

"I think I do. You've evidently been killing for years and you've always prided yourself on your secretiveness. But it must have been terribly frustrating to find out that someone else was garnering all the attention and headlines and yet was able to get away with her murder. You knew you were being smart to hide your kills, but it must have gnawed at you. You wanted everyone to know how smart you were. Smarter than that man who had killed Bonnie, the man you told Murdock was a superstar in everyone's eyes. You desperately wanted to be that man. So you claimed her death as your own kill."

"How clever you are. And perhaps that's why I was so drawn to make contact with you? Maybe I think by killing you, it will somehow validate the lie about killing Bonnie. It does make sense, doesn't it?"

"If your ego is as huge as I think it is."

"Of course, this is all supposition."

"Show me her grave."

"My dear Eve. She has no grave."

"But all these other children have graves?"

"Not all."

She moistened her lips. "You're lying."

He shook his head. "You haven't thought this through. I like to experiment."

"Where is Bonnie?"

"Do you really want to know?"

"Where is she?"

He said softly, "Ask the alligators."

Shock sent her reeling back on her heels. "You just want to hurt me. You're not telling the truth. You couldn't—" Yes, he could. Kistle was capable of doing anything evil under the sun.

"I could." He smiled. "You know I could. It's only a question of if the whim struck me. Most people are bound by all kinds of strictures. I've broken away from all those ties. You'd be surprised how free and powerful that makes you feel."

She dove for the rifle lying next to her.

Hot pain tore through her as a bullet pierced her left shoulder. She ignored it and rolled over as she grabbed for the rifle.

"Oh, no." Kistle's foot stomped down on the rifle. "Though I do admire your determination." He picked up her rifle. "Now lie still while I see if you have any other weapons. Make a move and I'll smash in your head with this rifle butt." His hands ran over her. "Clean. But then I wouldn't expect you to be loaded with firepower. It's not your area of expertise." He stepped back. "I could kill you now and I'd feel nothing but pleasure. No guilt, no regret. But you'll find that wound I gave you is nothing, a trifle. I barely skimmed your shoulder. Do you know why?" He didn't wait for her to answer. "Because you wouldn't care enough. I'll have to up the stakes to get the response I need from you." He moved back into the trees. "It has to be Joe Quinn, I think."

She struggled to her knees. "No!"

"You could always stagger after me and try to stop me. That would be amusing. You wouldn't have a chance, of course. You're wounded and you have no weapons. You must know by now how good I am. No, you'd better wait here. I'll bring him to you."

"Kistle." She got to her feet. "You can't—"

Kistle was gone.

And he was going after Joe.

You wouldn't have a chance, of course. You're wounded and you have no weapons.

But as he'd said, the wound was minor,

and she could go back to the boat and get Joe's Magnum he'd left with the rifle.

There's always a chance, you bastard.

She reached under her windbreaker to compress the wound. She flinched as pain shot through her. It hurt, but the good news was that it didn't appear to be gushing blood. Maybe Kistle was right and it was only a flesh wound.

She started back toward where the boat was moored.

SOMEONE WAS IN THE BUSHES ahead.

Joe froze and drew his .38. He couldn't see anything even wearing his infrared goggles, but he had heard a whisper of sound.

Kistle?

But it could also be Eve. He didn't trust her to stay away from the island. He'd only hoped he could get Kistle before she made a move.

Get off the ground and get a better view.

He shinnied up a blackgum tree towering next to him. Come on, Kistle. Move.

Nothing.

But there was someone there.

A bullet plowed into the branch next to him!

From where?

From the left of that patch of bushes. He snapped a quick shot.

"Close," Kistle called. "You have good judgment, Quinn. Another two inches and you would have had me." The last sentence had been several yards to the right. He was on the move.

Joe swung over to the next tree.

"I just encountered Eve Duncan. It was very interesting. I shot her as she knelt by her daughter's grave."

Joe went rigid. He had to be lying. Kistle just wanted an answer, a response, so that he could gauge his shot. Joe wouldn't give it to him.

Kistle chuckled. "You didn't rise to the bait. I didn't kill her. I'm waiting to do that when I can be sure of optimum satisfaction. I was thinking about killing you. But I think I'll go and retrieve Laura Ann instead. That will hurt Eve and you'll have to follow and come out of hiding to save the poor child." His voice was fading away. "Two for the price of one."

Joe muttered a curse and began to climb down from the tree. Laura Ann had been on the other island, so Kistle must be heading for the bank where he could get across. Kistle knew every inch of these islands. He'd be traveling with speed and surety.

Joe would have to avoid any traps and move very, very fast.

FIFTEEN

HE SAW HER!

Miguel could barely make out Laura Ann on the water, clinging to the bole of a cypress tree. She was very little and the huge tree was dwarfing her small body.

"I'm coming, Laura Ann," he called softly. "I see you. I'll be there in a minute."

She didn't answer. Perhaps she thought he was Kistle.

"My name is Miguel Vicente. I'm a friend of Eve's. You talked to her on the phone, didn't you?"

She still didn't answer, but he thought he heard her sob.

"I'm going to get you out of the water. The roots of that tree are too big for me to get close to you in this boat, so I'm coming in after you."

"Don't jump in the water. He'll hear you."

"Kistle?"

"No." She pointed to the bank. "I heard him come into the water. I've tried not to make any noise. It's too dark to see, but I think he's watching me."

Holy shit.

Laura Ann couldn't see in the darkness, but with his goggles on Miguel could. An alligator at least twelve feet in length was hovering near the bank. God knows why he hadn't attacked.

"Laura Ann, can you try to climb that tree you're holding on to?"

"I already tried to do it. It's too slippery. There's slimy stuff around the trunk."

And Miguel wouldn't have time to swim to her and then pull her back with him to the boat before that prehistoric monster was on top of them.

"I'm going to have to get in the water."

"No."

"Don't be scared. Our ugly friend won't even know I'm swimming toward you." He hoped. He took his knife from his sheath. "Here's what we'll do. When I get next to you, I want you to let go of the tree. I'm going to give you a boost past that slick part of the trunk and throw you up as high as I can. Then you scramble up to that first branch."

"Will I be able to do it?" she asked doubtfully.

"A girl who could get away from a bad man like Kistle? Of course you can do it." He just hoped he'd be able to do his part with these damn hands. "You only have to be ready when I get there."

"Okay."

He carefully lowered himself over the side of the boat. No splash. No vibration in the water. Take it slow. Keep an eye on that triangular snout that could bite a man's arm off in one snap. Pray. Yes, definitely pray.

One yard.

Two yards.

He could hear the little girl's hoarse breathing, but she wasn't sobbing or screaming. That's a good girl, keep it together and we might get through this.

One more yard to go.

And then his leg hit the roots of the cypress and started a shock wave in the water.

"Shit."

The alligator was moving away from the bank!

He reached Laura Ann in seconds. "Up!" He took her by the waist and threw her up the tree. "Grab it, dammit."

She grabbed, but her feet were slipping again.

"Hold on." He started to climb the tree.

Too late. The alligator was right beside him, mouth opening.

He stabbed his knife into the alligator's mouth and left the knife sticking in its jaw. Hell, it probably didn't hurt the reptile more than a mosquito bite.

Then Miguel was scrambling up the tree toward the first branch, where Laura Ann was clinging.

He heard the snapping of jaws below him, but he didn't look down. Laura Ann was sliding down toward him. He grabbed her and held on as he wrapped his legs around the branch. "It's fine," he said. "We're safe." Big lie. The alligator didn't look like it was going anywhere and Miguel could see the snout of another alligator in the water a short distance away swimming toward them. Evidently their first attacker had invited a guest to dinner.

Laura Ann was clinging to him with all her strength. "What . . . if the branch breaks?"

He wished she hadn't asked him that. "I'll think of something. I can always fight them off. I'm very strong."

She looked down at the alligators and then back at Miguel. "I think they're stronger." Her gaze went to his bandaged hands holding her. "And your hands are all bloody already."

Damn, she was right. He'd broken the stitches and the blood was staining the bandages. The colonel was going to murder him.

He suddenly chuckled as he realized what he was thinking. If the branch broke, it didn't really matter how angry Montalvo was going to be.

"You're laughing." The little girl had raised her head and was staring at him with sudden indignation. "I don't think this is funny." Her eyes were glittering. "I'm scared. That man, Kistle, said he'd feed me to an alligator."

"I don't think he has trained alligators. I think this one is strictly on his own."

"I know that." She buried her face in Miguel's shoulder. "Are you scared too?"

Poor kid. She had been through hell in the last couple days and she was showing more guts than a lot of men he knew. "Very scared." His hand gently stroked her hair. "But maybe we can make it through this together. I don't believe this branch is going to break. You don't weigh much." But he had felt the branch give a little when he'd pulled himself up on it. They might be on borrowed time now. "I'll wait for a few minutes until my cell phone dries out a little and then try to call for help. If it doesn't work, we'll just sit here and either wait for those alligators to go away or until my friend comes to get us."

"Is Eve your friend?"

She wasn't shaking quite so much now. "Yes, but I was speaking of my friend Montalvo. We've been together for a long time and I tend to think of him first. I was just a young boy when he found me in the jungle."

"Were you lost?"

"Yes." There were many ways of being lost, so it wasn't a complete lie. "It's easy to get lost. Aren't there stories in your fairy-tale books about children getting lost in the forest?"

"I don't read fairy tales anymore. Mama says that it's better for me to face what happens in the real world."

Miguel glanced down at the alligators swimming below them and turned her head on his shoulder so that she couldn't see them. "I don't think that a little escape from the real world is too bad. Maybe your mother wouldn't object if you thought of something a little distracting at the moment."

"What?"

"Well, I don't know any fairy tales. My father didn't approve of them either." Unless they appeared in one of his cocaine hallucinations. "But after I went to Montalvo I used to read books from his library. I found one about Tarzan and the apes." That should be okay to talk to a kid about. At any rate, it was as close to squeaky clean as Miguel's background provided. "Tarzan was lost alone in the jungle too.

Just like me. Then this big, ugly ape found him and took him home."

"Like Montalvo?"

Miguel grinned at the thought. "Exactly like Montalvo."

NO QUINN.

No Kistle.

Montalvo moved silently through the underbrush. He could feel the familiar tension and exhilaration that always gripped him when he was on the hunt. He'd already explored the east side of the island and now he was moving west. There couldn't be much more territory to cover. This was a small island, not like the acreage in Clayborne Forest.

He could smell the rotting vegetation underfoot mixed with the sweet fragrance of water lilies floating on the nearby water. No scent of sweat or soap, salt or musk. He hadn't really expected it. Both Quinn and Kistle would have made sure to rid themselves of those telltale signs.

But Eve was no soldier. He had made her go shower in the jungle in Colombia to rid herself of that clean scent that clung to her.

Eve.

He immediately banished the thought of her. Don't think of Eve now. If he managed to get Kistle, then there would be no danger to Eve. It was the only way to—

The cell phone in his pocket vibrated.

Shit. Not now.

He looked at the ID. Miguel.

He punched the button. "What is it?" he whispered.

"Two alligators, one tree, me, and Laura Ann." The phone was crackling. "No, I think one of the alligators got bored waiting and swam away. But I believe we could still use some assistance. This branch is a little unstable."

Damn it to hell. "Where?"

"Off the north side of the island."

"How bad is it?"

"Laura Ann is a few inches away from me."

"And you don't want to scare her."

"That's right. Though she's amazingly resilient. I'm sorry to spoil your fun, but I really think you should take care of plucking us out of this tree before you go back to—" The cell phone crackled and disconnected.

No choice. Montalvo thrust his cell back in his pocket. If Miguel thought the situation required an SOS, then it must be deteriorating rapidly.

He set off at a trot toward the north.

THE BRANCH CRACKED AGAIN AND began to slowly give way.

"Oops." Miguel scrambled to pull the little girl higher and closer to the trunk. But the break was too close to where they were huddling. Could he manage to get to that higher branch? Not likely. Maybe.

He'd have to try.

"Laura Ann, we're going higher." He tightened his thighs around the branch and inched carefully forward. "Listen, if we happen to take a dunking, I want you to swim for the bank. Don't wait for me. Don't look back. Don't stop. Montalvo will be here soon."

"No. I won't leave you." Her arms tightened around his neck. "They'll eat you."

"No, they won't. I'm practically a superman. You saw how I fought off that alligator.

Alligators have no real family feeling. Maybe if I wound one, that other alligator will come back and attack him."

"Will that work?"

"Of course it will." The branch was splitting, the pale fibers gleamed in the darkness. It wouldn't hold much longer. "But we'll try to get to that other branch before I—"

"For God's sake, Miguel. What are you doing?"

Relief so intense it made Miguel almost light-headed poured through him as he saw Montalvo swimming toward the boat Miguel had abandoned to come after Laura Ann. "I'm being a hero. But evidently not very well. I'd get in that boat fast. We seem to be fascinating this alligator, but his buddy may come back. And there are too many underwater roots for you to get that boat close to the tree, if that's what you plan on doing. Could you nudge this alligator out of the way?" He added, "Quickly, please?"

"Nudge?" Montalvo pulled himself onto the boat. "I don't think there's any question of nudging. I'll have to get off a couple shots that will take him down."

"Good idea. Isn't it fortunate they're not an endangered species in this swamp any longer?"

"Get *rid* of him," Laura Ann said through her teeth. "Now."

"She's growing impatient. Smart girl. Did I tell you how remarkably intelligent she is?"

"I'll have to get close enough to shoot him in a vulnerable spot. A bullet wouldn't puncture that tough hide. The eye, I think . . ." He was rowing, drawing nearer. "Get her on a higher branch."

"It's not that easy. I've been trying."

The branch dipped another two inches.

Laura Ann cried out, her arms tightening to a stranglehold around Miguel's neck.

"Shh," Miguel whispered. "My friend is here. He'll help us. He's very smart."

"Montalvo?" she asked shakily. "The one who's like the ugly ape?"

"Ape?" Montalvo maneuvered the boat at an angle. "After I get you out of there I think we'll have to talk, Miguel."

"It was actually complimentary . . . sort of," Miguel said.

"I can imagine." He was drawing a bead on the alligator under the tree. "That branch is holding by a few splinters of wood. Don't even breathe."

"I won't," Miguel said hoarsely. "Who needs oxygen?"

The alligator was turning toward Montalvo's boat as if sensing danger . . . or fresh meat.

Montalvo shot it in the eye.

But the alligator moved in the last second and the bullet only skimmed the edge of its eye. The alligator exploded into action, its powerful tail whipping in a fury of pain and rage. It struck the trunk of the tree with desperate force.

And the last splinters of wood holding the branch broke.

"The bank," Miguel yelled to Laura Ann as they hit the water only yards from the wounded alligator. With all his strength he threw her toward the island. "Swim!"

"Shit." Montalvo gunned the boat and sent it between the little girl and the alligator. The alligator crashed into the boat, rocking it wildly. "Miguel, go after her. I don't know how long I can distract him."

Miguel hesitated.

"Go!"

Miguel struck out for the bank.

JOE'S FISTS CLENCHED AS HE SAW the alligator ram Montalvo's boat again, striking it with that massive tail and spinning it sideways. Dammit, one more hit and Montalvo could be in the water. From where Joe was standing on the bank of Kistle's island, he could see Montalvo desperately trying to focus his rifle, but it was all he could do to keep the boat afloat.

Let Montalvo work it out for himself, Joe thought. Miguel and the little girl had safely reached the bank of the other island. Joe had other things to do. Kistle must be close now. He might be just up ahead watching this same disaster scenario Joe was looking at.

He started to turn away.

No, dammit, if Kistle was watching Montalvo, then he'd be a sitting duck in that boat. Kistle had already told Joe he was going after Laura Ann. He'd have to take out the men who stood in his way to get her.

The alligator's tail struck Montalvo's boat again. Again. And yet again. Whirling it like a top. If Kistle didn't kill Montalvo, then the alligator would when the boat capsized.

Damn it to hell.

Joe jumped into the water and swam toward the boat. "Montalvo!" He took out his machete and cut his arm. "I'm leaving a blood trail. When I get close enough for the gator to smell the blood, he'll leave the boat and come after me. You'll have time for one shot." He added grimly, "It had better be a good one."

"It will be." Montalvo fought off another reeling blow to the boat and managed to right it as it almost tipped over.

Joe kept the machete ready as he drew closer to the alligator. Any minute now.

Yes!

The alligator was turning, gliding away from the boat.

Joe splashed the water in invitation.

"Come on," he whispered. "Come and get me, ugly."

The alligator was swimming toward him.

"I've got him in my sights," Montalvo said. "Get out of there."

"Three more yards," Joe called. "I don't want him going under the water after me."

One.

Protruding silver eyes glittering.

Two.

Snout opening, teeth gleaming.

Three!

"Now!"

Joe dove underwater as the alligator was almost on him. Fast, deep, he swam under the belly of the alligator.

He didn't hear Montalvo's shot. He wasn't about to wait around to find out if he'd gotten the gator. If he hadn't, Joe had to swim for his life.

He didn't surface until he was near the bank.

Montalvo's boat was only a few yards away. "You'd better get on board. There are more alligators than our late friend in these waters."

"You got him?"

"Yes." Montalvo reached down a hand to pull him onto the boat. "Have you no trust? I told you I'd make the shot."

"If you wanted to make it."

"I wanted to make it," he said quietly. "You literally gave your blood for me." He turned the boat toward the bank. "Though I'm puzzled why you did it."

"So am I," Joe said curtly. "We have to pick up Miguel and Laura Ann and get out of here. Kistle will be able to pick us off from any vantage point on the north side of the island. I was following him when I saw that damn alligator. Kistle probably saw you too. He set Laura Ann up on that island as bait, but she spoiled his fun. But now he's got what he wanted. We're prime targets."

"Then let's get going. Have you seen Eve?"

"No. And Kistle is unpredictable. I have to get back to Kistle's island before he changes his mind again and goes after her."

THE MOON HAD COME FROM behind the clouds and its light was bright enough that Kistle didn't even need his night goggles to sight down his rifle.

Excitement was racing through him. He couldn't believe it. It was all working out as he'd originally planned it. He would have all of them! The child and Miguel were huddled together in full view on the island and Quinn and Montalvo were in the boat only a short distance away. He had only to pick and choose. The power of life and death was his again and he was drunk with the taste of it.

Pick and choose . . .

He'd have to kill the men, of course. It was too dangerous to do anything else. But he might be able to just wound the child so that he could have her to play with later. He couldn't bear the thought of not breaking that little bitch. He'd have to shoot her first or they would rush to protect her. Yes, that was the thing to do . . .

A rustle behind him!

He whirled to see Eve Duncan emerging from the trees. He relaxed. No real threat. She was almost staggering and there was a patch of blood on her windbreaker. She was wounded and he'd taken her weapon. She was just a desperate woman trying to save the people important to her. It might even make the kills richer to have her witness them. "Just in time. But I'm in a little hurry so I can't talk to you." He gestured with the rifle. "Come here. I don't want you behind me where I can't see you if you rush me. Every shot has to count."

"Shot?" Eve tensed as her gaze followed his across the water to the island. "Oh, my God."

He chuckled. "That's the way I feel. Like God loosing a lightning bolt. I thought I'd have to work much harder to set this up again, but providence took a hand. Now come and stand beside me and watch."

Eve moved slowly until she was a few yards away on the bank. "Don't do this, Kistle."

"You know that I will. The child first."

"Always the children," she said bitterly. "Like Bonnie."

"Yes."

"Did you kill Bonnie, Kistle?"

"I could have killed her."

"Did you kill her? Is she here?"

Kistle smiled maliciously. "I told you where you could get your answer." He moved to the edge of the bank and lifted the rifle to sight on Laura Ann. "Now don't make a move or the shot to her arm will go into her head. I want her to keep you company for a while."

"Wait."

"I can't wait. Quinn and Montalvo are already heading to pick them up. They'll be moving fast and I—"

Agonizing pain as his hand shattered as it moved toward the trigger.

He was shot, he realized incredulously.

He stared in disbelief at Eve Duncan standing a few feet away, pointing a Magnum at him. The bitch had shot him!

Another blast of pain as another bullet tore into his arm.

His rifle dropped to the ground.

No!

He dove to get it.

Pain in his back. She'd shot him again.

"Bitch," he screamed. "You can't do this to me."

"Yes, I can." She was coming toward him. Her face was hard and totally without mercy. With her toe she pushed him from the bank and into the water. "Ask Bobby Joe and Laura Ann. Ask all of those children you buried on this island. Ask my Bonnie."

He was sputtering, water in his eyes and his throat, pain wracking his body. "I'll get away. You can't stop me." He started to swim with his good arm. "I'll come back. I'll kill you all. No one can stop me."

"You're wrong." He looked back to see her standing on the bank, gun lifted, pointing at his head. "I can stop you." Her finger was slowly pressing the trigger. "Ask the alligators, Kistle."

His head exploded as the bullet shattered his skull.

EVE DROPPED THE GUN AND SANK to the ground. She felt cold and she couldn't take her gaze from the place where Kistle had disappeared under the water.

She had killed him and was feeling no remorse. All those children, all the cruelty and savagery that he had let loose in the world. She would call Joe's cell in a minute and tell him what had happened, but first she had to pull herself together.

Even after making the call, she couldn't seem to stop staring at the water.

Joe jumped onto the bank from Montalvo's boat ten minutes later. "Go on," he told Montalvo. "Get the kid and Miguel back to the dock. I'll take care of Eve."

"She seems to take fine care of herself."

Montalvo turned the boat. "But I envy you the opportunity."

Joe didn't answer as he fell to his knees beside Eve. "You've got blood on your jacket. You didn't mention you were hurt."

She shook her head. "No. He shot me, but he made sure it was a flesh wound." She smiled crookedly. "He wanted to make certain that it wouldn't interfere with what he planned for me later." Her stare shifted back to the water. "I killed him. I don't regret it. Monsters like him shouldn't be permitted to live."

"You're right, I'm just sorry that it had to be you who did it." Joe took her in his arms. "I'm still a little wet, but I want to hold you. Okay?"

He was damp, but his skin was warm from the hot summer breeze and she nestled closer. She needed warmth right now. "Megan was right. I saw the graves. So many . . ."

He was stroking her hair. "Bonnie?"

"He said that she wasn't there." She closed her eyes. "I don't know, Joe. He lies . . ." No, it was past tense now. He was dead. She had killed him. "I could never trust anything he told me. He wanted to hurt me, to make me think I'd failed again."

"You didn't fail. Laura Ann is safe."

"Yes, she's safe." Her eyes opened. She had to think of that one true positive. No, there was another one. Kistle would never be able to kill another child. "We should get back to Megan."

"Did she bandage your shoulder?"

"No, when I went to the boat to get your gun she was sitting there like a statue. I couldn't get her to answer me. I don't believe she even knew I was there. I just put a bandage on the wound and took off. I had to find Kistle." She pushed him away and stood up. "I have to get back to her. I have to make sure she's all right."

Joe got to his feet. "She was probably safer than any of us, staying in the boat."

Eve shook her head as she remembered Megan's face that last moment before she had gone after Kistle. "I wish I could be sure of that."

EVE'S FIRST THOUGHT WAS that Kistle had somehow found the boat and killed Megan.

Megan was no longer sitting upright but lying huddled beside the seat.

"No sign of a wound. But she's unconscious." Eve checked Megan's pulse. "She's ice-cold and her pulse is thready."

"Shock." Joe jumped into the boat. "We've got to get her back to the dock. Was she this bad before?"

"After Bobby Joe?" She shook her head. "I don't think so. This is . . ." She didn't know what it was. But Megan's almost coma-like state was scaring her. "She kept saying there were too many. I saw what it was doing to her. I made her come to the island anyway."

"Stop the guilt trip," Joe said curtly. "She came because she thought she should do it. She's a strong woman and you wouldn't have been able to browbeat her into doing anything. It's done and we have to do damage control. At least she doesn't have a bullet in her like you do."

"Small favors," Eve said wearily. "It wasn't her war. Though she still looks in worse shape than I feel. We don't even have anything to drink or blankets to cover her to fight that shock."

"It will only be twenty or thirty minutes

back to the dock. As soon as we get under way, we need to call Phillip Blair and have him have an ambulance at the dock when we arrive." He cast off. "Can you drive the boat?"

She nodded. "This wound is barely a scratch."

"Then change places. I'll hold her and try to give her my body heat." He took off his shirt and drew Megan to him. "You always said I was a furnace."

"Yes, you are." Eve started to back the boat away from the island. "But I wasn't sure you'd want to share anything with her."

"Then you were wrong," he said shortly. "I'm not sure what the hell went on with her tonight, but I know what she did was for you, not herself. I don't want her checking out and making the nightmare any worse for all of us."

Checking out. Surely Megan wouldn't die because of this night. But what did Eve know about the trauma the other woman had suffered? There was no doubt Megan Blair was in dire straits and people did die of shock.

She looked back at the island where all those children had met their end. Had

Kistle lied again? Was Bonnie one of those children buried there? One of the voices that had sent Megan spiraling downward until she crashed and splintered? She didn't know, but she knew that Megan needed more than body heat and the medical care that waited for her on the dock.

I don't know if you're there, Bonnie. If you are, then you know Megan tried to help you. Or maybe you're not there but the others are holding on to Megan. Things were terrible there on the island and everyone was hurting, so maybe you don't realize that you're taking Megan with you. Let her go now.

Help her.

SIXTEEN

PHILLIP BLAIR WAS WAITING when they arrived back at the dock.

His fists clenched when he saw Megan.

"My God," he said unsteadily. "What the hell have you done to her?" He held out his arms as Joe carried Megan from the boat. "Give her to me."

"Where's the ambulance?"

"It should be here any minute. Give her to me."

Joe transferred her to Phillip's embrace. "It's shock. She wasn't wounded."

"Maybe not physically. How do you know what you did to her? My wife spent years in an institution fighting those damn voices. And you made Megan go searching for them. I told you to take care of her."

"We didn't make her go," Joe said.

"Yes, we did." Eve got out of the boat. "No, *I* did. I didn't force her, but I used every way I could to persuade her. I wouldn't take no for an answer." She stood before Phillip. "So if you want to blame someone, blame me."

"I do blame you." He looked at the blood soaking her shoulder. "But Megan wouldn't blame you. She'd want to fix your damn arm." He turned away. "So you'd better come along to the hospital with us."

"HOW ARE YOU?" MONTALVO MET Eve as she was coming out of the emergency room. "Any problems?"

"No, they cleaned it, bandaged it, and sent me on my way. After telling me that I had to make a report to the police department because it was a gunshot wound. How is Laura Ann? They told me she was in a room down the hall."

"Bruises, scratches, and hungry. The bastard didn't feed her." He smiled. "But she felt much better after she talked to her mother on the phone. She's on the road now, driving down to pick up her daughter."

"That's good. After what Laura Ann has been through, she'll need her mother close for a while."

"Right now Miguel seems to be filling the maternal role. She won't let him out of her sight."

"How are his hands?"

"Bad. The stitches are torn out and he's having to have shots to fight infection from that swamp water. We'll have to start all over."

"That's too bad. But he did save that little girl. I don't think he could have made any other choice."

"No. And they seem to have formed a bond dangling in that tree over those alligators. He doesn't mind playing surrogate mom for a while and he'll be able to keep the media away from her. They're bound to get the news anytime now that she's been found. Where's Quinn?"

"He dropped me off and then went directly to the local police department to make a report on Kistle's death and what they're going to find on that island." She shuddered. "I don't even want to think about the scope of that burial ground." But she would think about it for the rest of her life. There would be no forgetting one minute of this night. "I asked him not to mention Megan Blair's part in this. She's been through enough and sure as hell doesn't need the kind of notoriety this would bring her. I don't even know what all this did to her. She's still unconscious and the doctors didn't like her condition when we brought her into the emergency room." She shook her head. "They couldn't understand why they couldn't bring her back. I could tell them why. But they wouldn't believe me." She moved down the hall. "I'm going to her room and stay with her until she regains consciousness." She made a face. "If Phillip Blair will let me near her. He wanted to take a hatchet to all of us when he saw what I did to Megan."

"You didn't do it," Montalvo said.

"Of course I did. I saw what happened to her with Bobby Joe and I went right on. I was willing to put her through that hell. Oh, granted, I didn't know that she wouldn't just be facing one death but all those others." She said unevenly, "But,

God help me, I might still have done it. So what kind of ruthless bitch am I?"

"Driven, obsessed, desperate," Montalvo said gently. "And, yes, ruthless. It goes with the territory. But you're also very giving and have moments of being damn wonderful."

"Bullshit."

He smiled. "Go on and start your vigil with Megan. This isn't the time for me to talk to you. But my moment will have to come, Eve."

"No, it doesn't. I don't want to—" She broke off as she looked at him. He was still dirty and bruised and it reminded her of all he had gone through tonight for her and Laura Ann . . . and Bonnie. She nodded slowly as she moved down the hall toward Megan's hospital room. "We'll find a time to talk."

MEGAN'S FACE HAD NO COLOR and she looked very fragile in the white hospital bed. She was hooked up to an IV.

Phillip Blair was sitting in an upright visitor's chair beside her bed.

"How is she?" Eve asked.

Phillip shrugged. "I don't know. I don't think those doctors know either. We're all just waiting. Are you okay?"

She nodded. "Though I'm surprised you'd ask. You obviously have no kind feelings toward me." She grimaced. "And who could blame you? Certainly not me."

"No, it will take a long time for me to feel anything but resentment toward you. Megan is my family. We've been together since her mother died when she was fifteen." He gave her a cool glance. "I'm very protective of my family."

"And I respect you for it. But you don't have to protect Megan from me right now. All I want to do is stay with her until she wakes."

"Why?"

"Because I like her more than any woman I've met in a long time. Because I hurt her. Because I'm worried sick about her. Is that enough reason?"

He didn't speak for a moment. "Maybe." He nodded at the other visitor's chair. "Sit down."

She dropped down in the chair. "Thank you."

"Don't thank me. I have an ulterior

motive. Megan's going to want reassur-
ance when and if she comes out of this. I
have to have answers."

"Answers," Eve repeated. "What are
you talking about?"

"She was probably very upset before
she collapsed?"

"Of course. It was horrible for her."

"And did she touch any of you?"

Eve tried to remember. "I reached out
and held her hand at one point. Just for a
minute, and then she pulled it away."

Phillip muttered an oath. "Dammit, I
knew it would happen. Anything else?"

She shook her head. "Joe held her on
the way back from the island. She was unconscious and in shock."

He frowned. "I think that's probably all
right. No emotional contact."

"I don't know what the hell you're talking about."

He glared at her. "You wouldn't have
had to know anything if you hadn't per-
suaded Megan to go into that swamp."

"Look, she did go, and that's past history. There's nothing I can do about it. Now,
why are you on edge about my touching
Megan?"

He didn't answer.

"Phillip, I'm exhausted, I'm worried, my nerves are shot, and I've no intention of letting you say something like that and ignoring it. This weird phobia Megan has about touching people has been popping up since I met her. I've hurt her enough tonight. I'm going to know if I somehow managed to accidentally hurt her again."

He looked back at Megan. "She's the only one who has the right to talk about it."

"Tell me, dammit."

He wearily leaned back in his chair. "She wouldn't be the one hurt. It wouldn't matter so much to her if she was the one to take the hit. When she's under extreme emotional tension, it's sometimes dangerous for her to touch anyone."

"How?"

"Megan is not only a Listener. In the last few months she's discovered she has another psychic gift." He smiled sardonically. "Though she thinks of it more as a curse. She found out that she's a Pandora."

"Pandora?"

"Another term would be a facilitator. She can release the dormant psychic talents of those around her. She doesn't know exactly how it works, but she thinks it's triggered by extreme emotion and she has to touch them. That's why she isn't practicing medicine right now. She can't take the risk."

"Risk?"

"Some people can't accept the release. They can't handle it." He paused. "There have been . . . deaths."

She shook her head incredulously. "This is totally bizarre. I've never even heard of anything like that."

"Neither did Megan. Imagine how she feels."

"I have to imagine," she said flatly. "Because I can't believe it."

Phillip shrugged. "That's your privilege. You asked, I answered. But is it any more unbelievable than the fact that she's a Listener? You seem to have accepted that premise."

"That's . . . different."

"Because you've been a witness and gone through the experience with her. She was hoping you wouldn't even have to know she was a Pandora. But you touched her and that means we have to be on watch."

"You're saying I might die?"

"I'm saying that in two cases the subject went mad and that resulted in death. In another case there was no ill effect and he seems to be handling the gift." He made a face. "Though he'd rather go back to the way he was before."

"And that came just from touching one of these Pandoras?"

"She thinks that's the trigger. She can't be certain. As I said, this is new to Megan. She doesn't know any of the nuances. The releasing of the talent occurred after she touched the subjects during a moment of intense emotionalism. At first she wouldn't even accept that she was the one responsible."

"I wouldn't either."

The corner of Phillip's lips lifted in a half smile. "Because you may be very much alike. Megan has always been practical and levelheaded. Then her life was turned upside down and she's been trying to get it back on track. She loved being a doctor. It's killing her to not go back to medicine. It's the measure of how much she believes that she could hurt her patients that she refuses to take the chance."

"There has to be another explanation."

"And I hope we all find it. Until that happens, I'd just as soon you stay close so that I can keep an eye on you."

"To see that I don't go off my rocker?" she asked dryly. "And what great psychic gift am I supposed to develop?"

He shrugged. "Whatever talent is latent in you. Telepathy, mind reading, healing. I understand some psychics are supposed to be able to predict the future, communicate with the departed, and find lost objects."

"And you believe these things are possible?"

"I know some of them are possible. I've experienced the benefits of one of them."

"Which one?"

He shook his head. "I promised I wouldn't talk about it."

"How convenient." She gazed back at Megan's face. Dear God, she wished she'd regain consciousness. "And how long am I supposed to be under this surveillance?"

"I don't know. I understand sometimes the subject shows signs of the release of talent at once and then in others there's a delay. We don't know how long that delay might be. We just don't know enough about it. Megan has been planning on investigating any other possible Pandoras she can find to try to find out answers. You didn't give her the opportunity before you pulled her into that swamp."

"Pandora . . ." Eve thought about the name. "The mythological woman who opened the box and let out all troubles into the world?"

"It depends on what myth you read. Pandora kept hope in the box, why not other virtues?"

The lady with the box.

What had Bonnie said about the lady with the box?

Don't let her hurt you, Mama. Don't let her hurt me . . .

The lady with the box. Pandora.

"What are you thinking?" Phillip's eyes were narrowed on her face.

"Nothing important."

How could Megan have hurt Eve? She was the one who had damaged Megan.

Unless this bizarre story of Megan's being a facilitator had a small basis of truth.

"Don't be so worried," Phillip said gently.

"Megan would be the first to tell you this talent is wildly erratic. She's worked with patients for years and there was no sign of any change in them. It's just that we have to be careful."

"And Joe wouldn't be affected by this craziness?"

He shook his head. "Extreme emotion is one of the necessary elements. Megan was unconscious. No, you're the one we have to watch."

Don't let her hurt you, Mama.

Poor Megan, Eve thought, she didn't want to hurt anyone and she was caught up in this tornado of guilt and pain. She reached forward and touched Megan's hand. "I think you've drawn a blank this time. I'm feeling perfectly normal," she whispered. "And I'm sure you'll be relieved to hear about it. So why don't you come back and we'll talk?"

Megan didn't stir.

Phillip pushed back his chair. "I'll go get us a cup of coffee. Sandwich?"

Eve shook her head. "Not now."

She settled back in the chair and waited for Megan to wake.

EVE WENT OUTSIDE THE HOSPITAL and called Joe on her cell phone six hours later. "Megan's still unconscious. I'm going to stay with her until she wakes up. What's happening?"

"Media all over the place. I've filled out the report on Kistle." He paused. "I said I'd shot him while attempting arrest."

"Then you'd better change it. I'm going to tell the truth."

"Hell, they'll give me a medal. There's no reason for you to be involved."

"Except the truth."

"We'll talk about it later. I called Jane and told her what had happened. She's pissed."

"Of course she is. We knew that would be a given."

"I'll be at the hospital as soon as I can. I have to take the police to the island and let them—" He stopped.

"Open those graves," she finished, and then went on with an effort, "Show them the memory box, Joe. It had names on most of his damn souvenirs. Are they going to let the media go with you?"

"No," he said curtly. "I've told them they can either have me to lead them to the island or the media. No one is going to be allowed on that island until every one of those bodies has been exhumed. I promise you, Eve."

"That's good. Those parents don't need a media circus going on while they're trying to cope. I just visited Laura Ann. Her mother was there with her in her room and she seemed fine. We don't know what the effect of that horror will be down the road, but she's tough. I think she'll make it." Laura Ann might have memories and nightmares all her childhood, but at least she was alive and would have a childhood. Not like those children on Kistle's island. "I've got to get back to Megan. Call me when you get through at the island, Joe."

"Right." He hung up.

She put her phone back in her pocket and went back inside the hospital. Joe wasn't finished with the island and he'd probably be hours out there with the police.

She wasn't finished either. She had been worried about Laura Ann's memories, but what about her own? There were still unanswered questions that had to be answered.

And the most important one might have to be answered by Megan Blair.

MEGAN WAS STILL UNCONSCIOUS when Eve reached her room.

Phillip looked up. "The doctor came by and checked her vital signs. He said he might have to call in a neural specialist if she doesn't respond. He says there could be some underlying problem. He doesn't know what else to do."

"She told me once that she thought those bouts of unconsciousness were sort of like hibernation so that her mind could heal."

He shook head. "This is so deep it's almost a coma."

"She had a lot of wounds to heal." Eve was saying words of comfort, but they were only words. She was as scared as Phillip. "Why don't you take a break? Go back to the hotel and shower and change. I'll stay with her until you come back."

He shook his head.

"Go on. I'll call you the minute she wakes up."

He hesitated and then stood. "I'll try to

be back in an hour, but I might be longer. I'm going to call someone who might be able to help her. Grady's in Tanzania and I might have trouble getting through to him."

"Grady? Tanzania's half a world away. Are they close enough so that he'll drop everything and come to her?"

"There's nobody closer to Megan. In more ways than one." He headed for the door. "He'll be on the next flight home."

Eve watched the door close behind him. Even if this Grady flew to Megan's side, she didn't see how he could help. Well, Phillip thought Grady could do something, and they were clutching at straws. Heaven knows Eve couldn't think of anything to do for her.

MEGAN OPENED HER EYES a little over an hour later.

"Eve?"

"Thank God," Eve said.

Megan's gaze drifted around the room and then came back to Eve. "You again? This is getting to be a habit." Her voice was slurred. "And it's not one I want to get into."

"I don't blame you." Eve blinked back

tears. "I'd avoid me like the plague from now on."

"It's a thought," Megan said. "Laura Ann?"

"Safe. She's here at the hospital and her mother is with her."

"That's good. Kistle?"

"Dead."

"That's even better. So much evil . . ."

"I'll be right with you." Eve pulled out her cell phone. "I promised to call Phillip and tell him if you woke." She dialed the number and when he picked up she said, "She came out of it two minutes ago. Her speech is a little slurred, but otherwise she seems okay."

"Thank God."

"That's what I said."

"I'll be right there."

Eve hung up. "He's on his way. I think he likes you a little."

"He's my family," Megan said simply.

"What about this Grady Phillip was trying to get to fly here from Tanzania? Phillip said you were close to him."

Her eyes widened. "Phillip called Grady? He shouldn't have done that."

"He was scared. *I* was scared. This didn't seem like the last time. Even the doctors here at the hospital were uneasy."

Megan was silent a moment. "No, it wasn't like the last time. This was different. It was as if I were breaking apart inside."

"I'm sorry." It wasn't enough, but Eve didn't know what else to say. "I'm very grateful."

"I didn't do it for you. I did it for Laura Ann," Megan said. "And for those kids that bastard murdered. He had to be stopped."

"But I brought you into it."

"Yes, you did." She sat up in bed. "I need to go and take a shower. Then I want to get out of here."

"They're not going to release you until a doctor signs off on you."

"Will you go tell someone I'm okay and set the wheels in motion?" She swung her legs to the floor and then had to wait a moment until she had strength to move. "I feel a little woozy."

"That's not surprising. Why don't you wait for—"

"I'll be okay." She carefully got to her feet. "If Phillip comes back before I get out of the shower, will you tell him that I'd love it if he could pick me up a hamburger and hot chocolate?"

"I'll call him back and tell him to bring it with him."

"Thank you." Megan was moving stiffly across the room. "It's not really for me. Phillip just feels better if he can give me comfort food. I imagine he was pretty upset."

"That's an understatement." She paused. "You're moving like someone who's been run over by a truck. Are you sore?"

"I feel as if I were thrown into a cement mixer and then spit out. They tore me apart."

Eve tried to restrain herself. Give her time. Don't ask the question.

She did it anyway. "I need to know if it was—"

"Not now, Eve." Megan opened the bathroom door. "I'll talk to you later. I know what you're going through."

And she should have been more patient, Eve thought, as the door closed behind Megan. She'd acted like a selfish bitch, when Megan was barely able to function. She owed the woman a debt and she needed to help, not interrogate, her.

She took out her phone and dialed Phillip Blair again.

SEVENTEEN

THE HOSPITAL RELEASED MEGAN four hours later and she opted to go back to the motel with Phillip rather than start immediately back to Atlanta.

"Eve will drive me back to the motel," Megan told Phillip as they left the room. "I'll meet you in the suite. Okay?"

"Okay." He turned to Eve. "You keep an eye on her."

She smiled. "I'll do it. Are you satisfied you don't have to keep an eye on me now?"

"Ask Megan. But it's been over ten hours and I'd think that would be safe." He held out his hand. "I like you, but I don't like what you did to Megan. Don't do it again."

She shook his hand. "Good-bye, Phillip. I hope we meet again under kinder circumstances."

"But I notice you're not promising anything," Phillip said. "I'll see you back at the hotel, Megan."

Megan watched him go toward the elevators before she turned back to Eve. "He told me that he felt compelled to tell you about me and this Pandora business. He shouldn't have done it."

"He seemed to think that there was some kind of risk. And he wasn't sure when or if you'd be conscious to deal with it."

"I understand why he did it." She started down the hall. "He's a responsible man. But since nothing happened I would just as soon have not had you know about it. It sounds like something from an X-Men movie." She glanced at Eve. "You don't believe it, do you?"

"It's difficult."

Megan shrugged. "I felt the same way. I had to be convinced. But since you're not affected, you can mark it down to the ravings of just another nutsy psychic and forget about it."

"You're not nuts. You led us to that island."

"So I'm not nuts as a Listener, but I'm completely bonkers as a Pandora." Megan held up her hand as Eve opened her lips. "It's okay. I'm not hurt. I'd feel the same way. No, I couldn't feel exactly the same way. I never had a child of my own, so I can't know your desperation. But I think I can empathize." She changed the subject. "Do you mind if we drop in and see Laura Ann before we leave? I'd like to see with my own eyes that she's well."

"I can see why. You went through hell for her and you've never even met."

"You're not to tell her how I helped. She wouldn't understand." She shook her head ruefully. "None of us understand, do we? What room is she in?"

"First floor, 28B. I paid her a visit after they finished with me in the emergency room." She added curiously, "This is a hospital, very high-stress. I'd think you'd be overcome with voices."

"I've learned to block them. It's only

when I lower the barriers that they can overwhelm me."

They met Nina Simmons walking out of Laura Ann's hospital room. She was smiling and appeared ten years younger than the first time Eve had seen her.

"I was going to come to see you." Laura Ann's mother gave her a fierce hug. "You gave me back my baby. Any favor. All you have to do is ask."

"You don't owe me anything."

"Yes, I do." She stepped back. "I'll find a way. But now I have to go and spring Laura Ann out of this place so that we can go home." She hurried down the hall.

"Seeing her face was almost worth everything." Megan's gaze followed Nina Simmons until she disappeared.

"Yes, that's how I feel," Eve said as she opened Laura Ann's door.

Laura Ann was dressed and sitting on the side of the bed when they walked into the room. "Eve." Her face lit up with a smile. "I'm going home. Mama is downstairs signing papers so they'll let me out."

"And she let me stay and say good-bye." Miguel came out of the bathroom carrying a pink posy bouquet in a glass container. "I thought I'd put water into this vase so that she could take it home with her."

"It's very pretty," Eve said. "I'm sure your room at home will be overflowing with flowers when word gets out that you're safe."

"But none will be as wonderful as this one," Miguel said. "I gave it to her." He handed the little girl the vase. "Did I not choose well, Laura Ann?"

"I like yellow flowers better," Laura Ann said. "But I guess it's okay."

"Is that gratitude for you?" Miguel asked. "I face alligators for her and she spurns me. I hate to see what you'll be when you grow up."

"What does spurn mean?"

"Reject. Send away."

"I didn't spurn you." Laura Ann was frowning. "I just like yellow—and you said you wouldn't go away. When we were in that tree, you said you wouldn't leave me."

"And I didn't."

"And you're not going to leave me now. I won't let you."

Eve quickly stepped between them. "I'd like you to meet a friend, Laura Ann. This is Megan Blair. She was on the island searching for you too."

Megan smiled. "Hello, it's good to meet you. I'm sure you're very happy to be going home."

"Yes." Laura Ann was still frowning at Miguel. "You promised."

"You'll be going back to school. You'll have your friends. You'll never miss me," Miguel said gently. "But I promise if you ever run into a hungry alligator again I'll be there."

"I want you to— My daddy promised he'd be around too. But after he left Mama and me, he never came back." Her lips firmed determinedly. "You *have* to come and see me. And I'm not going to ever see an alligator again. I don't like them."

He smiled. "Okay, when we go to the zoo we won't visit the reptile house." He paused. "If you have time for me, I'll probably be around Atlanta for a while. I messed up my hands and I'll have to go back to have them taken care of."

"They were bleeding." Laura Ann was looking at his bandaged hands. "You did it on the tree when you pushed me up."

"May I see them?" Megan asked. "I'm a doctor."

Miguel turned so that the little girl

wouldn't be able to see and held out his hands. "Sure. Though you probably can't do anything more. The doctors in the emergency room here cleaned me up and gave me a shot. They told me to go back to the specialists."

Megan quickly unwrapped the bandages on one of his hands. "They were probably right. I'm not as qualified as the specialists who operated on you." She took one look at the wounds and shook her head. "Ugly. It needs very delicate surgery and even then it might take years to heal properly." She rewrapped his hand. "Who did your first surgery?"

"Smith Lowe at Emory."

"He's excellent." Megan reached into her purse and drew out a business card. "But there's a man I'd like you to see." She was scrawling on the back of the card as she spoke. "His name is Jed Harley and he may be able to help you."

"What hospital is he with?"

"He's sort of a consultant and moves around a lot. Right now he's working at St. Jude's in Memphis. I'll call him and ask him to come to Atlanta to look at your hands." She handed him the card. "You'll see him?"

He shrugged. "Why not? Montalvo has had me seeing every specialist in the Southeast. What's one more? Thank you."

Megan shook her head. "No. Thank *you*, Miguel." She went to the bed and brushed her hand caressingly on Laura Ann's cheek. "I have to go now," she said softly. "I know I'm not as important as Miguel, but I live in Atlanta too. I have a friend, Davy, who is younger than you, but maybe you could put up with him if we all went to the aquarium. He wants to see the penguins."

"So do I." Laura Ann's eyes shone with excitement. "They take your picture with them, you know."

"I didn't know. Suppose I call your mother next week and we'll see if we can get together." She shot Miguel a glance. "We may even let Miguel come along. I don't think the penguins can hurt his hands."

"Hands aren't that important. I saw that movie *Happy Feet*," Miguel said. "Maybe they can teach me to dance."

"That was only pretend," Laura Ann said in disgust. "Don't you know anything?"

"I guess not. You'll have to teach me."

He sat down in the chair. "I learn quickly. Ask Montalvo."

"The ugly ape." She was smiling again. "He didn't like me saying that, did he?"

"I'm afraid you have a streak of mischief," Miguel said. "I must speak to your mother about it."

"And you don't?" Eve said dryly. She gave Laura Ann a hug. "Good-bye, Laura Ann, I'll see you in Atlanta. Maybe you could come out to the lake and meet my daughter, Jane's, dog, Toby." She moved toward the door. "Good-bye, Miguel. Take care of those hands."

Megan waved and joined Eve as she walked down the hall. "I can see how Laura Ann survived Kistle. She's a tough little kid. Miguel may have his hands full. She seems to have forcibly adopted him."

"He can take care of himself," Eve said. "And he obviously likes her or he wouldn't put up with it. Miguel is only as soft as he wants to be." She glanced at Megan as they went out the exit into the parking lot. "Do you really think your consultant can help him?"

"We'll have to see. I think Harley's success rates are exceptionally high." She got into the passenger seat of Eve's SUV. "It's starting to rain. Dammit, that's all the police need to cope with on the island."

Eve backed out of the parking space. After a few minutes she asked, "Can you still hear the voices?"

"No." Megan gazed at the fat raindrops falling against the windshield. "I'm too far away. Maybe if I didn't block them, I might be able to do it. Ordinarily I'd say that I was free, but this was different."

"You said that before. How?"

"I brought them with me," she said. "That's why I couldn't wake up. They were inside me, tearing me apart with their sadness. The other times when I was unconscious, I didn't feel anything. This time they were still there." She shook her head. "As I said, I empathize with you and all the other parents who lost those children, because now I feel as if I've lost them too."

They drove in silence for a while before Eve finally said, "If you can empathize, then you know what I want to ask you. May I ask it now?"

"You want to know if one of the voices was Bonnie's." She paused. "I've been thinking about it ever since I woke up. It could have been. There was such a cacophony of sound, of voices." She shook her head. "But I don't recall and I believe I would have recognized Bonnie. I knew how much it meant to you to find her."

Eve felt a wild surge of disappointment. "Kistle told me that she wasn't buried on the island."

"I'm sure that isn't all the son of a bitch said."

"He said . . . alligators."

"What a monster. He chose the most horrible scenario he could dream up and handed it to you." Megan shook her head. "Even if she wasn't buried there, if that's where he took her life, I'd hear her voice."

"You don't think she's there." Eve pulled into the motel parking lot. "I told him that I thought he was claiming credit for a kill he never made. It made him furious." She moistened her lips. "I killed him, Megan. I was afraid that somehow he'd wriggle away and go on slaughtering. I pulled the trigger four times to make sure he was dead."

"Good. I don't know if he killed your Bonnie. You'll have to wait until they finish searching. I know he killed those other poor kids on that island," Megan said. "And if I'd been able to do it, I would have sent the bastard to hell myself."

Eve parked as close to the motel as she could get. "You're going to get wet." She tried to smile. "And Phillip told me to take care of you."

"A little rain won't hurt me." Megan didn't move to get out of the car. The rain was pounding, enveloping them in a cocoon. "Don't ask me to do it again, Eve."

Eve's eyes widened in shock. "I wouldn't do that."

"Yes, you would. If you come up empty. If they don't find Bonnie on that island. You couldn't help yourself." She gazed out the windshield. "And I'll turn you down, Eve. Not because of what I went through. I could take that, I think. But you couldn't take it. It would kill you."

"No, it's what I want most in the world."

"When we started out, I told you that I wouldn't do it except for Laura Ann. I told you not to try to find her through me. I could see what would happen."

"I'd have my Bonnie back."

"You'd have a horror to live with for the

rest of your life," Megan said. "Because if I found her, you wouldn't be able to leave it alone. You'd want me to share exactly how she died and you wouldn't leave me alone until I told you."

"No."

"Yes. You love her, you'd want to share her death as well as her life. If someone else finds her, then you'll probably never know. But I'm the one who could destroy you. I won't do that."

"You're wrong, Megan," Eve said unsteadily. "I'm not that weak."

"No, you're strong. I admire you more than anyone I've ever met. But you've had your share of nightmares and I'm not going to give you any more."

"I wouldn't ask you to—" She closed her eyes and tears rolled down her cheeks. "God help me, I would. I'd find a way to make you help me. Don't do it. Don't let me hurt you."

Megan's arms were suddenly around her. "I won't." She rocked her gently. "It's going to be okay, Eve. You'll find her. I know you'll find her."

Eve lifted her head and drew a shaky

breath. "I know it too. Maybe I already have." She straightened away from Megan and smiled with an effort. "But it would be nice if that was a psychic prediction."

Megan shook her head. "No." Her hand reached for the door handle. "It's a prediction based on the fact that you're smart and strong and life can deal from the bottom of the deck for only so long. If you need me, call me." She opened the door. "Except for that one thing, Eve."

"Megan."

Megan looked back at her.

"There aren't words to thank you."

"Then don't try to find any." She jumped out of the SUV and ran through the rain toward the entrance.

Eve watched until she disappeared inside. She suddenly felt lonely. Megan's warmth and vitality still lingered with her. She was the most caring individual Eve had ever met and she didn't want to see her walk out of her life.

But she would try to let her keep her distance. She had begun by thinking Megan was the ruthless intruder, but it wasn't Megan who was the danger, it was Eve herself. It was really Eve who Bonnie had been warning her against. Megan was only the instrument.

The lady with the box. Don't let her hurt you, Mama. Don't let her hurt me.

THE RAIN WAS COMING DOWN in sheets and the police had covered the entire glade under makeshift tarp canopies that allowed them to move freely from area to area.

Grave to grave.

Joe was wet, his boots muddy, in spite of the yellow ponchos the police were issuing to the team who were exhuming the bodies.

Small bodies. Pitiful bodies. The sight wrenched him to the core.

And made him want to kill Kistle all over again.

"It's incredible."

Joe turned to see Montalvo standing behind him. Montalvo was soaked to the skin, raindrops running down his cheeks, but he didn't seem to be aware of it. His gaze was fixed on the rows of remains that had been exhumed. "So much pain . . . I envy Eve. I would have been proud to rid the world of Kistle."

"So would I." It was what Joe had been feeling. "What are you doing here?"

"The same as you. It's not finished. How many bodies have they found?"

"Twenty-two. They think there may be six more buried in this glade."

"Bonnie?"

"I don't know. Kistle told Eve she wasn't here." He turned away. "I've got to get back to work. They want to get this site clean before they let the media anywhere near it."

"I can see why. Where are they giving out the shovels and rain gear?"

Joe looked back at him. "I told you, Bonnie may not be here."

"But there are six other children who are buried here." He met Joe's eyes as he added quietly, "It's not finished for them either. Let's bring them home, Quinn."

Joe didn't speak for a moment and then he turned away. "You can get a poncho and shovel from the officer on the other side of the glade."

JOE CALLED EVE'S CELL three hours later.

She braced herself and then pressed the button. "Good news?"

"Bonnie isn't buried in the glade," he said baldly. "He had all the corpses labeled with their first names just as he told you. We found a body to correspond with every trophy in his damn memory box. It will take time to go over the entire island but she's not in the burial ground."

Disappointment tore through her. "No."

"As I said, he may have buried her somewhere else on the island." He paused. "Or he may not have buried her here at all. There was no Bonnie trophy in that memory box. We think that box was only for the island. We have to find any other souvenir box he might have had."

"Or he may not have been the one who killed her," she whispered. "But I was so sure this time."

"So was I." He drew a harsh breath. "God, I don't know if I can go on with this—" He stopped. "It may not be the end of the trail with Kistle. I won't give up yet. Go on back to the cottage. I'm going to go back to my precinct to make a report there. We think most of the victims were from Atlanta, and bodies will be sent to our medical examiner for identification and DNA tests. We won't know what kind of records to check until we find out how long ago they were killed."

"Publish the names Kistle had on his labels and I'll bet you'll be flooded with calls from parents with missing children." Eve shook her head. "What am I thinking? That would be the worst way to find out your child has been murdered. Until the last minute they'll be hoping that their baby is alive and happy somewhere."

"I'll be back at the cottage as soon as I'm through and I'll call you if I find out anything more. Will you be all right?"

"Yes." She made an effort. "Don't worry about me, Joe. It's not as if I haven't been disappointed before. Do what you have to do."

He muttered a curse. "How can I help but worry? How long can you take this? How long can I take it? It's been going on for—" He was silent a moment, but she could sense the tension and despondency charging the stillness. "I'll call you." He hung up.

She pressed the disconnect button. Yes, how long could Joe take it? she thought wearily. The desperation he was feeling was even more obvious than it had been before. She would go on forever because she could do nothing else. Bonnie was the beloved. She could no more stop searching than she could not draw breath.

But Joe may have reached the end of the line. Who could blame him? He could not share her love for Bonnie, only the pain connected with her death.

Don't think of it right now. Drive to the lake cottage and let the beauty soothe you as it has done for years.

Heal and think and hope.

Oh, yes, by all means hope.

IT WAS CLOSE TO MIDNIGHT when Eve arrived back at the cottage. It was too late to pick up Toby at Patty's, but she wished she had him with her. She felt lonely and uncertain and wanted a warm body to press against her.

"I'm sorry about Bonnie," Montalvo said.

She whirled to the porch swing where he was sitting. "You startled me." She turned on the porch lights. "How did you know about Bonnie?"

"I was on the island. I thought they might

need my digging prowess. I seem to have become an expert lately." He shook his head. "I could have done without that particular skill. It was enough to break my heart."

"Joe says she may still be somewhere on the island."

"But you don't believe it."

"I don't know. I want to believe it." She rubbed her temple. "What are you doing here, Montalvo?"

"I dropped Miguel off at the hospital and I came here to pack up our camp. I was afraid he'd try to do it himself if I brought him with me."

"That's right. I forgot about the camp. It seems a long time ago."

"And I wanted to see you before Joe, the conquering hero, appeared back on the stage."

She stiffened. "No, Montalvo."

"Yes, Eve." He held out his hand. "Come and sit down. You promised me my time with you."

That's right, she had promised him. That seemed a long time ago too. She slowly moved across the porch toward him. "I haven't changed my mind." She sat down on the swing beside him. "And I won't change it."

"You might. Time passes, life changes. But I'm not here to bulldoze you. Life has made another jog that changes the picture a little."

"What jog?"

He looked out at the lake. "Quinn saved me from a very nasty death. He didn't have to do it. God knows, he didn't want to do it. But the fact remains that he did do it. That puts me in a quandary."

"Why?"

"Because I find myself reluctant to be as ruthless toward him as I would ordinarily." He made a face. "Miguel tells me that he has to take care of me because I saved his neck. I laughed at him. It's absurd."

"Is it?"

"Yes. But I'm feeling a ridiculous sense of responsibility for Quinn. I'd never call myself an honorable man. Yet I have a code that I live by and it's getting in the way."

She frowned. "What are you saying, Montalvo?"

"I'm saying I have to let you go for now."

"You never had me."

He smiled. "I did in my mind. It was only a matter of time until I made it into reality."

"Bull."

He chuckled. "I love that bluntness of yours." He took her hand. "No, don't pull away. I deserve this. Now I'll tell you how it's going to be. I can't let you go entirely. We're much too close. So I've decided to become your Joe's best friend."

Her eyes widened. "What?"

"It won't be difficult. We have a good deal in common. I'm beginning to like him."

"I don't think it's mutual."

"Then that will be my new challenge." He was playing idly with her fingers. "I will be your friend. I will be Joe Quinn's friend. You'll both come to admire and rely on me. Isn't that a fine plan?"

"It's a fine fairy tale," Eve said dryly.

"And like all fairy tales it can have wicked twists," he said softly. "If I'm lucky enough to save Quinn's life at some point, then the story changes again. No more obligations. If he turns into a wife beater, then I kill him and we ride off into the sunset. You agree?"

"This is your fairy tale, not mine."

"But it's one that's going to make you

happy." He paused. "Because you don't want me to go out of your life any more than I want to go. Some people are meant to be together. Sometimes things happen or go wrong to change the order of things, but then we have to fight to put them back where they should be."

"I should be with Joe."

"Perhaps. But I'd be a fool not to position myself for any change in the wind."

She leaned back in the swing and looked at him. His dark eyes, the power of his body, the confidence that was sensual in itself. He was everything that was mature, charismatic, and seductive, and she felt the magnetism as she always did when she was with him. Dammit, it was forbidden and, therefore, all the more alluring. "It won't work."

"Yes, it will. I'm something of a chameleon and in six months you'll have forgotten I was anything but your staunchest ally and bosom friend."

She wouldn't forget. "It would be easier if you'd just go away, Montalvo."

"But neither one of us likes easy." He lifted her hand and pressed the palm to his lips. "You see how restrained I'm being?"

Restrained? She could feel the heat tingling in her palm and wrist. She jerked her hand away. "Good-bye, Montalvo."

He chuckled and rose to his feet. "Good night, Eve. I'll be in touch. Probably not with you, because you're too wary right now."

"And Joe's not?"

"Quinn and I understand each other." He headed for the steps. "In time we can bridge our differences."

"You're dreaming." She paused. "Why are you doing this? Why go to such lengths?"

"Miguel once asked me if you were worth it. I told him yes." He stood there at the top of the steps looking back at her. He added simply, "And I'm lonely. I find it difficult to come close to many people. I'd miss you if you weren't in my life. So I'm going to arrange it so that you stay."

She shouldn't be this moved. No one was tougher or more able to take care of himself than Montalvo. Yet she couldn't doubt his sincerity. "You know, this may boomerang against you. You say you're going to be Joe's best friend and yet you're planning on standing apart." She smiled. "I know Joe. There's no standing apart from him. It's all or nothing. You say that you understand him. You may find that you develop as much affection for him as you have for Miguel. Wouldn't that be funny?"

"No, it would not be funny." He lifted his hand in farewell. "But I'll take my chances. What's life without a little uncertainty?"

She watched him walk down the stairs. What a difficult man. He was full of complexities and character shadings that could keep you guessing and probing into infinity. This latest development had taken her completely by surprise. Was it calculating? Yes, but there had been that moment of vulnerability too. It was better not to think of Montalvo as vulnerable. With any luck he would be out of her life before long. In spite of his confidence in his success, it would be like climbing a mountain to overcome Joe's antagonism. Montalvo did have a certain sense of honor and she believed him when he said that he wouldn't interfere between Joe and her. If there was no other access, then the door would close and he would go away. She felt again that unreasonable pang of sadness. It was natural, when a force like

Montalvo moved out of your life, that you'd experience a sense of loss. It would go away.

She got to her feet and moved toward the screen door. She would go take a shower and change. Then she'd go through her correspondence and wait for Joe to call her.

And hope that there would be news of Bonnie.

EIGHTEEN

SHE STOOD WATCHING FROM the porch as Joe's car drove up the road three hours later.

He looked exhausted, she thought as he got out of the car. Why not? It had been almost thirty-six hours since either one of them had gotten any sleep.

"You shouldn't have stayed up. I would have woken you." He came up the steps. "I know what's important."

"I didn't want to go to bed." She tensed. "Tell me."

"No Bonnie. They're still searching the island, but they brought over some instruments from Jacksonville and there don't appear to be any buried bone fragments." He took her in his arms and buried his face in her hair. "God, I'm sorry."

"Me too," she whispered.

"And Bonnie's favorite song? We found a story in a Macon, Georgia, paper about Bonnie that mentioned it."

"And Kistle could have read it and remembered." Her arms slid around him. He was warm and hard and blessedly comforting. She could feel the tears welling, but she blinked them back. "But I think I was expecting it. When I saw Kistle's expression when he started backing away from telling me where Bonnie was buried, I was afraid that he'd been lying to me about everything." Her voice was muffled against him. "God, it's going to be hard to keep on searching after this, Joe."

"Then don't do it."

She shook her head. "Kistle wasn't the only name Montalvo gave me. There were two others."

"And you're already thinking about the next man on the list. I knew it would be like this. I don't know if I can—" He was rocking her in an agony of pain. "It was too bad this time, Eve. It almost killed you. And part of me died a little too. I *can't* care about Bonnie. I'm sorry but that's the way it is. I'm not sure I can watch you go through— I feel you stiffening against me. Don't *do* that."

She hadn't known she had been pushing him away. It was instinctive rejection because of the panic his words were bringing. "I can't help it." She kissed him and then stepped back. It was the last thing she wanted to do. She wanted to stay in his arms, convince him to stay forever. She couldn't do it. She didn't know how many times she'd unconsciously tried to sway him, keep him close. It wasn't fair to him. If she was hurting him, then she should stand aside. "And I can't help you with this, Joe." She added unsteadily, "It's got to be your decision." She moved toward the kitchen. "But don't make it exhausted and on edge. We'll talk about it tomorrow. I've made a pot of coffee. Let's just sit and talk and then go to bed." She poured coffee into a mug. "I made it decaf, but I don't think it would make a difference. We'll both sleep."

He nodded. "I saw that Montalvo's camp was gone when I drove in."

"Yes, he dropped Miguel off at the hospital and broke it down himself."

Joe looked down at his coffee. "He came up to tell you about it?"

"Yes, and to tell me how grateful he was that you'd saved his life."

"I should have let that alligator eat the bastard."

She smiled. "He also told me that you hadn't done it willingly."

"Damn straight."

"But he said it didn't matter and he was going to make himself your new best friend."

"What an ass." He took a drink of his coffee. "We've identified fifteen of the victims so far. We'll try to find case reports on the others, but we may be asking your help for a couple of them."

She nodded. "Though I might be able to ask Megan if she remembered any of the names of her voices. It could help."

"We'll take any help we can get." He gazed across the table at her. "Even Megan Blair's."

"You believed her, Joe. Maybe you didn't want to believe her, but you did."

"I believed her." He grimaced. "That

doesn't mean I'd believe her on another case. I'd step very carefully."

"I wouldn't expect anything else of you." She looked away from him. "But at least you're willing to accept that everything isn't exactly as it might seem to you. That's a small breakthrough."

"I don't know what I'd accept or not accept. My good sense is telling me that I shouldn't believe any of this. As I said, once I have time to analyze, she'd probably have a hard time convincing me."

"I doubt if it will come up. I don't think Megan's going to be involved in any other cases anytime soon. This one could have killed her if you hadn't kept her warm on the way back to the dock. She was in severe shock."

"What else could I do?" He downed the rest of his coffee. "Shower and then bed. Coming?"

Conversation over coffee, shower, bed; the familiar routines that made up their lives. She could sense the edge of darkness in him that could cut them apart, but he wasn't letting it surface. Not yet. So hold those beloved routines close. There was no guessing how long they would exist.

She smiled and got to her feet. "Always."

JOE WAS ASLEEP WITHIN minutes after he had hit the bed, but Eve lay awake. She should be as exhausted as Joe and she supposed she was. But the memories and sadness wouldn't go away. Memories and the worry about what was to come.

Joe would leave her. Perhaps not this week or this month, but it would happen. He couldn't stand the thought of continuing the search for Bonnie and she couldn't bear not to do it.

I can't *care about Bonnie. I'm sorry but that's the way it is. I'm not sure I can watch you go through—*

She could understand his pain, but she couldn't help him. The only thing she could do was wait and try to prepare herself for what was to come.

Her cell phone vibrated on the nightstand and she grabbed it to keep it from waking Joe.

Jane.

She slipped out of bed and left the bedroom before she answered.

"Hi, Jane, how angry are you?" she asked when she picked up.

"Not angry at all. Hurt. You know you shouldn't have lied to me."

"Yes," she said wearily. "It seemed the only thing to do at the time. I couldn't stand the thought of dragging you into that horror too."

"Why not? It's where I belong if you're there. Joe said Bonnie's body wasn't found."

"Not yet."

"I'm sorry. I know how much you're hurting."

"I'll be okay."

"How about Joe? He didn't sound very good when he called."

"It's difficult for him."

"I can see it." She paused. "When I was a little girl, I had to fight to keep from disliking Bonnie."

"Jane."

"Oh, I wasn't jealous. You gave me all you could. But she was a stranger to me and she was the one thing we couldn't share. And I was like Joe. I didn't like you being hurt."

"You never told me."

"I didn't want to hurt you. The only

reason I'm telling you now is to make sure you realize what Joe is feeling."

"I understand. We'll get through it."

"Yes, you will. I got through it and now I'm fine with the way you feel about Bonnie. But I can't see your face to tell if you're trying not to worry me. Sometimes I hate telephones." She added crisply, "But I'll be able to see you soon. I'm in New York between planes. I'm arriving in Atlanta in a couple hours. Will you meet me?"

"Jane, why didn't you stay in—"

"Because you're my family and I'm going to be with you. Now can you meet me?"

"Of course."

"Delta 231. I love you. 'Bye." She hung up.

Eve pressed the disconnect. The conversation had been disturbing. In her heart she had known that Jane had felt that Eve had not loved her as she did Bonnie, but Jane had always denied it. Now it was out in the open and they would have to face it. Yet Eve wasn't feeling apprehensive. It was almost a relief, and she and Jane were so close now that they could deal with anything.

Lord, it would be good to have Jane home. Just the sound of her voice made Eve feel more cheerful. She quietly opened the bedroom door and moved toward the bathroom to start dressing.

"WHERE ARE YOU GOING?" JOE asked sleepily as she came out of the bathroom. He rose up on one elbow. "It's still dark outside."

"Go back to sleep." Eve bent and gave him a quick kiss. "I'm going to the airport to pick up Jane. She called me from New York where she's making a connection."

"I thought I'd convinced her to stay in Paris." He yawned. "She probably hopped the next plane."

"More than likely. She wasn't pleased that we'd lied to her."

"I lied to her. You didn't."

"It's the same thing."

"Is it?"

She smiled. "Oh, yes. United we stand . . ." She brushed her lips across his forehead. "I should be back in a couple hours. I'll stop at Dunkin' Donuts and get a supply of sinful sweets for breakfast. Maybe they'll be a mellowing influence on Jane." She headed for the door. "Though that's a tough one. Jane is definitely not mellow."

"Like you," Joe said. "And donuts never fazed you, Eve."

"Maybe I'll develop a liking for them. You're right, I could use a little mellowing too." She waved her hand and was gone.

Joe slowly lay back down as he heard the front door shut behind her.

Mellow. Eve didn't understand the concept of mellow. She was storm-driven, with flashes of humor and affection that filtered through the clouds.

And he didn't know how long he could survive living in the center of that storm. He would destroy himself and he could destroy Eve. She'd had tragedy enough in her life and she didn't need to deal with the bitterness and fury that was tearing him apart. She would never give up her search for Bonnie and he could never feel anything but frustration and despair whenever he thought of Eve's child. The bitterness would grow and eventually it would make him walk away from her. But not before he might have hurt her beyond healing.

Don't think about it. Eve was with him now and for a little while there would be peace. That would change, the search would start again. He'd decide then whether he'd try one more time.

He closed his eyes. Try to sleep. In a few hours Eve and Jane would be back and he needed to pull himself together so that Eve wouldn't know this conflict was so near the surface. He didn't want to hurt her before he had to do it . . .

OPEN.

"No!"

Megan sat upright in bed, her heart beating so hard she thought it would jump from her chest. She swung her legs to the floor.

"What is it?" Phillip had opened her bedroom door and was frowning with concern. "You called out." He turned on the light and moved toward the bed. "And you're crying."

"Am I?" Megan wiped her cheeks on the back of her hands. "Just a nightmare. I'm sorry I bothered you, Phillip."

"You didn't bother me." He dragged the easy chair up to the bed. "And it's natural that you'd be upset. It's the first night home after that god-awful experience. What were you dreaming about?" He paused. "The island?"

"Not exactly." She drew a deep breath. "It was . . . strange. It was the voices." She got out of bed. "I'm going to get a glass of water." She held up her hand when he started to speak. "No hot chocolate. Water. Just give me a minute. I'll be right back."

She drank a full glass of water and then leaned against the vanity and took deep breaths. She would have to go back to Phillip soon, but she needed this moment to herself.

Open.
Hear.
See.
Pushing.
Open.
Voices.

Just lingering words from the voices in the nightmare. But they were words she couldn't remember hearing from the voices of the children on the island.

Yet she had a panicky feeling that she should remember them.

Hear.
See.
Open.

She wiped her face with a cool washcloth. She had to get back to Phillip before he became any more concerned.

He was frowning when she came back and slipped into bed. "I feel better. Go on to bed, Phillip."

"Soon." He leaned back in the chair. "You've had nightmares about voices before, but I don't remember you getting this upset. You're usually . . . sad."

"This was different."

"You said that about the shock trauma you went through this time. Is this a residual effect?"

"Go back to bed, Phillip."

"Nope." He smiled. "You wouldn't let me go to the island, but I'll be darned if I'll be closed out of helping with the fallout. You're uneasy and we're going to talk it out."

"I'm not uneasy. Well, maybe I am. But it doesn't make any sense. The Listening was terrible, but everything could have been worse if that damn Pandora had kicked in. It didn't. I didn't hurt Eve. There's no reason for me to—"

"What were the voices saying?"

"Hear. See. Open." She ran her hand through her hair. "They kept pushing. I wouldn't answer and they wouldn't give up. I fought and fought, but they kept pushing. Couldn't they tell I wasn't with them any longer?"

He frowned, puzzled. "Then where were you?"

"What?" Then she realized what she had said. "I don't know where I was. I just wasn't— Oh, my God."

Phillip leaned forward. "What is it?"

"That was the time when I was unconscious." Panic was rising within her. "I didn't remember when I came out of it. But that was why I wouldn't come back. I was struggling, fighting, and they kept coming at me."

"The children?"

"Yes, the children. I thought Listening was only echoes. Maybe it is. But those echoes wanted to be heard. They couldn't reach me. They couldn't make me open my mind and listen to them. So they kept pushing and pushing."

"It's over, Megan," Phillip said gently. "And all that's left is a nightmare. We can get through those together."

He was right. Of course he was right.

No, he wasn't.

Dear God.

"You don't understand," she whispered. "Even though I was unconscious I was upset. I was fighting. I was struggling for my life and sanity."

"What are you saying?"

"Pandora. Facilitation. I was probably more emotion-charged while I was unconscious than I am sometimes when I'm awake. You know emotion is always the key. Dammit. Dammit. Dammit." She jumped out of bed and grabbed her cell phone from the bedside table. "I've got to call Eve Duncan."

"She's safe, Megan. Nothing happened to her all the time she was with you at the hospital. No sign of a release of latent talent."

"We don't know that for certain. All the rules are screwy, since I was in an emotional state while I was in shock. That's not supposed to happen. How do I know how much of this facilitation crap I was radiating while I was unconscious? It could have been less but steady. Would that cause an extended delay in any latent talent to show itself?"

"Or dilute it completely."

"I'm not that lucky." She found Eve's number in her cell phone. "I've got to warn her."

"It's the middle of the night."

"Then she can stay up and worry along with me."

Hear. See. Open.

"I still think that you have nothing to worry about. Calm down. You'll scare her."

"Yes, I will." She pushed Eve's number. "But she has to know. It's my fault. I should have figured it out before. I can't let her face it blind. Maybe she can help . . ."

THE CLOCK ON JOE'S NIGHTSTAND read 5:20 A.M.

Eve and Jane should be coming home anytime now with donuts in hand. He might as well have coffee ready for them. He wasn't sleeping anyway. He got out of bed and slipped into his robe. The morning was cool, although by noon it would be stifling hot even here on the lake.

The dawn was just starting to break and the hall was dim. He started the coffee and set out cups and creamer.

See.
Hear.
Open.

Joe froze. What the hell? The words had

come into his mind out of the blue. No sense. No connection. Lord, he must really be tired.

He went out on the porch to wait for Eve and Jane. He strolled over to the railing and looked out at the lake. Sunset and sunrise were always the most beautiful here. How many hundreds of times over the years had he and Eve come out here to watch the dawn unfurl its brilliance? It was a memory that was so poignant that it—

See.

Hear.

Open.

What on earth was happening to—?

"Hello, Joe."

He whirled toward the porch swing.

A little girl was curled up on the swing. "I've wanted to come to see you so many times, but I couldn't do it. I'm so happy I can do it now."

In the dimness of the porch she was only a blur, but she couldn't be over seven or eight. The nearest house was miles away. How had she gotten here? "Who are you?" he asked. "You shouldn't be here. Where's your family?"

"Coming. But I hope you're my family

too, Joe. You closed me out for so long, but something . . . happened. You're open to me now."

Hear. See. Open.

"Yes, that's right, Joe."

"No, it's not right. None of this is right. You should go home. Your parents must be worrying."

She shook her head. "You know that won't happen. You know who I am."

"The hell I do." The dawn rays were gradually banishing the pool of darkness surrounding the swing, touching the little girl's curly red hair and small face with light. He couldn't take his eyes off her. This was crazy. Yet he didn't feel crazy. He felt a weird sense of . . . peace. "Who are you?"

"It's going to be all right, Joe. I promise you."

"Who are you?"

The sunlight was now surrounding her as had the darkness before, revealing the Bugs Bunny T-shirt she was wearing.

"Why, Joe." Her luminous smile lit her face and reached out to touch him, embrace him, enfold him in love. "I'm Bonnie."